LOOKING TO SCORE

CORALEE JUNE
CARRIE GRAY

Looking to Score

Copyright © 2020 by June Publishing

All rights reserved.

No part of this book may be reproduced in any form or by any electronic or mechanical means, including information storage and retrieval systems, without written permission from the authors, except for the use of brief quotations in a book review.

Editing by Helayna Trask with Polished Perfection

Cover design by Black Widow Design

❀ Created with Vellum

For all the bold people who read motivational quotes in their spare time and embrace the yoga pants.

1

My breakfast consisted of Klonopin and Diet Coke.

I didn't need an alarm clock. My quarter-life crisis woke me up at the ass crack of dawn with a slight panic attack and a craving for carbs. I didn't give in, though my damn mouth watered at the idea of a toasted bagel slathered with cream cheese. I ignored the temptation and feasted on cardio instead. Fucking delicious. And for dessert, I did an online manifestation meditation video guided by an Instagram influencer with big breasts and a bleached smile. She was good. By the end of the video, she had me half-convinced I could manifest the perfect life and the perfect man.

Apparently, if you genuinely believed that your pussy deserved to be thoroughly fucked, then mother universe or Oprah would dropkick that motherfucker right into your lap. And I lived by that.

I rolled my razorblade-thin shoulders back, threw my strawberry blonde hair up in a bun, and slipped on an oversized shirt and some navy LivyLu yoga pants before going out into the kitchen to greet my roommate, Shelby. "Morning," I said in a painfully cheerful way.

Shelby was barely awake and fumbling through the kitchen in search of coffee. "Why did I move in with a morning person?" she groaned.

"Because you are a strong, independent woman who likes to challenge herself," I replied sarcastically. "You took a chance on a Craigslist ad, and the universe gave you me. It's quite serendipitous."

"You're watching those manifestation meditations again, aren't you?" she asked.

"I'm going to manifest a more positive conversation by not responding to that." Shelby and I had a unique relationship. When I transferred to the University of Texas for the summer semester, there weren't any housing options for a last-minute transfer student. I checked Craigslist on a whim and ended up moving in with her the next week. We were opposites in every way that counted. She was a few years older than me, and a local photographer. Shelby was impulsive and disorganized. She wasn't unmotivated, per se, she just couldn't keep set on one particular thing. She changed her mind like the Texas weather and had the financial freedom of a trust fund to do whatever she wanted.

She didn't even need a roommate. Her skyrise condo in the heart of Austin was easily worth more than my entire undergrad degree. She just wanted the adventure of "sharing her life with someone" and got me. I wasn't sure if she regretted that whim or not, but I'd take advantage of my oversized room and walk-in closet for as long as she'd let me. I wasn't exactly hurting for money either. My dad was an executive for Plotify, a music streaming service, but he wanted me to get at least a semblance of the college experience—which meant a healthy dose of ramen noodles and a strict allowance every month.

"Well, if we're talking about the universe, Mercury must be in Gatorade or something, because my vibes are all off. Like literally, I ran out of batteries for my vibrator last night and I'm ovulating, so you know I'm horny as hell," Shelby said. I rubbed my temples. There was so much wrong with that statement that I didn't know where to begin. "Did you use the last of the coffee?" she complained, with a loud sigh.

"Nope. My body is a temple," I replied. "I don't do instant coffee."

"A temple of anxiety meds and Diet Coke," she snapped back. Damn, she was on the struggle bus this morning. I made a mental note always to keep the kitchen stocked with caffeine.

She continued to wrestle with the kitchen cabinets, looking for her instant coffee. I personally didn't understand her obsession with the crap. It tasted like fermented dirt— and I might have known what it tasted like because I stole the last of it just yesterday.

"Are you sure you didn't take it?" she asked again. This time, she spun around to scrutinize me, boring those mud-brown eyes into mine as she twisted her bright, box-dyed, red hair on her finger. I gave her frumpy black pajamas a once over before answering her.

"Positive," I lied, making her huff in annoyance and drop the conversation. This was payback for stealing my Burberry sweater last week and spilling a strawberry margarita all down the front. That overly-sweet sugary shit was hard to get out.

"Do you have class today?" she asked. I raised my eyebrow. She probably didn't even know what day of the week it was.

"Yep," I said distractedly, eyeing the bright green apple on the kitchen island. "First day of the new semester."

"Nice," she replied half-heartedly. I continued to stare

longingly at the Granny Smith apple on our kitchen island, mentally calculating its nutritional value as Shelby continued. It looked to be about seven ounces. One hundred and two calories. Twenty-four grams of carbs. If I skipped the bus to class and jogged for about twelve minutes, it would be enough to burn it off.

Shelby was rambling about something, but doing mental food math took all of my brainpower. My stomach growled, and I reached for my water bottle to take a drink. "Amanda," Shelby said, drawing my attention back to her. "Did you listen to a word I said?"

No. I didn't. But Shelby took it personally when she felt like I was ignoring her, so I lied. "Yep."

"So you don't mind? Awesome! It won't be full nudes. I'm thinking a couple of shots of him in a towel and—"

"What?" I cut her off. I wasn't exactly sure what I'd agreed to. Shelby sighed in annoyance before explaining.

"I found the perfect subject for my next exhibition. It'll make a huge statement about the human body and resilience." Her voice had that faraway quality to it that she usually got when she spoke of her art.

"So basically, you found a hot guy with a six-pack and lured him here for a photo shoot."

"You know me so well," she deadpanned. "He's an athlete actually. I'm going to do some commentary about how we sell our bodies for higher education. It'll be great." Shelby waved her hand for emphasis, and I forced myself not to roll my eyes at my eccentric roommate.

"Well, I'm supposed to start my internship today, so I'll be late."

"Perfect," Shelby replied. "Can we use your room? The layout in there is perfect for my lighting kit and—"

"Absolutely not."

"Right. Right," Shelby said with a tight smile and a wink.

She was totally going to take nude photos on my bed. My door didn't have a lock on it, either. I was just about to yell at her when I saw my phone ringing. Mom.

"I gotta go to class," I told Shelby, swiping the apple off the countertop.

"Yeah, yeah. Get out of here so I can go nap," Shelby relented.

Once I was outside of my apartment, I quickly answered my cell phone and made my way down to the street. "Hey, Mom."

"I need your help hiding a body, no questions asked," she hissed into the phone. I could hear people chatting in the background, and I snorted.

"Did Lacey McGuire try selling you anti-aging cream again?" I asked with a chuckle.

My question released the floods of her fury. "That bitch had the audacity to tell me that I could look fifty again with a proper skin care regimen," Mom snapped with a huff. "I'm forty-fucking-seven! I mean seriously, last month she was selling diet pills. I heard her garage is filled with boxes of pyramid scheme shit."

Mom hadn't worked since I was born, and filled her life up with three things: my dad, me, and gossip. Her hair was so big because it was, in fact, full of secrets. She was a midwest prom queen grown up to be a Silicon Valley housewife. She drove a Range Rover, attended goat yoga, and called me every other day to complain about her friend circle. I fucking loved her.

"That's insane," I replied.

"You're telling me. Do you want to know what else is insane? How fucking skinny you look. I saw your Instagram post yesterday. Have you just not eaten at all this summer, Amanda?"

I cringed at her statement. I knew what photo she was

talking about. I'd snapped a shot of me reading a new self-help book at the lake. I guess my legs did look a lot thinner. Diets were such a slippery slope. I read once that if you developed an eating disorder while you were fat, you were a success story. If you developed one while skinny, you were sick. I didn't know what I was or what I had or what the fuck I was doing with my life, but I did know that I was avoiding shit.

"I've just been trying to get healthier," I explained. "Ever since the incident, I just…" My voice trailed off. We both knew what I was going to say. Traumatic experiences tended to make you rethink everything. In the spring, I was an overweight alcoholic. Now, I was…something else. A health nut obsessed with improving her life. We only had one body, after all. And I was all too familiar with how life can change in an instant.

"Just be safe, okay? I'm going to come to visit you soon. Your father and I are worried."

I knew Dad was worried. He started having groceries delivered to the apartment last week and threatened to drag me back to California if I didn't take advantage of this fresh start. He pulled quite a few strings to get me here. I needed something new. A new place. A new outlook on life.

"Okay. I miss you guys," I sighed, squeezing the apple in my palm.

"We miss you too, baby." I could hear the emotions in her throat. We'd never been this far from one another, and she was worried about me. I hated that I needed this, but being at home just reminded me of everything. "Now today is the first day of the fall semester, right? Are you nervous? It'll be different than summer classes. And when do you hear about your internship?"

I smiled, thankful that we were back to chatting about other things. "I find out today about my placement. Since I transferred in the summer, they had to scramble to find me something. I'm guessing Dad helped?" I prodded.

Mom laughed loudly, the sound like expensive bells hanging from a booming church tower. "Your father did not Lori Loughlin shit for you. Despite your excessive extracurriculars," Mom began. Excessive extracurriculars was a politically correct way of saying I spent every night drunk off my ass and bouncing between frat houses back in California. "You have an amazing GPA and awesome recommendations from your professors. Everyone was shocked when you—"

"Okay," I interrupted. My whole purpose for running here was to escape what I'd done, not dig it up every time I spoke to my mom. I could hear her huffing on the other end of the line. "I'll let you know about my placement and how the first day of school went. I love you," I said while speed walking on the sidewalk past crowds of people. My stomach was rumbling, aching for some food.

"Okay, baby. Go do great things," she said.

I hung up the phone with a smile on my face. A homeless man on the street was playing a battered and scuffed violin. His eyes were closed, and he had a look of pure joy on his face. His skin was burnt from the hot Texas sun, and his clothes were dirty with various holes in them. I paused for a moment to listen to the haunting song he expertly played before placing my apple in his box.

2

"We couldn't find you a placement for your internship."

My advisor was leaning back at his desk, thumbing through papers. I had been waiting outside of his office for our appointment for two hours. I'd expected that the first words to leave his mouth would be an apology, not that.

"Excuse me? What do you mean you can't find me a placement?" I asked. "My program requires an internship for graduation. I've already arranged my Public Relations courses around this schedule. This is the final step to graduating early. What am I supposed to do for an entire semester?"

My advisor, whose name I think was Luis Tuesday or some shit like that, let out an exasperated exhale, as if my freak out was dampening his mood. "I looked at your schedule. Have you ever considered Sports Media?"

I shook my head. "I don't know anything about sports. I want to work with artists." My dad's love of music had definitely been passed down to me. The whole reason I was looking to graduate early was so I could start working with him. His streaming service just formed an agency that focused on promoting independent artists. The future of the entertainment industry was through the indie community, and I wanted to lead that division for him.

"I'm good friends with the head football coach. Since all the other internships were taken, I was wondering if you'd be open to working with one of the players on his image."

My eyebrow rose. Working with a football player? It wasn't exactly on my projected career path, but that could work. In Texas, football was God, and that multi-million dollar stadium was church. They attended religiously. It was an entire thing—a thing I didn't particularly care for. But, if I did a good job, it was a networking wet dream. Working with the football team could open a few doors. Yeah, I could get excited about that.

But still. I didn't know what this would entail. "I don't know if I'm qualified for that. I've catered all my courses to brands and musicians."

"I think you'd be surprised how much crossover there is," Mr. Tuesday began. "Public relations is about creating and maintaining a positive image—in this case, for the athletes or sports clubs they represent. You'll be responsible for coordinating the seamless flow of favorable information about this player. Monitoring his social media. Keeping him out of trouble and out of the news. Fans are more likely to buy tickets, purchase merchandise, and fill stadium seats when there's a public interest, and right now, the good wholesome Bible Belt of Texas is not amused with our star running back."

"What's the damage?" I asked.

Mr. Tuesday slid his phone across the desk to me, and I picked it up, frowning at the social media feed I saw there. Picture after picture showed a tall, muscular guy with bulging muscles and thick lips in compromising photographs. He was kissing random girls and doing keg stands. There were even a couple of him cupping his junk. This was a media clusterfuck of epic proportions. He was kind of hot, though, if you were into that kind of thing.

"Doesn't the coach have rules about this?" I asked. "Is there a scholarship on the line?"

"He does. But Oakley Davis is a god. There's never been a player like him. He knows he can get away with anything because there is no one that can match his talent or his mother's wallet, you understand?" I resisted the urge to roll my eyes. I never understood why a large bank account made you immune to rules. "Coach Howard's contract is up for consideration this year. He wants to keep his job, which means he needs to keep Oakley playing."

"And what am I supposed to do?" I asked, sliding the phone back across the desk. From the looks of it, Oakley Davis needed a complete overhaul of his image. It was the type of job that would require a lot of hours and a lot of patience.

"Do what you've been taught to do—polish his image. Find opportunities to put him in a more favorable light. I've taken the liberty of enrolling you in the Intro to Sports Media class. It's a freshman course, but it'll help you this semester. Coach Howard will be grading you. He's your boss. Keep him happy with Oakley's progress, and you'll graduate early just as you planned."

I chewed on the inside of my cheek. I still didn't know. Working with Oakley truly was a fantastic opportunity, but it wouldn't give me the learning experience I'd envisioned. I wanted to work with people already in my field, not teach myself how to babysit a grown-ass man.

"If you don't want to take this on, we will have to try again to find you a placement next semester. It'll push you back, but you'll get it done."

I shook my head. I wanted to be done with college. I took

eighteen hours this summer because I was ready to leave school behind. I worked my ass off to graduate early, and I didn't want all of that to be for nothing. I was ready to start my career and my life.

"Fine. I'll do it. But I want Dr. Haynes to mentor me through it." My voice sounded strong, but I was nervous as hell. Dr. Haynes ran the Public Relations department and was well-known in the PR world. He had the most connections and would be invaluable to learn from. If I had to do this, then I was going to get a glowing recommendation from the top professor at this school, dammit.

"I'll see if Dr. Haynes has room in his busy schedule. You aren't asking 'cause you have a crush on him, right? His last TA became a little obsessed, so I have to ask."

Dr. Haynes was a hottie, a total silver fox. I'd only seen pictures in the campus newsletters, but holy fuck. I could learn a lot from that man. "No," I choked out. "I just want to make sure I have a good mentor and the support of Coach Howard. From the looks of it, Oakley Davis will require a lot of work, and I want to be set up for success."

"Of course," Mr. Tuesday replied, though he didn't sound convinced. I didn't really care. I was doing the university a favor. Most universities had PR reps for the campus, but if they wanted to assign an intern to their star player, then they must be desperate.

I briefly wondered why Oakley was willing to throw his life away. I mean, how hard was it to keep your social media clean and stay sober? Did he not want to become a pro? Most guys on the team at this school were using the university's influence as a stepping stone to the NFL. I didn't know sports, but it didn't take a genius to see that there was something else going on.

"I'll make sure you have all the resources necessary to do this," Mr. Tuesday said, drawing me out of my thoughts. I was already trying to think of how I'd help him. Maybe he needed to sign up for some charities. It would be easy enough to get his photo in the newspaper, kissing a baby or something. "Practice ends at seven tonight. Coach Howard said he would introduce the two of you afterward."

"Great," I said unenthusiastically. "Thanks for finding me something." I had never been to the stadium before. I had a general idea of where it was, but I made a mental note to look it up.

"I only want what's best for the students," Mr. Tuesday replied before pulling a Twinkie out of his desk, opening it, and shoving the entire thing in his mouth. Disgusting.

I excused myself without a word and let out a long exhale in the hall. Glancing down at my phone, I quickly found all of Oakley's social media accounts and followed him so I could start researching my client.

He was hot. I wasn't going to deny it. But as I scrolled through every feed and tag and ridiculous comment, I grew sick to my stomach. Oakley's wild life felt all too familiar. It was like staring at my old self. This was going to be a challenge—for more reasons than one.

Coach Howard was a short man with orange skin and chiseled muscles. He looked like your typical coach, with a university-issued polo shirt tucked into khaki pants. His tennis shoes were tied so tight that I wondered if any circulation could get to his toes. He was about my height but still somehow managed to look down at me.

"Are you the intern?" he asked when he caught me standing outside of his office. Their practice had been over for forty-five minutes. I had arrived about fifteen minutes early since I wasn't sure exactly where his office was, so I had been standing there for about an hour. I smiled to hide my frustration. Was no one punctual on this campus?

"Amanda Matthews," I said while shooting my hand out in greeting. "It's very nice to meet you." Coach Howard looked down at my hand and reached out to grab it, squeezing a little harder than what was necessary. Based on my initial observations, I sensed that he was the type of man overcompensating for something. It wouldn't surprise me at all if he drove a big lifted truck.

"I'm assuming Mr. Wednesday told you everything that would be expected of you?"

Oh shit. I thought his name was Tuesday. I racked my brain, trying to remember if I ever called him by his name. I couldn't remember. He never corrected me, so I probably didn't? Oh well, I could obsess about it later.

I pulled out the folder from under my arm and started flipping through the notes I made earlier this afternoon. I wanted to be prepared, considering Coach Howard would be the person to decide my grade.

"I want to do a complete overhaul of his social media, sign him up for some charity events, and shift the focus to his talent on the field—"

Coach Howard's snort interrupted me. "Oakley is the cockiest, self-absorbed, selfish, pompous, belligerent asshole I've ever met. If I had a decent second-string running back, I would have kicked him off my team last year when he was caught having a threesome in the locker room." My eyes widened. My mouth dropped open in shock. "Oakley doesn't care about anyone but himself. You can type up pretty little reports, but it would take an act of God to get him to cooperate. Period."

It was an act of God that got me here. Maybe I could squeeze one more miracle out of the big guy. "I've got it handled," I replied in a curt tone. "Why don't we skip ahead to the introductions so I can get to work, hmm? I will send you a detailed email outlining my *pretty little report* for you to reference," I added in a sickly sweet tone. I knew how to talk to men like Coach Howard. I just had to keep my cool and do my job. Then graduate. Easy, right?

"Good luck," Coach answered. "He disappeared from practice early, saying he had a *prior commitment*." Coach plopped down at his desk and scratched his head. "He's probably balls deep in some unlucky coed right now. That boy's dick is going to fall off one of these days. When you see him," Coach continued, wagging his finger at me, "tell him that he owes me another hour of practice."

I couldn't believe this. The University of Texas was one of the most prestigious schools in the state—hell, in the country. People were dying to get in here. There was no way Oakley was *that* good. There were always better players waiting to prove themselves. I didn't know anything about football, but even I knew that.

I should have excused myself, but instead, I sat down. "Why is Oakley still on the team?"

The coach rolled his eyes and asked, "Why do you care?"

"If you want my help, I need all the information. You and I both know you wouldn't put up with this shit unless you were forced to," I replied.

His brows shot up in surprise as if he weren't expecting me to ask that. Coach leaned over his messy desk and lowered his voice. "You're a smart girl. Let's just say Oakley is *very* protected by higher-ups that want to see him succeed. One might even say they have no other choice but to keep Oakley happy."

I nodded and wrote a quick note in my planner, then stood up. "I'll find him and pass along the message. When is your next practice?"

"Oh six hundred in the morning."

Perfect. I loved to start my day early. "We'll be there."

He snorted. "Mr. Wednesday said that I'd be monitoring your progress? I'll be watching you. I suggest you go ahead and plan on being here another semester because Oakley Davis is hopeless."

I smiled. "I'll keep that in mind." I loved it when people underestimated me. It made proving them wrong that much more rewarding.

I walked out of his office with my head held high and my shoulders rolled back, making sure to pour confidence in my steps as I left. I looked like I had my shit together. I was getting a fucking A, come hell or high water.

But the moment the door closed and I was out of his line of sight, I squeezed my eyes shut and frantically picked up my phone, desperate to figure out where my client was. I pulled up his Instagram and checked his story.

Shit. Damn. Hell. Sonofamotherfuckingbastard.

He was clutching a towel and taking selfies in someone's bedroom. The pink bedding hinted that it belonged to a girl. I took in the motivational poster on the wall and then gasped when I saw a purple vibrator left on the nightstand. Mother. Fucking. Shelby. He was in my apartment. He was with *my* roommate.

Guess she found batteries for her vibrator.

I clicked through his story and paused when he playfully dropped the towel to cup his junk. I saw a flash of peen. Like, full-on flesh baton. It was quick, but there was no denying Thor's hammer hanging out there for the world to see. I skipped back to double-check.

Yep. That's his dick.

His massive elephant dick.

It was only a split second, but I knew that girls could screenshot slips like it was one of those fucking shoot out duels in the Wild West. His cock was probably already in spank banks all over campus.

Oh my lanta. Oakley was a sexy bastard. The way he bit his lip had me flushing. I skipped to the next post and frowned.

Headed to Longhorn Sports Bar for drinks.

I closed my phone and started heading out of the Athletics building and toward the bus stop. This wasn't bad. Leaked nudes sometimes *made* a career—Kim Kardashian was proof of that. But this didn't exactly promote the good wholesome vibe the school wanted.

I quickly ran through options, tapping my foot on the concrete and waiting for the bus to arrive. The quicker I got to him, the better.

3

It had been four months since I'd set foot in a college bar. I braced myself for the memories I knew would hit me like a punch to the gut. Outside, the Austin city lights illuminated the grime-filled sidewalk. I stared at the entrance for a moment, mustering up the courage to put my big girl panties on and waltz inside like the bad bitch I was.

It took ten minutes for me to feel like said *bad bitch*. I was a medium bitch. An over-easy bitch.

The second I walked through the front door, the stench of perfume and beer assaulted my senses. I curled my lip, and my stomach rumbled at the sight of plates filled to the brim with bar food. Hungry college students who weren't worried about their slowing metabolism were devouring appetizers dripping with bubbling grease. I nearly drooled at the sight of a pitcher of beer and nachos. Fucking hell, I hated my diet.

This place was my ultimate weakness. Just a few months ago, I would have confidently stepped up to the bar and ordered a whiskey sour. Now, I was trembling.

I swallowed those nasty little nerves crawling up my throat like bile and walked up to the bar. I needed something in my hands. "Sparkling water, please. With lime," I ordered once I could flag down a bartender. I tipped the hipster dude pouring drinks extra well to overcompensate for feeling embarrassed about my order. This was more of a beer and cholesterol type of place.

With my glass in hand, I made my way over to an empty table and looked around. It was surprisingly crowded for a Monday. The start of the semester brought on a flood of camaraderie and excitement. Students were greeting and hugging one another with broad smiles and loud squeals as if the summer break was more of a year-long sabbatical instead of two short months.

I felt a twinge of jealousy. There was no one here excited to see me. I didn't get to hug my friends and pose for reunion selfies. Maybe if I were back in California, a few people would politely smile if I walked into a room, but here I was invisible. Most of the time, I liked that, but tonight it felt a little more lonesome.

I took a sip of my refreshing, fizzy drink and sighed in fake satisfaction as it slid down my throat. *Fuck*, I wanted some vodka. Something to dull the chatter in my teeth—something fulfilling, but the sparkling water would have to do. I was here for a reason.

It didn't take me long to find Oakley Davis. In the corner of the large bar was a loud group of people cheering and slapping each other on the back. The guys were tall and muscular, obviously athletic. Some of them wore football shirts or other athletic wear, and the girls surrounding them were dressed up in tight little dresses, strappy high heels, and expertly applied makeup.

I recognized Oakley the moment I saw him. It wasn't his signature dark hair or the way he towered over everyone else that made him stand out—though his classically handsome appearance helped—it was his very essence, his energy. He had this carefree power about him that was intoxicating to watch. The entire room seemed to shift to accommodate his presence. Girls craned their necks to stare at him, and guys nudged closer for the opportunity to rub elbows. When his drink was empty, another one replaced it immediately. When he said a joke, everyone laughed at it, like the world was at his fingertips.

He looked like the type of guy to cum down a girl's throat in some frat house bathroom and expect gratitude. As if letting her swallow his Taco Bell-and-vodka flavored jizz was some sort of gift from God. I was not amused. It was like watching a documentary on Antarctica: fascinating to watch, but I wouldn't be freezing my tits off to experience it any time soon. Oakley was, like, literally the worst kind of privileged.

His ego was huge. Gigantic. Heavy. I could already tell that he was a complete douchebag based on the way he treated his coach, but seeing him here, in action, furthered that belief. I started to wonder what exactly I had gotten myself into and if I could do this.

His strong jaw could cut granite. His defined Adam's apple that bobbed whenever he swallowed down large gulps of his beer would forever be ingrained in my mind. He had a sense of swagger that couldn't be duplicated. It was in how he spoke to people. It was also in the way he wore casual clothes that perfectly fit his body with name brands that cost more than some people's rent.

Oakley even occasionally stopped to take photos with fans. He took requests, going as far as to pose in football stances or with his arms draped across a girl's shoulders. It seemed almost expected. He didn't seem annoyed by the attention—he thrived on it. Oakley Davis was a big fucking deal.

I watched him toss back drinks without a care in the

world. I wasn't sure how long he'd been here before I got here, but he wasn't showing any signs of stopping after the fourth pint. Sorority girls with tequila in their shot glasses rubbed their breasts against his chest in the crowded area. He looked down at them with cocky pleasure but didn't entertain anyone specific.

It wasn't until someone jokingly asked him to sign her tits that I decided to intervene. It was important to watch him and get a feel for his presence, but now I had to do my job. From now on, autographing boobs was off the table.

As I walked over to him, I couldn't help but think how much my life had changed over the last few months. Before, I probably would've been trying to get his attention for entirely different reasons. I would have been wearing Spanx and an uncomfortable dress that clung to my body like a second skin. Just a few short months ago, I would've worn heels and caked-on foundation and smoky eyeshadow just to feel a little bit pretty. I would've ordered a couple of pitchers of margaritas for myself and drowned my insecurities so that I could be the life of the party.

Now, I was still wearing the leggings I put on this morning, and my blonde hair was thrown back into a messy ponytail. I couldn't even remember the last time I wore makeup. I knew that image was essential to be in the PR business, but I just couldn't be fucked to impress anyone anymore.

As I made my way through the thick crowd, people barely looked at me. It was like I was invisible—something I used to fear but now welcomed. And it wasn't until I elbowed a girl in the ribcage to introduce myself to Oakley that someone noticed I was intruding on their party. "Whoa," a guy with olive skin and rust-colored hair said. I had seen him in quite a few of Oakley's posts on Instagram, so I assumed that they were friends. I quickly scanned my thoughts to remember his name. Ah, yes. Dale.

"Excuse me," I said politely with a smile.

"Whoa, whoa, whoa. Where are you off to, hmm?" he asked while positioning himself in front of me. His breath reeked of cheap beer. I nervously tucked a stray strand of hair behind my ear before answering him.

"I need to speak with Oakley Davis," I asserted, trying to sound professional despite our environment. Dale frowned for a moment, then quickly schooled his face into a smirk. I stored the brief crack in his relaxed appearance away to think about later. I wasn't really a fan of frenemies and needed to protect my client at all costs.

"I can introduce you," he offered. "But fair warning, you're definitely not his type."

I didn't honestly give a single fuck if I was Oakley Davis's type or not. But I *was* curious about what his friends thought about him. If they were quick to loosen their lips and talk shit about their teammate, I needed to know. Any information I could get on the school's star running back was useful, so I entertained Dale for a little longer.

"And why exactly do you think I'm not his type?" I asked, crossing my arms over my chest.

He looked me up and down in a single sweltering swoop. I felt my cheeks heat, and I took the lingering moment to stare right back at him. Dale was kind of hot. He didn't command the room quite like his teammate, but there was a playful energy about him that felt authentic and genuine. Dale was confident; his blatant staring was proof enough of that. He was also flirtatious. "Don't get me wrong, you definitely look the part. Blonde hair. Blue eyes. Legs for days, and lips any man with half a testicle would lose his shit over." As he spoke, he took a step closer.

"I sense a *but* coming on," I replied, making him laugh. Dale's dark chuckle made my skin buzz.

"But you brought your backpack to a bar. I can see your copy of *Seven Habits of Highly Effective People* sticking out of your bag. You have a pencil tucked behind your ear, and you carry yourself with confidence. You didn't even bother getting dressed up when you came here, which means you don't have to try hard to make your presence known." That wasn't exactly true. I just had a preference for comfort if I had to walk all over campus. "Oakley Davis likes easy girls that aren't smart enough to call him on his bullshit, so if you're looking to hook up with him, you're better off finding someone else."

I didn't let Dale see me falter. Although his words had affected me, I didn't know how I felt about him pinning me down with baseline assumptions. "Well, good thing I'm not here to sleep with him. I'm here for work. I'll just go introduce myself, thank you," I replied with a wink, excusing myself before Dale could say or do anything else. I couldn't put my finger on it, but there was something off about him.

Oakley was laughing with a short blonde girl when I walked up and introduced myself. I stared at his side profile longer than I should have. His jawline was impeccable. "Oakley Davis?" I asked before clearing my throat. Oakley turned to look at me, with confusion evident on his face.

"That's me," he declared. God. Even his voice was sexy. Low and rugged. I cleared my throat again, begging a sense of professionalism to course through my veins. What the fuck was wrong with me? Justin Bieber once had dinner at my parents' house—when I was fucking fourteen and overwhelmed with hormones. If I could handle the Biebs, I could handle a cocky football player. I was a grown-ass woman.

I opened my mouth to introduce myself but stumbled

when Oakley gave me a long, sensual perusal, similar to what Dale had just done. It was like the blonde at his side was long forgotten.

But this felt different. This was like disarming a gun. I was standing there with my finger hovering over the trigger to my career, and he emptied the chamber at my feet. His dark eyes looked like deep pools of honey with specks of gold. A shadow of scruff covered his jaw. His hands rested on his chest, the veins in his arms thudded as he dragged his gaze up to my thighs, my stomach, my breasts, my chest, and finally landed on my lips. I shivered, then shook my head. Nope. Nope nope nope nope.

"I'm Amanda," I choked out while thrusting my hand out to shake his. I felt stupid. Oakley grabbed it with a grin and squeezed before pulling me closer. I tried snapping my palm back, but he wouldn't let me. And up close, I breathed in the spicy scent of his aftershave and the booze on his lips. What the fuck was wrong with me?

"It's nice to meet you, Amanda. Have I seen you before?"

I looked up at him through my thick lashes and shook my head free of the lust once more before pulling back. The pheromones this asshole was giving off were fucking with my ability to form coherent words and make good choices. "I'm a new student. A public relations major," I said, hoping it would lead us into the part where I got to tell him I was his new publicist.

"Public relations? I think I need some help with my image," he rasped, stepping closer. His hold on me felt hot. I was trapped in his orbit.

"Oh?" I asked. I couldn't help myself. Was he genuinely self-aware about his issue? I wasn't sure what was worse: a client who didn't know any better or a client who didn't care.

"There's this rumor going around," he began before releasing my hands and sliding his own to my hips. I knew right then that I should have stopped him and drawn a clear line of appropriateness. But I didn't. Nope. It was like my vagina took control of my mouth and slammed that sucker shut. "Do you want to know what that rumor is...baby?" The pause before the nickname sobered me some. Oh my God, this bastard couldn't even remember my name. From five fucking seconds ago. It was hard to tell if that was a reflection of his view on women or if it was the booze. He swayed a bit as he spoke. His eyes were heavy from drunkenness—fucking hell.

I nodded. "People are saying I have the biggest cock in Texas." Was this guy serious? No. He couldn't possibly be serious. "Is that something you could help me with?"

Oh my lanta, he was serious. He grabbed another shot from a nearby table and slammed it. Any more and he'd be passed out on the ground. "I suppose I could help. The first step would be to stop sharing nudes," I replied dryly. His face lit up.

"So you've seen it?" he asked, as if proud. I guess he had a right to be. His dick looked lethal. It honestly was brag-worthy, but as his publicist, I probably shouldn't think about how it hung mid-thigh and looked like it could put an eye out when hard.

"I don't think there is a girl on campus that hasn't," I deadpanned.

Oakley must have finally caught on that I wasn't amused, because a slight sense of clarity poked through his drunken haze. "What was your name again?" he asked.

I sighed in annoyance while peering around the room. Other girls were glaring at me for hogging the prime real estate. "Amanda," I replied. Yeah. He was definitely drunk. There was no way I was letting him go home with anyone tonight.

"Amanda," he slurred. "How about you come home with

me? I'll let you ride my face until I'm drowning in your cum. Then"—he leaned closer to brush his whiskey lips against my ear—"I'll fuck you until the entire city of Austin can hear your moans."

Okay. Oakley Davis was a pro at dirty talk. My panties were like the San Marcos river, and my nipples stood at attention. Damn. Even drunk, he was a charmer.

Obviously, this wasn't the right setting for a professional meeting. Right now, my only priority was getting Oakley home. "Sure," I replied. My lack of enthusiasm made him pause. "I'd really, uh, like to be fucked, please," I choked out awkwardly. A couple of people nearby snorted at my lame attempt to seduce him.

He chuckled. "I'll order us an Uber to my place."

He pulled his phone from his pocket and struggled to unlock it. I memorized the code.

6969

What a fucking tool.

"One more shot before the road?" I asked with a grin while handing him a glass.

"Bottoms up!" he slurred, tossing it back.

With any luck, he'd be passed out before we even got to his place.

4

Oakley was snoring. I stared at him like a fucking creeper while he slept. His shirt was crumpled on the bed next to him, and his pants were halfway off, leaving his skin-tight black boxer briefs on display. My eyes lingered on the tight bulge that looked like it was about to tear through the fabric. I allowed myself to indulge in just a moment of fantasizing about what I saw during towel-gate on his Insta yesterday. Hell, it was better than indulging in that double chocolate caramel brownie. Right?

The sun hadn't even risen yet, but I knew we only had a few minutes until he needed to get up and head to practice. It was time to snap out of it. Oakley had an early morning practice, and he was going to make it if I had to drag him there myself. "Rise and shine, princess," I called out in a cheery tone.

I waited. And waited. Nothing. Oakley didn't even stop snoring. The steady rise and fall of his chest just annoyed me. I walked over to the bed that we definitely did not share last night and timidly poked him. Again, nothing.

Come on, Amanda. You're waking up a football player, not

playing Jenga. "Oakley, get up," I said more firmly as I shook him awake.

"You ready for round two, baby?" he asked through a thick haze of alcohol breath and cockiness. He obviously didn't have a clue that he passed out about five minutes after we got out of the Uber last night. I blushed as I remembered him trying to do a striptease as he fell into bed. I didn't sleep at all last night. I took advantage of having unsupervised access to his cell phone and his room, and got to work, pausing only for a quick nap on his chair.

In five hours, I managed to clean up his social media, change all his passwords, and sync his calendar to mine so I could make sure to attend all of his activities. I also sent an email on his behalf to Coach Howard, apologizing for leaving practice early and promising to make up the hour. There were a few privacy laws broken, but all in all, I didn't really give a fuck. If Oakley had a problem, he could bring it up with his coach.

"There would have to be a round one in order to experience round two, and I'm not sure your morning whiskey dick is up for the challenge," I deadpanned, scrolling through his email.

He sat up in bed, eyebrows raised as he looked at me. "Who are you?"

"Amanda Matthews, your new publicist," I replied, taking off my reading glasses and handing him back his phone. He grabbed it out of my palm and immediately peered at the screen. "There is an email from Coach Howard validating my claims. I cleaned up your social media, deleted your apps, and changed your passwords. I'll give you access again once I'm convinced you won't share any more photos of your dick."

"What the fuck?" he groaned.

"You have ten minutes to do whatever you need to do to

get your ass out the door for practice," I said in what I hoped was a convincing tone.

"I don't have to listen to you," he argued, scratching his head.

"Yes," I began. "You do. If you won't do it because your spot on the team is in jeopardy, then you'll do it because I found poems you wrote to your high school girlfriend, and I'm not afraid to share them."

He swallowed. "You're bullshitting me. Who even are you?"

"Your breasts are like playdough, molded perfectly for my large hands," I recited, eyebrow arched. When I was going through his phone, I wasn't expecting to find prime embarrassment for blackmail, but luck was on my side. *"Your flowery pussy smells like pistachio ice cream."* The poem was bad with a capital B. He stared at me like he was still trying to understand what was happening, and his eyes widened when he realized I wasn't bullshitting him.

"I was fifteen when I wrote that. You can't just break into people's personal property," he argued.

"When I think about coming inside of you, I get hard as a baseball bat," I added. "I will say your dirty talk *has* improved." He finally shook his head and started to get out of the bed. I watched his back as he walked into the bathroom, and I snuck one last look at his tight end, then looked down at my own phone.

Two new texts. One from my mom and one from Shelby. Shelby wanted to know why I didn't come home last night—she made sure to include a suggestive winky face. My mom was still seething about Lacey implying that she looked over fifty. Apparently, Lacey slipped some samples into her mailbox. I didn't bother replying to Shelby, and I had just sent a reply to my mom, telling her where Lacey could stick it, when Oakley came back out looking ready for practice. I didn't know what football players wore to practice, so I was just guessing.

"Ready?" I asked.

"I'm going to practice. But only because I need to have a conversation with Coach. I don't want or need a fucking publicist."

"Your legs are as long—"

"Enough with the teenage poetry. I was fifteen. Fifteen! Let's go," he replied, looking pissed and still a little confused. Since Oakley lived in an apartment on campus, the practice stadium was only about a five-minute walk. As we were walking out of his building, I debated whether or not I could trust him to get himself to practice.

"Do I need to make sure you get to practice, or are you capable of getting there on your own?" I asked. I mean, there was only so much trouble he could get into at the ass crack of dawn, and I had to get back to my place so I could shower and get ready for my own classes.

"I think I can handle it," he growled. "I'm feeling pretty motivated to talk to the coach. I think he should know about the girl that broke into my apartment and started blackmailing me."

I grinned. "You invited me over last night, don't you remember?" I watched him scowl as he tried to recall the moments leading up to this instant. "And yes, please do. Also, be sure to mention that I got you scheduled with the physical therapist for this afternoon. I saw that he's been trying to get you to talk to the specialist about your shoulder, and booked you an appointment online. Their online scheduling system is very convenient."

He fumed, and the vein in his forehead throbbed. "You're fucking insane. And I'm too hungover to do something about it right now, but I *will* get to the bottom of this. You have no idea who you're fucking with."

I smiled. Despite my feeling exhausted, pissing off Oakley Davis made the late night worth it. I felt alive. This was better than my morning manifestation meditation. "Practice hard, and maybe I'll give you your Instagram login back. I know you like the attention."

"Fuck you," he growled. His chest heaved as he looked me up and down. He was so angry that he looked wild. I met his stare with an equal level of determination.

"It'll be a pleasure to work with you," I replied with a polite smile.

He stormed off, and I watched him disappear around the corner in the direction of the practice building. I went toward my home with my mind reeling about everything I needed to get done, but when I got to the next intersection, I sighed in resignation and turned in the opposite direction of my apartment, toward the Athletics building. I didn't trust Oakley Davis one bit.

"You can't do this. I woke up to some strange chick in my room, going through my phone," I heard Oakley complain as I walked toward Coach Howard's office.

"Sounds like a typical night for you," Coach replied with a chuckle.

I couldn't hold back the quick snicker that escaped my lips. I slowed my steps, composing myself, and then leaned in to listen to their conversation before making my presence known.

"I did not consent to this."

"And I don't give a fuck. You've been reckless. Belligerent. You put this entire program at risk. Just because you don't care about going pro doesn't mean that you can fuck off all season. You might be good, but you're not good enough to act like this. The university wants to see you get your act together, and they aren't afraid to exploit a public relations intern to do it. Now suit up for practice." The coach dismissed Oakley. I have to say, it was super fun for me to hear Oakley get his ass handed to him.

I cleared my throat and walked into the office just as Oakley was about to leave.

"Good morning, Coach Howard! Oakley Davis hand delivered and on time for practice, just as promised!" I said in my most chipper voice and flashed the coach a colossal smile. "I trust that you've got it from here unless you need me to type up that report for you?"

Coach Howard glared at me and then barked, "Oakley still owes me another full hour of makeup practice. I'll be impressed when you make that happen." That was Oakley's cue to storm out.

"Un-fucking-believable," he snarled as he practically stomped out of the room.

I turned to follow, and the coach called my name and handed me a piece of paper.

"If you are going to have a snowball's chance in hell, you are going to need this," he said as he gave me a dismissive wave. After I left the coach's office, I looked down and saw that he had given me a schedule of practices, games, and other various things that Oakley was expected to attend.

I started the walk back to my apartment when I spotted a cute little coffee shop. I figured one small skinny, low fat, no sugar latte wouldn't hurt. I promised myself I would only drink half anyway, and I needed the caffeine boost if I was going to make it through the day. That would be sixty calories and eight grams of sugar. If I power walked, I could easily burn that off. After ordering, I sat down and loaded Oakley's schedule into the new shared calendar that I had created on his phone earlier this morning, complete with alarms that would go off when he needed to start getting ready and when he needed to leave.

I immediately got a text, and when I saw Oakley's name flash on the screen, I couldn't help but think of him lying in his boxers this morning, and I could feel the heat creeping up my face.

Oakley: What the fuck did you just do?

I smiled to myself as I typed back.

Amanda: Oh good, you found where I programmed my info into your phone! And aren't you supposed to be practicing?

I could almost see how pissed he was when his phone blew up with calendar notifications. Imagining him annoyed as hell gave me a deep sense of satisfaction. I didn't wait for his response and sent another message.

Amanda: According to the schedule, your last practice gets out at 7:00 tonight, I'll see you then.

I clicked the button to lock my screen and got up to head home, leaving my latte on the table untouched.

5

I was unstoppable. The universe was my fucking oyster. I was so tired that even the seven dollar concealer I splurged on two months ago couldn't hide the dark circles under my eyes, and my hair was so full of dry shampoo it felt like a fire hazard, but nothing could get me down. Not a single thing.

In one day, I managed to get Oakley to practice and completely overhaul his Instagram image. Coach Howard even sent me half of a compliment via email at 10:06 in the morning. It was backhanded and attached to a formal request to stop emailing him updates, but I took the "good" and rolled with it.

Not to mention, Mr. Wednesday got me an advisory slot with Dr. Haynes. *The* Dr. Haynes. I was so stoked to be learning from the absolute best I could hardly contain my excitement. I was headed to a meeting with him right now.

My life felt like endless chips and salsa and a large pitcher of margaritas without the calories. It felt like having a good hair day minus the good hair. I was going to fucking rock this internship.

I didn't know what the big fuss was. Oakley Davis was easy to handle, and I was totally slaying the first day of my internship. And now, I was going to impress the pants off of Dr. Haynes and get a kickass letter of recommendation from one of the leading experts in our industry.

Manifest that, motherfuckers. I couldn't stop fist bumping the air.

I knocked on the door to Dr. Haynes's office and smoothed my hair nervously while waiting for his invitation inside. I felt a flutter of nervousness and couldn't wait to devour his brain. There was no shame in my zombie game.

"Come in."

I twisted the handle and smiled.

Dr. Haynes's office was smaller than I expected. The walls were lined in overflowing bookshelves, and his desk was organized chaos. It was cozy and helped to calm the rush of nervous excitement I was feeling. At least until I saw Dr. Haynes, that is. Holy. Shit. Seeing his pictures did not prepare me for this.

Even though he was sitting, I could tell that he was tall, at least six feet, and had a commanding presence. His thick silver hair was a little bit longer on the top than the sides and perfectly styled. I had a sudden impulse to run my fingers through it. His chin was dotted with salt and pepper stubble that played into his boyish charm. When he stood up to greet me, it was clear that his abs were rock hard under his button-down shirt and perfectly cut blazer.

"Hi. I'm Matthews. Amanda. Umm...Amanda Matthews," I stammered. Great first impression. Super professional.

"Miss Matthews. Thank you for meeting with me this morning. I heard you had a late night," he greeted me. Were the bags under my eyes really that bad? Just as I was silently cursing myself for not taking the extra five minutes to put on foundation, there was a knock on the open door, and Oakley burst in uninvited. What in the actual fuck was happening here? I thought this was a one-on-one meeting?

As Oakley shot me a smug look, Dr. Haynes said gravely, "Mr. Davis, thank you for joining us. I wanted to address your concerns with Miss Matthews so that we can all feel comfortable moving forward." He gestured for us to sit in the chairs on the opposite side of his desk.

Shit. What? Shit. All of the confidence I had just moments before was gone. I didn't know where this was going, but I knew it wasn't good and the world was definitely not my fucking oyster anymore.

"Thank you, Dr. Haynes. I guess I just didn't realize how *personal* having a PR rep was going to be," Oakley replied in an equally somber tone. Even though I didn't really know him, I could tell that he was laying it on extra thick.

Shit shit shit.

"I mean, we had a good time and all last night." He put a lot of emphasis on *good time*. I half expected him to start waggling his eyebrows. "But waking up to find that the girl you brought home the night before is going through your phone feels so violating," Oakley finished while giving me a disapproving look. I could tell he was really enjoying this. Oh. My. God.

"Yes, I understand how it would feel that way. Is there anything you would like to say, Miss Matthews?" Dr. Haynes asked.

I wanted to say that Oakley was totally used to waking up with randos, this was not a new thing for him. But, instead, I tried to compose myself and said, "I'm sorry. It was a lapse in judgement. It won't happen again. I just wanted to get him home safely from the bar, and when I had access to his phone—"

"She asked me if the rumors about my large dick were true," Oakley interrupted, *definitely* laying it on thick.

I blushed and resisted the urge to hide behind my hands. "That is not true," I argued.

"I mean, you're hot and all, but are all clients supposed to sleep with their publicists? I just didn't know this was normal. And the things she asked me to do last night. It was really strange."

Dr. Haynes's brows shot up in shock. "No, that is not normally condoned," he said while picking through papers on his desk.

I stammered, "We did not—"

"This is a safe space, Mr. Davis," Dr. Haynes cut me off. "If you need Miss Matthews to leave so you can file a complaint, I can arrange it."

My heart fucking stopped. A complaint? Forget graduating early, this could mean I never graduate at all. After everything I had been through, I could not believe that graduating college and my future in public relations was being seriously jeopardized by one stupid fuckboy.

"I mean," Oakley drew out, leaning forward. He stroked his chin, thinking it over. I was already planning on calling my father's lawyer to fight this. Fuck. Fuck. Fuck. "It was all consensual. I thought it was weird she kept wanting to read me her poetry while we fucked. And even weirder that she called my dick Mr. Snuggles."

I choked. I legit choked on invisible air, spit and anger for this asshole. I was so mad I couldn't even breathe. They both stared at me as I sputtered and coughed. "I did not!!"

"Settle down, Miss Matthews. Mr. Davis has a right to speak!" I had never been so embarrassed in my entire life. Well, I could think of *one* time. But I buried that shit four months ago.

Oakley gave both of us an Oscar-worthy somber look. Like I actually traumatized him. "I'd still like to work with Miss Matthews in a professional capacity. She's obviously good at her job. But I'd like to create clear boundaries so both of us are successful."

Motherfucking liar lying pants of motherfucking volcanic fire.

"Of course. I'll discuss those boundaries with Miss Matthews so we can work together professionally moving forward, Mr. Davis. Thank you for coming in. Can you please give Miss Matthews and me the room so that we can discuss the standards expected of her?" Dr. Haynes dismissed Oakley. I felt my face turn red and wished the floor would swallow me whole. This is definitely not how I thought this meeting was going to go.

"Of course. Thank you for listening to my concerns."

Oakley got up and exited the room but made sure to smirk at me just before leaving. I imagined strangling him in his sleep. And the second the door clicked shut, Dr. Haynes let out a low sigh. "Now where is my ethics packet..."

WHEN I LEFT Dr. Haynes's office, I had a slew of things to do. I had to watch a video about sexual harassment, write a four-page paper about ethics, and I had an overall feeling of shame. It was brutal, and he didn't even let me get a word in about what really happened last night. The hottest and most well-connected professor on campus thought I was a poetry-reading deviant that liked to nickname dicks while doing bedroom aerobics.

Oh my lanta!

"That was a good meeting, don't you think?" Oakley asked with a grin. I hadn't seen him leaning against the wall near Dr. Haynes's office, but the moment our eyes met, I clenched my fist. I had to repeat a quick calming mantra in my head just so that I wouldn't throat punch the university's star football player.

"We did not sleep together!" I growled. "You were too drunk. You literally passed out, and I had to make sure you didn't choke on your own vomit all night."

He rolled his eyes like he thought he was fucking invincible. I had to walk away before I smacked the smug look right off his face. The last thing I needed was to add assault to my sexual pervert rap sheet. To my surprise, Oakley started to walk with me.

"What are you doing?" I snapped at him.

"Since we are going to be spending so much time together, I thought you might like to give Mr. Snuggles a chance to get to know you better," he practically purred. "Or, better yet, give me back my damn Instagram password." I knew he was just trying to get a reaction out of me. So in as calm of a voice as I could muster, I politely told him to get fucked.

I spun on my heels, prepared to stomp off back to my apartment and come up with a way to get back at Oakley, when he grabbed my wrist and spun me around to face him. My free hand collided with his chest, and I looked up at him with a gasp. "This doesn't have to be so *hard*," he rasped, migrating his hands to my hips.

Fucking hell, he was hot. But I knew guys like him. Hell, I'd fawned over plenty of men that played this role well. Attractive. Well-connected. Panty-meltingly sexy. It was predictable and painful to watch. I didn't give a rat's ass if he wanted to throw his reputation and future away. I had plans to work with talent that had integrity. I was the garbage woman in his dumpster fire of a career, and there was no way in hell that I'd let him burn me alive with him.

"I know we got off to a bad start," I began, taking a step back. I needed distance from him if I was going to establish myself clearly. The scent of his cologne was too tempting to form coherent statements otherwise. "I know you don't care about your career. Or your image. Or your grades. Or who you stick your dick into. Or—"

"Does this have a point?" he asked with a frown.

"Yes," I said, smoothing my shirt. "It does." He tilted his chin up and stared at me with defiance, but the playfulness from earlier had disappeared from his gaze. "I really need this internship. I really need to graduate early and get out of here. I'm going to keep you organized, keep you out of trouble, and make your life easier. I am sorry for my intrusiveness this morning, but I *will* do whatever is necessary to pass, regardless of what you want."

He licked his lips, and I glared at the movement. Why the hell did this dude have to be so distractingly sexy?

"I look forward to the challenge," he replied before storming off.

You and me both, asshole.

6

It had been exactly ten days after my shitshow of a meeting with Dr. Haynes. Ten days, seventeen manifestation meditation videos, one ethics paper, and three M&M's later, I was finally starting to make some progress. I was sitting at the kitchen island, denying tag requests on Oakley's Facebook from Ashleigh *Delta Delta Drunk* and debating on a fourth M&M when Shelby walked in.

"Damn, you're working again? It's Friday night. Have you slept or done *anything* at all since getting this internship?" she asked with a sly smile.

"Not really. I have to wake his ass up for practice every morning. And if I'm not chasing after him to make sure he doesn't do live videos showing off his cock, then I'm following up with Coach Howard on his progress and assuring Dr. Haynes that I'm not reverse cowgirling my client."

"That sounds like a lot of work."

I let out a sigh. "Yeah, it is."

"You know he takes you for granite, right?" she asked, walking to the pantry. "I mean, I heard rumors that he was about to be permanently benched this season. His senior year! Could you imagine?"

"Granted," I replied. "He takes me for granted, and yes, I know. There's coffee next to the peanut butter." I kept talking as she fished around in the pantry. I didn't understand how she had coffee so late at night. It was almost ten o'clock. Didn't she want to sleep? "I don't think he really believes that his position on the team is in jeopardy. So to him, I'm just the annoying girl who won't let him have any fun."

"Granite, that's what I said," Shelby replied. "I have to get ready for a shoot," she added and then walked out of the room, calling out over her shoulder as she left, "He may be a giant douche, but he sure does have a big cock!" I rolled my eyes and smiled. Seventeen manifestation videos was the magic number to be able to find it funny that the reason the whole university knew the size of Oakley's cock was thanks to the pictures she took in *my* apartment.

Despite my complaints, Oakley had actually been somewhat behaving over the past week and a half. I wasn't exactly sure what changed, but maybe he realized that doing what he was supposed to was better than having my crazy ass around. And, bonus, he hadn't been bothering me either. For the most part, we mutually tolerated each other. I sent him super fucking professional texts to make sure he stayed on track, and he showed up to workouts and practices just to avoid having to see me. I even got a half-assed "okay, I'm impressed" from Coach Howard.

I think Dr. Hottie's opinion of me was improving too. We'd had two more meetings where I managed to not make a complete ass of myself. We had come to an unspoken agreement that, unless there were more complaints, we just weren't going to talk about what happened during our first meeting with Oakley. I was starting to feel like maybe I wouldn't fail out of this internship and fuck up my life...again. I checked my step tracker to see where I was for the day so far. Four M&M's was about seventeen calories. I laced up my shoes and headed out the door to run the stairs in our building.

I was just about to start my workout when my phone rang. I sighed before checking the caller ID. Asshole Davis was calling. Lucky me.

"Hello. How may I help you?" I answered, using the customer service voice I'd perfected while working at a call center last year.

"Amanda?" he asked. Oakley sounded out of breath and nervous. "I need your help."

I listened to the background and frowned when I heard loud music and chatter thudding in dull echoes through the phone speaker. The music sounded like that weird German electronic dance shit. "What's wrong?" I asked as I walked down the stairs and outside. My heart was racing. What had he done now?

"You're my publicist, right?" he asked. It was the first time he'd sounded unsure since I'd first spoken to him. The absence of cockiness in his voice made me even more apprehensive.

"Yeah?" I responded, kind of wishing someone else was his publicist instead.

"Well, I have a fucking mess for you to clean up. I'll text you the address." Oakley hung up, and I grumbled to myself as his text came through.

He was at a frat house. Perfect.

I HELD my breath the entire Uber ride to the frat house, having no idea what I was about to walk into. It was a little unsettling hearing Oakley sound like anything other than an arrogant ass.

What the fuck had happened? The driver pulled up to the curb to let me out, and there were two drunk sorority girls sitting on the front lawn by the bushes. Drunk Girl One was holding Drunk Girl Two's hair while she threw up. Oh gross, was that a fucking mushroom? Not only were they emptying the contents of their stomachs on the lawn, but their bodycon dresses were rolled up to their hips, flashing their neon thongs to the world.

Been there, done that. Solidarity, sister.

I walked past them into the house, scrunching my nose at the scent of sweat, booze, sex, and vomit. The bass was so loud that I could feel it vibrating in my teeth, and it was so crowded that I could barely push through. I used to live for this kind of party. It just wasn't a fun night if you didn't puke, sit on a random guy's face, or post twenty-three pictures to Instagram to prove you were #LivingYourBestLife. Now, I just wanted to find Oakley and get the hell out of here.

I walked into the next room. Standing on my toes, I tried to pick Oakley out of the crowd, but it seemed that a requirement to get into the frat was to be tall and muscular. Everybody looked the same and was blending together. This was starting to feel impossible. I was about to walk into the next room when I felt a hand on my shoulder. I turned toward it and ran right into Dale's chest. Smooth, Amanda.

Dale looked like every other cookie cutter frat daddy in this place. He wore boating shoes, and his button-down shirt was drenched in sweat from all the bodies slammed up against one another. His red hair was pushed back, like he'd been running his nasty-ass, greasy hand through it all night, and there was a bead of sweat perched on his plump upper lip.

"Come with me," Dale shouted over the music. I couldn't tell if he was drunk or not, but the cup in his hand was overflowing with beer. I followed him silently, mostly because he wouldn't have been able to hear anything I said anyway. He led me up the stairs and then down a hallway. It was quieter upstairs, so I started to ask Dale what was going on. "Where is Oakley? If this is some fucking prank, then I'll sign him up for volunteering on a Sunday morning, so help me Orlando Bloom." I abruptly stopped, my voice coming to a complete halt when he opened the door.

The room was predictably messy, with dirty clothes and empty beer cans strewn across the stained carpet. There was what I assumed to be a sorority girl crying on the bed, her head in her hands and her brown hair falling forward like a curtain around her. Oakley was standing uncomfortably a few feet away from her. Oh fuck.

I immediately went to her. "Are you okay?" I asked, kneeling at her feet. Her head popped up, and I noted the smeared mascara trailing down her cheeks. A series of scenarios went through my mind. If Oakley hurt her, I'd end him. Client or not, there were certain lines I refused to cross—supporting a rapist was one of them.

"I just want to go home," she choked out. Her voice sounded rough and clogged with emotion.

I looked up at Oakley and Dale, who were standing with their arms crossed and uneasy expressions on their face. "What happened?"

"Chantell here is sixteen," Oakley grumbled. My eyes widened. Sixteen? Holy shit.

"You didn't—"

"No!" Oakley snapped. "We were making out, then she just started crying. I didn't know she was underage, I swear." Staring at Oakley, I tried to gauge if he was telling the truth. His clothes were wrinkled, but he didn't look like he'd just attacked the pink fortress.

I turned back to Chantell with a grimace. "Chantell, are you…"

"I didn't mean to drink so much. My parents are going to kill me," she sobbed, this time even louder.

"When is your curfew?" I asked.

"Two hours ago," she croaked back. "I just wanted to make my boyfriend jealous. He cheated on me last week with Tammy fucking Tabernackle. As if fucking that stupid whore is something to brag about."

"Jesus fucking Christ," Oakley groaned at my back. I stood up and let out the breath I had been subconsciously holding. My mind was racing as I mentally went over what needed to happen. First, I needed to calm Chantell down. Then, I needed to figure out a way to make sure that she wasn't going to lie to her boyfriend or anybody else and say that she and Oakley had been about to bop squiddles. And lastly, I had to start on damage control, who saw what and who were they telling?

I took a deep breath and turned my attention back to Chantell. I sat next to her on the bed and started rubbing her back in what I hoped was a comforting gesture. I didn't have any actual siblings, but I had done this a thousand times, comforting my drunk sorority sisters back in California. "Chantell, sweetheart," I cooed. "Everything is going to be ok. I'm going to help you. Your parents don't need to know about tonight, ok? Do you have a friend you can go stay with?"

"Uh-huh," she sniffled.

"Ok, good, that's a good start." I spoke gingerly. "Text your friend and let them know you're coming. What's her name?" I asked.

"Jessa," she told me. After she texted Jessa, I took her phone and scrolled through until I found her messages with her mom. I didn't trust Chantell to text her mom convincingly while she was so upset. I quickly tapped out something I thought was believable and hit send. Chantell seemed to be calming down.

"I'm going to get you an Uber. Make sure Jessa is waiting for you so that she can sneak you to her bedroom without her parents seeing. You need to drink tons of water. Dale, go get her some water." Dale scoffed at me, but he left the room. I prayed to the flying spaghetti monster that he actually remembered to go to the kitchen, get the water, and bring it back.

I got the notification that Chantell's driver was here. I helped her to her feet and started walking her down to the front. Oakley moved like he was going to try to help. "You've done enough," I snapped at him. "Wait here for me to come back. Don't move, we're not done."

We ran into Dale on the staircase. I grabbed the bottle of water he was holding and handed it to Chantell as I clumsily guided her back through the crowded party, past the formerly puking sorority girls who were now the *passed out* sorority girls, and into the car. It looked like she had sobered up quite a bit, and she thanked me profusely for helping her. I wrestled with my inner self trying to decide if I should try to manipulate a drunk high school junior into keeping quiet. But ultimately, I figured that she had more to lose by talking about her drunken night at a frat house than we did if it came out. So I shut the door and wished her good luck. Now to deal with Oakley.

I stormed upstairs and found him sitting on the bed where Chantell was just crying. "So what have we learned from this?" I sang in a sickly sweet tone while sitting next to him.

"Check the ID of every girl you want to bone?" he asked.

"Or you could just not fuck random strangers at parties.

This could have been bad, Oakley. Forget your career, a pretty boy like you would not do well in jail."

He scrubbed his hands down his face with a sigh. "Fuck," he cursed. "Thank you. That could have really been bad."

Fuck, indeed.

"No shit, Sherlock. I know we're in this awkward stage of hating each other and not really wanting to work together, but I think tonight taught us a valuable lesson." He turned to look at me, his expression full of annoyance. Tough shit, asshole. I didn't want to be here any more than he did.

"And what is that?"

"You're a fucking hot mess. And you need me," I said matter-of-factly.

He rolled his eyes. Hard. "Fine. You *did* come in handy tonight. And it's actually kind of nice that you organized my calendar. Even though the alarms piss me the fuck off, I haven't been late to class in a while. Though the meditation and breathing exercises are a bit much," he replied begrudgingly.

"Practicing mindfulness is good for your mental health," I preached.

"Is that what you do? Because I do not want to sip from whatever Kool-Aid put that stick up your ass," Oakley growled.

I could have punched him in the jaw. "Careful," I began. "That stick just saved you from going to jail," I reminded him, and I hoped he didn't fucking forget it.

He stood up and stretched his hands over his head and rolled his neck in a stretch that had me salivating. "How about we go grab something to eat? We can start over or something, okay?"

My stomach growled at the mention of food. I didn't really want the temptation of a restaurant, but the opportunity to put this feud behind us was too good to resist. "Okay, I'm down," I replied with a fake smile.

Oakley looked me up and down, wiping his hands on his pants, as if he were trying to figure me out. "Okay. Let's go, Solver."

The nickname made me pause. "After you, Problem."

7

Watching Oakley eat was disgusting but oddly fascinating. Did he even chew? I guess when you worked out and practiced a sport like he did, you didn't really need to watch your calorie intake. I must have been staring, because he paused long enough to notice that I hadn't even touched my grilled chicken sandwich in the time he had devoured his fries and half his burger. "You gonna eat?" he grunted in my direction.

"Yes. But I like to take the time to enjoy my food. My body is a temple," I replied as I picked a piece of chicken free from the bun. That seemed to satisfy him, and he went back to his burger, although he seemed a little more mindful that I was watching him.

"How did you know what to do with that girl? Have a lot of practice getting drunk when you were in high school?" he asked. He looked at me and grinned like the thought of me having a scandalous past was hilarious. He had these really fucking sexy dimples when he smiled like that. Dimples that made me think of what it would be like to kiss him. What it would be like to kiss down his chest and follow the ripples down into his abs with my tongue.

"Well?" he asked, snapping me out of it.

"Umm…" I stalled. "I'm sure I had the same amount of fun as everybody else did," I replied, not really wanting to get into the details in a diner in the middle of the night. I took a bite of my sandwich so that my mouth was full.

Oakley snorted with laughter. "Yeah, I bet you were the life of the party," he teased. "Did you follow everybody around, telling them shit like 'the things you put on the internet last forever' and 'make good choices'? Is that how you got interested in being a publicist?"

His assumption of me was exactly why I moved to Texas and started over. I didn't want to be the party girl anymore. He might have been my first official job as a publicist, but my first true image overhaul was myself.

I debated on letting him continue to think of me that way, but maybe we could connect a little more if he understood that I wasn't just trying to cramp his style. I was a living, breathing example of what could happen if you took things too far, and I had to live with the consequences of my actions for the rest of my life. I let out an exhale and pulled out my phone to find a video I should have deleted ages ago. I honestly kept it in a secret file on my phone to remind myself how sloppy I used to be.

"This was me," I replied with a cringe before sliding my phone over to him. He grabbed it and positioned the screen so that we could both see what was happening. I took a deep breath and hit play.

The video started off out of focus and jerky but then stopped on a very, very drunk me wearing only a red lacy bra and jeans, sitting in a bathtub, my muffin top on full display. There were towels lining the inside of the tub and dried vomit in my hair. There was a lot of giggling from my "friend" Legacy who was taking the video. "Giiirrrrrrllllll," drunk me slurred. "I just wanna dance. NO! I gotta daaance. WOOOOO!" The tiny me on the phone screen then stood up in the tub and started gyrating her hips.

I could hear Legacy calling to some other friends who were at the party. "Guys. Amanda is TRASHED. Get in here!" Soon there were at least three more people crammed in that bathroom.

My new audience was just in time to see me try to twerk and then start violently throwing up. All over myself. Again. I managed to stumble out of the tub and sit on the bathroom floor. I aimed for the toilet but went in a little too hard and slammed my head on the toilet seat. When I was finally done puking, I turned my head to the side on the toilet seat and looked up at one of the guys in the bathroom. "Hey, baby. Wanna a blowie?" trashed me called out to a chorus of laughter as the video stopped.

I locked my phone screen and couldn't bring myself to look at Oakley quite yet. He wasn't saying anything, so to break the tension I said, "I learned later that I bruised my face and broke the toilet seat." I snuck a quick glance at Oakley to try to see what he was thinking. To my surprise, he wasn't laughing and he didn't look disgusted with me either.

"So that's why," he mused while scratching his jaw. I watched him think over the very embarrassing video before prodding him to continue.

"Why what?" I asked.

He smiled a bit as he wrapped his large, veiny hand around his drink. "Why you're so anal."

My nose scrunched up at that term. "I'm not *anal*," I spat.

"No? You send me a daily email of everything I need to do at exactly seven in the morning. Even on the weekends." I pursed my lips. He wasn't wrong. But that didn't mean I was anal. Did he *not* just see the awful video I'd shown him? "You also coordinate your purse to your outfits. You try really hard to look like you threw your clothes together, but we both know you have designer sneakers on with laces color-coordinated with your yoga pants."

I didn't have to look down at my Nike shoes to know that he was absolutely right. "So what's your point then?"

"My point is, you were such a mess that you went in the extreme opposite direction. You must have really fucked up to have gone to such extremes, and something tells me it wasn't this video that made you move across the country."

My mouth dropped open. How did he know that I moved? The sly look on his face made me feel like I was a math problem he wanted to figure out, and I didn't like it one bit. My father might have paid a lot of money to keep my *discretions* out of the media, but that didn't mean they were impossible to find. Anyone at my old school would happily supply the evidence of what I'd done. I needed to deflect.

"I could say the same about you," I began as he took another bite of his meal. His eyes remained trained on me as I spoke, and I had to pause and lick my lips.

"Oh?" he finally replied, with his mouth full of burger. He lost hot points when he spoke with his mouth full. Maybe I should just keep feeding him every time we were together. He was absolutely disgusting while stuffing his face, and it helped keep me sane and my panties dry.

"People don't party as hard as you do unless they're trying to escape something. I mean, yeah, it's college and we're all stressed to hell and want to drink the anxiety away, but you take it a step further. Why?"

This question hit close to home, mostly because I felt its truth in my soul. I wasn't running from anything too traumatizing, I was just overcompensating for my low self-esteem. Drunk Amanda liked to have fun. She didn't care what anyone thought. She ate her feelings and knew that if she couldn't be the prettiest girl in the room, then she'd be the loudest, drunkest, sloppiest, and funniest.

He set down his burger and eyed me for another long moment, then wiped his greasy hands on his chest. "I'm not running from anything," he argued and then nodded at the waitress, asking for our check.

"Are you sure? Coach Howard hinted that the university needed to keep your family happy," I prodded.

He gritted his teeth. Oh yes, talking about his family was definitely a sore spot. I made a mental note to prioritize research on them. For purely professional reasons, of course. It wasn't like I was trying to figure him out. "I don't have fucking Mommy issues, if that's what you're insinuating," he growled.

"I'm not saying you do, I'm just saying—"

He cut me off before I could get to my point. "Just because you showed me your sloppy drunk video doesn't mean I'm going to open up to you about my family life." I let out a sigh and he continued. "I appreciate your help tonight. That was a fucking close call, and even though I like to have fun, I definitely don't want to end up in prison. I'll start being more aware if you stop trying to psychoanalyze me. I'm just a college kid making the most of his senior year."

At that last sentence, his face turned into a full-on smolder. I could feel his heated gaze all the way down to my purring vulvarine. Shit. Why couldn't he keep talking with his mouth full of food?

He dropped some cash on the table and peered at my full plate for another moment. "I'll start listening more. But you're gonna have to learn to hang. Part of my brand is being a local celebrity. This town is full of fans that want to see me at parties and bars. It's seriously cramping my style having you tell me where to go and what to do."

It made sense. He was like novelty ice cream: Everyone

wanted a taste. And being seen in public was part of his role on the team, and as his publicist, it was my job to also fill stadium seats. "Fine. I'll do better about bridging the gap," I replied. I'd have to start low-key carding every girl that came up to him.

He tossed me another smile. "And if you ever wanna give someone a blowie…"

I rolled my eyes. Somehow, I knew that was coming.

"Not in a million years, asswipe."

8

My clock said that it was 5:17 a.m. It was way too early—even for me—but I couldn't sleep. Most of my night was spent tossing and turning. I spent fifteen minutes debating whether or not I wanted to get up or try going back to sleep. Ultimately, I decided to get in a morning jog. I had a meeting with Dr. Haynes today, and I needed to work out some, uh...*tension* and clear my mind.

As much as I hated to admit it, I hadn't been able to stop thinking about Oakley since we went to dinner the other night. I started to grab shoes with laces that didn't match my yoga pants just to spite the presumptuous asshole, but right before I left, I dashed back in my room and put on the right ones. Dammit.

While jogging down the crowded streets of Austin, my mind ran wild. I never understood why some people said working out cleared your mind. It just made mine go crazy. I thought about everything: what I was going to wear today; what homework I needed to do; Oakley's smile; my meeting with Dr. Haynes; Oakley's abs; my paper due in marketing; Oakley's di—

"Lady! Watch where you're going!"

I sidestepped a pedestrian carrying a large box and headed back to my apartment. I made sure to slam the door for a good morning jolt for my still-sleeping roommate, then headed to my bathroom, stripped, and jumped in the shower.

The hot water felt good on my screaming muscles. I may have hit it a little too hard on my run. The calories I'd burned blistered across my mind. I mentally tallied my daily intake. I thought about the lack of sleep I'd gotten and what self-care I could do to feel human again. Maybe I could squeeze in a few chapters of the new self-help book I just bought: *Girl, You Fucking Got This*.

And then I thought about Oakley. What wasn't he telling me? I couldn't understand what was so bad about his family that he didn't want me to know. I was certain that the information wouldn't be difficult to find with a little digging, but for some reason, it felt wrong. I wanted to hear it from him. My mind wandered from his family being Scientologists to porn stars until my fingers were so pruny I had to get out. I got dressed, grabbed my bag, and headed out the door. If it was even possible, my mind was more clouded than it was before my run.

I made it to Dr. Haynes's office a few minutes early. I pulled out my phone, hoping to see a text from Oakley, but saw one from my mom instead. She sent me a picture of a teacup pig wearing a bright yellow raincoat.

Mom: Do you think Dad will let me get one of these?
Me: Where would you even keep it?
Mom: Well in the house, of course.

It was like magic, my mom always seemed to know exactly what I needed. I smiled and made a mental note to call her later to talk her out of the impulsive purchase of a teacup pig. Then, I knocked on Dr. Haynes's door and waited.

"Come in," he ordered, and I let out a large sigh, then

opened the door and let myself inside. Dr. Haynes was wearing black slacks and a button up shirt that clung to his muscles. His hair was gelled back, and he wore thick-rimmed glasses as he thumbed through papers on his desk. "Have a seat," he said, gesturing toward the chair in front of him.

I sat down and started shuffling through my various binders in my messenger bag. Once I found the folder containing everything I needed to run Oakley's image control, I pulled it out and started sifting through pages. "The first game is this weekend, but it's an away game. We are gearing up for the home game next week. I'd really like to get him featured in some local publications in a favorable light. I've looked into a few charities, but no one wants to work with him. I had no idea how far his reputation reached."

"Good morning to you too, Miss Mathews," he replied with a chuckle. "I think you're onto something. It needs to be something that doesn't take too much time away from his studies or practice schedule, but also needs to be public enough that it improves public opinion."

I nodded. That was mostly the problem. Working around his crazy intense schedule was hard. I was surprised he managed to pass any of his classes leading up to this point. "I'll research some opportunities and email you a list of options later this afternoon," I replied. I was confident enough in my skills to steal my client's phone and take total control of his scheduling and social media, but I still felt like I needed reassurance from Dr. Haynes on Oakley's first big positive publicity event.

"I'm confident you can handle this, Miss Matthews. But I'm happy to provide some extra guidance," he told me. "I think you have done an excellent job in a very short amount of time. Especially after such a rocky start." Oh snap. That was the first time Dr. Haynes had brought up "the incident."

I thought we were just going to let it go. I fought the urge to literally hang my head in shame. "I can tell that you get your business sense from your father. How is he, by the way? I read in the New York Times that Plotify just implemented a new advertising stream that looks promising."

I didn't realize Dr. Haynes even knew who my father was, but I guess it made sense. You didn't become a leader in the industry without studying the major players, and my father was a giant in his field. "Dad is definitely leading Plotify into the future. I actually hope to work for him after graduation."

"I bet you do," Dr. Haynes said. "You'd be a fool not to. Plotify is one of the largest music streaming services on the planet. I know lots of undergrads who would burn their thesis papers for the kind of connections you have."

That statement left a bitter taste in my mouth, but I ignored it. Dr. Haynes wasn't necessarily wrong. "Thank you," I managed to squeak out.

"Anyway, I'm actually checking in with Mr. Davis a little later to hear his perspective on how things are going." Dr. Haynes looked at me, almost as if waiting to see if there was anything I wanted to confess.

"Great!" I said with all the confidence I could muster. "I'm looking forward to hearing any feedback that will help me improve."

Dr. Haynes seemed satisfied with that answer. He had a wrinkle that appeared in between his eyes when he really focused on something. It added to his appearance of sophistication. "Good. Let's touch base tomorrow morning. We can go over the volunteer opportunities you find, and we can have an informal performance review to help identify where you are really shining and see if there's anything we can do better. Have a good rest of your day," he said with a warm smile.

I left his office and immediately sent a text to Oakley.

Me: Hey!

Oakley: Hello?

I cringed. I didn't usually text him just to chat, so it was probably better if I just jumped right in.

Me: I heard you have a meeting with Dr. Haynes today. What are you going to tell him?

I stared at my phone screen and saw dots. Then nothing. I waited not so patiently for the dots to reappear. I needed to know if he was going to pull a stunt like last time. I didn't think he would, but we also hadn't really talked in the past couple of days since the party. He wasn't super happy with me for trying to press him about his family.

Oakley: Wouldn't you like to know.

Me: Actually, yes. I would. That's kind of why I'm asking.

I continued to walk out of the building, waiting for his response. Why couldn't he just give me a straight answer? It was like he enjoyed fucking with me.

Oakley: I should tell him that you put Life360 on my phone so you could track me. A bit invasive, don't you think?

Me: It makes following you easier.

Oakley: You sound like a serial killer. Or a stalker. Or both.

Well, if that wasn't a melodramatic response, then I didn't know what was. I stared for a long moment at my phone and debated on tracking him down so I could threaten him with bodily harm if he pulled anything. So what if I had his constant GPS location? Yes, I had a tracking app downloaded onto his phone. Privacy laws? Psh. His slipup at the party just reinforced the idea that he needed constant monitoring. He sent another text.

Oakley: Where am I now? ;)

I blew out a puff of air and checked the app. Sure enough,

he was at a sorority house off campus. I wouldn't be surprised if he was texting me while getting his Kappa Delta dick sucked.

Me: Be sure to check her ID first.

Oakley: Yes Ma'am.

I waited a good minute then pestered him again.

Me: So anyways, what are you telling Dr. Haynes? Remember, I know where you sleep.

Oakley: You would be a terrible serial killer. Text messages can be subpoenaed by the courts, you know.

I scoffed.

Me: The FBI agent monitoring your phone is probably thrilled by all the dick pics you send. Also I'm impressed you can spell subpoenaed.

Oakley typed and deleted a few times, and I watched the chat bubbles flash dance across my screen. Shit. Maybe I took things too far.

Oakley: I'm going to tell him the truth.

Me: And what exactly is "the truth?"

I was not in the mood for his mind games or trickery. I'd saved his ass at that party.

Oakley: Are you sure you want to know?

Me: I would. That's why I'm asking. Are you high? They have mandatory drug testing next week.

Oakley: You're doing a good job, Solver.

I let out a sigh of relief. Did this mean that he was going to give a good report?

Me: Thanks, Problem

I didn't feel like walking all the way back to the condo since I had a class in less than two hours. So I headed over to a local coffee shop to start researching some volunteer ideas for Oakley. I ordered a small Americano. *Eleven calories, thank you!* And after finding a big cozy chair, I pulled out my laptop and broke out my mad Google skills. "Volunteer, Make a

Difference" was the first result. I clicked the link and scrolled through. Community outreach, Meals on Wheels, and fundraising. There was also a link for high school outreach. After what happened at the frat house, I just noped right on by that one.

There were opportunities at the animal shelter. Puppies were cute. But not really enough publicity there. Unless we made a calendar? I involuntarily pictured Oakley, firefighter style, shirtless and holding a sweet little puppy for May. Maybe I could get Dr. Haynes to volunteer to be Mr. June? Also shirtless, but with a kitten. Meow!

As I was talking myself *out* of adding the calendar to my list of ideas to send to Dr. Haynes, something caught my eye. Senior outreach. As in the elderly, not this year's graduating class. That would be perfect! Oakley could go to the senior center for one afternoon, play some board games, help serve a meal, and keep the residents company. I could arrange for a photographer and a blogger from the university, and everything could be wrapped up in only a couple of hours.

I put the senior center at the top of my list, along with packing meals for starving children and Habitat for Humanity. I typed out a quick message to Dr. Haynes, including how I was excited to hear feedback from his meeting with Oakley, and hit send. I glanced at my Fitbit, both to see the time and how many steps I had taken so far. I had time to power walk to the cafeteria to grab a salad and then make it to my next class.

9

"This place smells like urine and perfume," Oakley grumbled while I slapped a name tag onto his muscular chest. I smoothed the sticker a little bit more than I had to and blamed the lingering touch on my lack of sleep the night before. I had three papers due and a test in sports management. Even though most of my time was allocated to this internship, my other classes were kicking into full gear too.

"And you smell like Cheetos and boxed wine," I replied with an eye roll and pulled away. "How late were you out last night?"

"I figured you knew. Weren't you up late watching the GPS on my phone?" I could have slapped the teasing grin off his perfect face. But I didn't.

Instead, I rolled my eyes again. He wasn't wrong. I wasn't *trying* to intrusively break our rules about space and privacy. Dr. Haynes made it clear that I needed to respect his boundaries and work within the constraints of his lifestyle. We were meant to clean up messes, not completely prevent them from happening. We could guide and inform but not control our clients—just control how the public perceives them. But that didn't mean I wasn't *constantly* refreshing his social media to make sure a sex tape wasn't leaked. How Oakley Davis partied this hard while staying in pristine shape was seriously a mystery to me.

"You got home two hours ago and still managed to show up on time. I'd say I was impressed, but we both know I set four hundred alarms on your phone. Are you even sober?"

"I'm sober enough," he purred, licking his lips.

The photographer and blogger were both running late. I should have called them this morning, but I supposed not everyone shared my appreciation for punctuality. "They told us to visit with"—I checked the paper in my hand before continuing—"Cassandra Kitchen? Her late husband played professional football. I figured it would be good for you to chat with her. Apparently Albert Kitchen was well respected in the NFL."

"Wait," Oakley interrupted, jarring my eyes back to him. It really wasn't fair how good he looked for having so little sleep. It took me two hours to get ready this morning. "Albert Kitchen? As in the..." He started spouting a ton of stats and football jargon that I was not interested enough to listen to.

"I guess?"

His lips stretched into a wide smile. "Sweet! Meeting his wife will be really cool. Think she has any photos of him?"

It was kind of adorable to see him acting like a kid. He was positively giddy. This was exactly the type of moment I wanted the photographer to capture. Where was he? "Hold on just a second, I'm going to try and get a hold of the photographer," I told Oakley and pulled out my phone. I found the email chain with his information. Nick Bell. I clicked Nick's phone number, and it started ringing.

"Yeah?" Nick answered.

"Nick? This is Amanda Matthews, Oakley Davis's publicist. I'm at the retirement center with Oakley. What's your ETA?" I asked, sounding politely irritated. I didn't see why it was so hard for everybody else to take their jobs as seriously as I took mine.

"I'll be there in about fifteen minutes," Nick answered and then hung up. I didn't have to repeat the same process with the blogger, because she had magically arrived while I was on the phone with Nick and was now practically hanging off of Oakley. What the fuck, girl, have some professionalism. I was more bothered than I should have been, seeing her flirting with Oakley.

She was beautiful with long dark hair and bright green eyes; it wasn't a mystery why she had Oakley biting his bottom lip like a cat in heat. She wore a University of Texas tee shirt with cut off shorts and wedges. She was hot. I could appreciate a pretty girl. I hated how I instantly compared myself to her. It wasn't healthy. In fact, it was something the old Amanda would have done. I shook my head and approached them both.

"Hi, Sara. I'm Amanda Matthews, Oakley's publicist. It's nice to meet you." Intentionally called her the wrong name. Damn, when did I become a jealous, petty bitch? Double damn, when did I become jealous? I really needed to get my shit together. Green was not my color.

"It's Brooke," she corrected me with a sour expression on her face. Oakley smirked at me, apparently finding the whole thing pretty funny. I wanted to stomp on his foot but remembered that he had a game this weekend. You didn't need toes to run, did you?

Brooke turned her attention completely to Oakley. "I'm super excited to be working with you, Oakley! It's just sooo amazing that you spend your time volunteering," she chirped, her bubbly voice matching her appearance.

"Nick should be here in about ten minutes," I interjected. "Then we can go meet Mrs. Kitchen."

"Oakley, let's use those ten minutes to give me a chance to get to know you better. That way, I can really give readers an accurate portrayal of their football hero! And if ten minutes isn't enough, I would be more than happy to meet up later. Maybe over dinner?" Brooke looked hopefully at Oakley.

Good God, Brooke. Get your shit together. "Great idea, Brooke! There's a table right over here where we can sit and talk while we wait for Nick," I told her with a big smile. No way was I going to let her try and flirt her way into a late night meeting. I needed this article to be perfect. Brooke's lips pursed into an actual pout. Brooke and Oakley, who had still not said a single word since I walked over, both followed me silently over to a round table and sat down.

She slowly crossed her legs and bit on the edge of a pen she produced from her purse as we settled in the chairs opposite from her. I glared daggers at her as Oakley's leg brushed against mine. "So tell me, Oakley, what made you decide to work with this specific charity?"

Oakley leaned forward and rested one of his elbows on the table top. "Well," he began, "both of my grandparents passed away before I could meet them."

I turned to stare at him, surprised by these developments. I had all of my grandparents still and was incredibly close to them. I couldn't imagine a childhood without Nana and Grandpa Dude—yes, his name was actually Grandpa Dude. "I guess you could say I just like the idea of seeing what I'm missing out on. I never got homemade cookies or twenty dollar bills snuck into my palm."

Brooke grinned like Oakley was the sweetest thing since cotton candy, and if I weren't completely charmed, I would have been rolling my eyes. "And who are you chatting with today?"

Oakley froze and reached out to grab my knee. I wasn't surprised that he'd already forgotten her name. "Cassandra Kitchen, wife of Hall of Fame recipient, Albert Kitchen!" I interjected on his behalf. "I think it'll be a really fun experience for everyone." Oakley squeezed my leg in appreciation and drifted his fingers teasingly toward my inner thigh. My breath hitched at the heated contact. What the actual fuck was he doing? I kept waiting for him to move his hand, but he didn't.

"And what do you have planned with Cassandra?"

"We're going to watch some old football footage," Oakley replied, running his middle finger along the inseam of my jeans. I chewed on my bottom lip to stop from screaming at him. "I thought she might like that."

Thought who might like what?

Brooke smiled with dreamy eyes that made me want to push away the table and show off Oakley's hand. He was like, maybe *three* inches from nature's Rubik's Cube. Maybe closer. Maybe I had no idea why I was suddenly obsessed with his fucking large ass hands. Why was he touching me?

I reached under the table and shoved him away, making his body jerk. The asshole covered his laugh with a cough, then brought his full attention back to Brooke, the pen biter. She hadn't even noticed; she was too busy tracing the lines of her collarbone and giving him a bedroom stare.

"Are you excited about the upcoming game this weekend?" she asked.

I turned to look at Oakley. His face turned serious, and he immediately threaded his hands together on the table top. It was the most intense I'd seen him since we'd met. "I think we have a solid team this year. We're bringing our all to practice, and I'm really looking forward to seeing that hard work in a game scenario. I think we are stronger than ever and ready to bring a championship home."

Brooke quickly jotted down notes. His answer was good. Encouraging. Everything that a publicist would want to hear. I was mentally high-fiving myself and playing out the scene where Coach was telling me how amazing I am and that he's sorry he was ever rude to me.

My phone buzzed, and I looked down to see a message from Nick.

Nick: Here

Some people might be put off by Nick's style, but I actually appreciated it. Short and to the point, no flowery chitchat to try and decipher. He walked through the door of the facility, and I immediately recognized him because of all the camera equipment he was carrying. I waved Nick over to the table and made all of the introductions.

"Hi, Nick, it's nice to meet you. I'm Amanda, and this is Oakley." Brooke glared at me until I added brightly, "And this is Brooke, the blogger who will be writing up the piece on Oakley." I really needed to get my head out of my ass and start being more professional. I didn't need to build a reputation of being difficult to work with. I silently vowed that from here on out, I was going to be super nice to Brooke.

"Is everybody ready to head over to our first meeting?" I asked. I looked at Nick and asked him if he could have his camera ready to take a couple of candid shots of Oakley meeting Cassandra Kitchen. I checked the packet and found the room number. After looking at the map, I started to lead the others down a hallway to the right. Nick took his camera out and started fiddling with it as we walked. I guess he was checking the lighting or exposure or something. I didn't really know anything about photography except that, to hide a double chin when taking a selfie, you were supposed to hold your phone up above your head. Nick would occasionally stop and look through the lens as we navigated the maze of hallways to get to Mrs. Kitchen's room. When we got to the right door, Nick checked a couple more things and said he was ready.

I told Oakley and Nick to go ahead of me and Brooke so that Nick could get some quick shots. Oakley knocked on the door, slowly opened it and said, "Hi, Mrs. Kitchen. I'm Oakley." He started to walk through the door, and I heard Nick's shutter click before hearing both of them scream, "OH MY GOD!"

My heart pounded, and I was instantly on high alert. The door was open, and both Nick and Oakley stood dumbfounded in the threshold. In the two seconds it took me to reach the entry to her room, I had convinced myself that the guys had just walked in to find Cassandra unresponsive and I was going to have to do mouth-to-mouth. We were at a nursing home, after all. I braced my hand on Oakley's back and shoved at him, trying to make my way through the door to assess the issues when moans filtered through to my ear.

What the fuck? Was she choking? Why was no one moving? Oakley's feet were like deep roots in the ground. "Move!" I yelled.

My voice seemed to shock both Oakley and Nick, because they started scrambling to get out of the way. It was like roaches were climbing up their backs with the way they were cringing. Nick's long, lanky limbs curled as he gagged and pushed Brooke to the side. Oakley started nervously laughing and shaking his head as he exited. A worn voice yelled, "Shut the door!"

I should have connected the dots. I should have known to run like hell. But I'm a stupid bitch.

I waltzed through the door like I was a fucking nursing major and not a publicist. And what I saw was the most intricate threesome I've ever seen in my entire life. Wrinkles on wrinkles on wrinkles. Cassandra wore leopard print lingerie and was currently being spit roasted by one man with hair growing out of his oversized ears and another man with dark skin and gray hair. Her mouth was full, so she couldn't tell me to get out. But I saw the fire in her eyes.

The two men bludgeoning the flaps started shouting.

"Get outta here!" the man with large ears grumbled. He sounded seriously out of breath.

"I'm not wasting the Viagra, John. You know they ration this shit out," the other said to his friend.

I threw my hands up to block the view. "I'm so sorry," I shouted while walking backward.

"Finally!" the man with large ears shouted.

The back of my foot hit a dip in the carpet, and I started falling backward. Two strong hands wrapped around me, pulling me to a hard chest to break my fall. I opened my eyes and let out a breathless thank-you when I saw Oakley holding me up.

He smiled as Brooke slammed the door to Cassandra's room shut. "Well, Solver," he grumbled, hovering his lips over my ears to whisper, "I think our first community service is going well, hmm?"

10

I was stress cleaning. Tomorrow, the article about our time at the nursing home was scheduled to be published, and I couldn't sleep; instead, I was scrubbing the bathtub at eleven o'clock at night. I couldn't get the image of Cassandra in gland-to-gland combat with the cast of *Grumpy Old Men* out of my head. Just thinking about it made me both cringe with embarrassment and want to bleach my eyes.

I took it out on my bathtub instead. I'm pretty sure I scrubbed until the enamel was coming off. Brooke wouldn't let me read what she was submitting, and not having control of the situation was driving me crazier than Britney Spears circa 2007. The "meeting" with Cassandra was definitely a shit show, but I think we managed to recover the rest of our time there.

Apparently, nobody told Cassandra we were coming, which explained why we walked in on her, well, *cumming*. She reached out that night to apologize and offered to reschedule, but I didn't think that I could ever look her in the eye again. I politely told her I would check our schedules and get back to her.

I finally took pity on my poor bathtub, rinsed it out, and hung up my teal rubber gloves for the night. I crawled into bed and was able to settle down after reminding myself that Nick got some great pictures of Oakley eating dinner and laughing with a woman named Ruth who completely embodied the word *grandma*. And surprisingly, Oakley bounced back from the incident rather quickly. He really shined with all of the residents and looked like he was enjoying himself. Brooke, however, looked a little pale the rest of the afternoon. Even though she didn't really care for me and I may have indirectly scarred her for life, I didn't think she would write something about Oakley that might affect his willingness to sleep with her. So at least I had that going for me.

My phone rang, and I quickly answered it, forgetting to check the caller ID. "Amanda Matthews," Coach Howard's booming voice said. Why was he calling me so late at night?

I pulled the phone away from my ear with a wince. "Hey, Coach. How are you?"

"Not so good, actually," he grumbled. Shit. Did Brooke release the article already? Was it bad? I was mentally doing damage control when he continued. "I need you to come with us to Oklahoma, Miss Matthews."

Oklahoma? All I knew about Oklahoma was that it was where that crazy Tiger King dude lived. I watched that show and made a decision to never go there. "Why?"

"We play Oklahoma University this upcoming weekend. Last time we went on a trip, Oakley slept with the head cheerleader from the opposing team and caused quite a social media stink."

"Why? It's not the first time he's slept with someone from the opposing school."

"No. But it's the first time that the head cheerleader was engaged to the quarterback, and photos of them...doing things...were leaked." I let out a sigh but welcomed the reminder that Oakley wasn't a good guy. It was easy to forget when he looked like a fucking Greek god. "If we could avoid any scandals, I think it'll boost ticket sales for our first home game."

I closed my eyes and let out a slow breath of air. I didn't want to go to fucking Oklahoma. And I definitely didn't want to spend my weekend watching Oakley chase pussy. "I don't know—"

"Dr. Haynes reached out to me this morning," Coach Howard interrupted me. I knew with complete certainty that this was the beginning of a threat. My grade was still very much in his hands, and if I didn't go, I just knew the report would be bad.

"Send me the information, and I'll be there," I replied.

I WAS SITTING at a table at the Jason's Deli at George Bush International during my hour layover. I opted to pay the one hundred and fifty-six dollars to fly to Oklahoma City instead of taking the bus full of loud, rambunctious football players. Having a little distance from Oakley also gave me the chance to plan for how I was going to keep him out of trouble.

I have never been to an away game. Actually, I had never even been to a home game either, so I really didn't know what to expect. I was hoping that this was going to be one of those situations where what I was imagining was way worse than reality. That the guys were going to be so tired from traveling, practicing, and playing that they would all just go straight to the hotel and go to sleep like giant, super muscular angels.

Oh, who the fuck was I kidding? Oakley was no angel, and after hearing the coach talk, I was starting to realize that this weekend might be my biggest challenge so far. I sighed and pulled out my phone to look up the itinerary for the weekend. Today was dedicated mostly to travel and getting settled into the hotel. Later tonight, there was a dinner planned for the team that I wondered if I could get out of since I knew Coach Howard would be there. Friday was a team breakfast, workout, practice, team lunch, a small block of free time, and then the game was that night. Saturday consisted of breakfast, and then the team would leave by bus, and I would head to the airport a little before noon.

I punched everything into my shared calendar with Oakley and finished up my fruit and yogurt parfait just as they started to call my flight. I was looking forward to the last little bit of time to myself, as I wasn't planning on leaving Oakley's ass alone for a single second. If the coach wasn't going to be there, I was. I even managed to get the hotel to give me the room right across from Oakley's.

As I waited for them to call my boarding group, my phone started ringing. I checked the caller ID and smiled while answering. "Mom," I greeted. "Any bodies to bury this weekend?"

"Where are you flying to?" she asked. "I saw a charge on your credit card." Her voice was a bit shaky and nervous. I couldn't blame her. We hadn't really had that much of a chance to talk over the last two weeks, and spontaneous activities were what landed me in Texas in the first place.

"I'm going to an away game in Oklahoma," I explained, my nose involuntarily wrinkling at the statement. I was certain that there was nothing wrong with the small state just north of Texas. I just honestly had zero desire to go there.

"A game? As in sinfully tight football pants, rah-rah, go team?" I laughed at her description.

"As in, I'm going to be making sure my new client doesn't

fuck anyone important or get drunk and end up in a bar brawl."

"I've seen photos of your client, Amanda, maybe you should keep him entertained in your room. They didn't make 'em like that when I was your age." She giggled nervously, and I tried not to imagine my mother lusting over Oakley's Instagram feed.

The airport called another group, and I grabbed the handle of my carry-on, then headed toward the gate. "Just be careful, okay? I'm so proud of you for taking what you were given and working with it. I just don't want you to backslide..."

I scrubbed my free hand down my face. "I haven't touched alcohol since that night, Mom."

She sighed, like that wasn't what she wanted to hear. "I just wish you weren't all or nothing. You never could have just one drink. Just one scoop of ice cream. Just one boyfriend..." I cringed. "And now you're in the nothing cycle. No fun. No freedom. No food..."

Her voice trailed off. If she thought I was about to admit that I was obsessively counting my calories, then she was losing her touch. I knew it would trigger a demand for me to come home. She wasn't wrong, I had an excessive personality. And if I couldn't have it all, then I wanted nothing. There was no happy medium.

"Look, I'm boarding the flight, so I gotta go," I said. "Love you. Byeee." I hung up the phone before she could complain anymore.

I had a football player to babysit.

Three hours later, I was sitting behind the wheel of my white rental car. Oklahoma University was just far enough that it made more sense for me to rent a car than to Uber. I punched the address to the Best Western into my maps and started the hour-long drive. I had never stayed in a Best

Western, and if I weren't such a dedicated publicist, I would have booked the nearby Hilton instead. But the team booked their rooms through their travel agency at a killer rate. I didn't have to stay at the same hotel as the team; Coach Howard had told me I could stay wherever I liked and the university would reimburse me up to the same rate the team was paying for their rooms. However, staying at the Hilton wouldn't allow me to keep a twenty-four-hour watch on Oakley. So Best Western it was.

I pulled into the parking lot, grabbed all my stuff, and started to head inside. I didn't see the team bus, which meant I could grab a quick shower before having to see anybody I knew. I felt super gross from the two planes and a long car ride. The guy behind the counter was very tall, and his name tag said Brian. He looked disinterested in his job and kind of annoyed that I walked in and interrupted whatever he was doing on his phone. He was probably watching Daddy porn.

"Hi. I'm Amanda Matthews, checking in!" I said cheerfully. "I called earlier and requested to be across from Oakley Davis."

"License and credit card," Brian replied.

I handed them over and smiled, determined to kill him with kindness. I've learned from all of my traveling that the people at the front desk had a lot of power over how your stay was going to go. Brian handed my license and credit card back to me along with my key cards.

"I just want to confirm that my room is next to Oakley Davis's."

"Sorry, ma'am, I'm not allowed to give out that information," Brian said lazily.

I was starting to get frustrated but didn't want to be a Karen and ask for the manager. I smiled and tried one more time. "I totally get it. But I'm his publicist. I'm traveling with the team and need to have my room either adjoining or across from his. I'm sure you'll see it in the notes if you look. His last name is Davis. First name Oakley."

"Wow, Amanda," I heard a familiar voice behind me say. "I knew you couldn't bear to be apart from me, but now you're bullying poor Brian here?" I turned around to see Oakley trying to stifle a laugh.

I held my breath and braced myself for his annoying push back. The moment I felt his heat at my side and breathed in his woodsy cologne, my second heartbeat reminded me that it had been a few months since I'd been laid. "Hello, Mr. Davis," I replied, trying to keep a sense of professionalism.

"Sorry about her attitude, Brian. Sometimes she takes our little games a bit *too* far," Oakley replied as he wrapped his arm around me. I almost shrugged him off, but I was curious to see where he was going with this and admittedly liked the feel of his muscular arm pulling me closer.

"My girl and I like to role play, and this weekend, she's my...*publicist*," Oakley explained with a wink and one-handed finger quotes. "The tension has been building up, ya know? I think after the big game, we will finally—"

"Continue that statement and I'll give you a groin injury," I interrupted.

"Fuckkk," Oakley playfully rasped. Poor Brian just looked at us with a confused expression. "I love when you talk dirty to me, babe."

He leaned in and chuckled against my neck. Fucking asshole. Just as I pulled away, Oakley addressed Brian once more. "No need to give us separate rooms. She really wants to keep an eye on me, and I think the best way to do that is to put us in the same room. Don't you think, babe?"

Oakley winked at me, and I could have slapped that smirk off his face. I knew this was a challenge. He wanted to see if I'd call his bluff and disappear to another room. Fuck that. If he wanted to share a room, then by golly, we were gonna share.

"Sounds good, schnookums," I replied, poking at his side and turning to Brian. "He loves that nickname. I can't wait to wake up in your arms at five a.m. tomorrow."

11

I was lying in a bed with Oakley Davis. I couldn't sleep. My eyes refused to shut.

And I had to fart.

I peeked over the pillow barrier I had built between us and was fairly certain Oakley was asleep—like ninety-three percent sure. I was kicking myself for letting him goad me into sharing a room with him. On top of not being able to fart, walk around without makeup, or wear my ratty-ass, comfortable-as-hell, stained sweatpants, I could only imagine what the coach was going to say when he found out.

I was contemplating getting up to go to the bathroom to fart while running some water when Oakley let out a snore. I had forgotten that he snored. It was really soft, and I found it soothing. It reminded me of my childhood dog, a pug named Charlie. She slept with me until the day I left for college. Listening to Oakley snore and thinking about Charlie relaxed me enough to snuggle down into the bed and let out a, thankfully quiet, toot. A little air poof.

I went back to worrying about what Coach Howard was going to say, and then pictured what sexual harassment webinar Dr. Haynes would make me take, because if the coach knew, he was for sure going to tell my mentor. I was pretty sure that sleeping in the same bed as your client would violate all kinds of ethical boundaries. Even if it was *his* idea —especially if it was his idea.

I rubbed my temples, trying to release some of the tension, and realized that the snoring had stopped. I turned to look in Oakley's direction again and found him staring back at me with half open eyes. We just stared at each other for a few moments, then Oakley broke the silence. "Hey, Solver. What are you doing up? Am I just too sexy for you to sleep?" he asked, his voice groggy.

"No," I replied. "I'm just not a very good sleeper. Go back to sleep, we have a super busy day tomorrow. Well, today. I'm going back to sleep too," I said softly, hoping to convince him to go back to sleep. I rolled over on my side and stayed perfectly still with my eyes closed.

"You know what I think?" he asked. "I think you're hungry. You barely touched dinner."

I opened my eyes and gnawed on my lip. He wasn't wrong. I was surprised he'd even noticed. That stupidly persistent rumble in my stomach was getting impossible to ignore. It was easy to focus on other things when I was managing Oakley's schedule and focusing on my senior coursework. But late at night, it was harder to pretend the emptiness in my stomach wasn't bothering me.

"I think you should mind your own business," I growled, tucking the blanket under my chin. I felt the mattress shift, and Oakley got out of bed. I squeezed my eyes shut when I heard him padding across the carpet. What the hell was he doing?

Heat traveled over my body, and when I popped my eyes open, I was met with his dark stare. "Hey there, Solver. How about you eat a protein bar?" he asked with a smirk, then slowly unwrapped the high-calorie protein treat. I watched his slow hands unveil a dark chocolate granola goodness that had the ability to make me horny for food.

"Did you just moan?" Oakley asked.

"Uh, no. Who does that, that would be weird," I lied. I totally moaned. Oakley brought the granola bar almost to my lips and hovered. The chocolate was just an inch away, wrapped up in his fingers. There was the tiniest bit of chocolate that started to melt on his index finger, and I imagined licking it off. I moaned again. Oh shit. I coughed to try to cover it up.

"Get that out of my face; I don't even like chocolate," I told him as I pushed away his hand. I don't think I was super convincing since people who don't actually like chocolate don't stare longingly at it.

Instead of moving away, Oakley chuckled to himself and launched his big, hard body onto the bed, straddling me above the covers. "What the fuck, Oakley?" I groaned.

"Just a little bite won't hurt, Solver," he joked, leaning over with the granola bar.

"This is ridiculous, Problem," I growled.

"If it's so ridiculous, then you won't have a problem eating a small bite." Oakley's breath feathered over my skin, and he rubbed the chocolate down my cheek and onto my neck.

"Wh-what are you doing?" I asked.

"All this talk is making me hungry. Can't let this go to waste." Then, Oakley's flat, wet, hot tongue drew a trail of heat down my neck. "Mmm," he moaned against my thudding pulse. "Chocolate."

All of my muscles tensed up, begging for more. My body reacted instinctively to the feeling of Oakley's tongue on my neck. I couldn't move or speak, I just lay there wanting to feel Oakley on my skin again.

I came back to my senses when Oakley let out a laugh, staring down at me with a twinkle in his eye. He had seriously beautiful eyes, and there was no doubt that the asshole was definitely enjoying teasing me. I tried to play it cool, but I think it took me just long enough to recover for Oakley to see what his touch did to me. *Come on, Amanda, shake it off,* I thought to myself as he put the bar back up to my lips. The chocolate was barely touching, so soft I wouldn't have known it was there if I weren't looking at it.

Oakley asked suggestively in a soft, low voice, "Are you sure you don't want just a *taste*?"

I don't know what possessed me to nip at Oakley like a crazed chihuahua, but one second he was teasing me with food, and the next I was sinking my teeth into his wrist and growling like I had rabies. "What the fuck!" he yelled. I let go and shoved him off of me. The hard sound of his body hitting the ground made me cackle in amusement. "Ouch! My arm! You broke my arm!"

I shoved the blankets off of me and sunk to the floor, my humor completely gone. We had a fucking game tomorrow. He couldn't play with a fucking broken arm. "Oh my God, oh my God, oh my God."

His arms shot out like a snake about to strike, wrapping around my middle and tugging me down to the hard hotel carpet that probably hadn't been properly shampooed in years. Was I lying in dried cum? Probably. Was Oakley still holding me? Absolutely.

"What are you doing?" I asked, squirming away. The sleep shirt I wore was rising up, up, and up. The edge of my sports bra was showing, and pretty soon I'd be mewing like a kitten.

"You sure are a feisty little thing," he said in a low voice, licking his lips.

I shuddered involuntarily, thinking about his tongue on my magic skin ball. "You are such a jerk!" I tried to say as offhandedly as I could. "I thought I was going to have to explain to the coach how your arm got broken and exactly what I was doing in your room in the middle of the night." I tried to redirect, although the wetness in my panties wasn't quite ready to move on.

"Explain what?" he asked innocently. "What *exactly* do you think is going on here?" His devilish smile sent a new wave of heat down my body.

I absentmindedly pulled on my sleep shirt to make sure I was covered. It was a habit I kept from when I was forty pounds heavier and about one thousand times more uncomfortable in my own skin. Oakley's eyes followed my hands to my thighs as my fingers played with the hem of my oversized Backstreet Boys tee shirt.

Oakley's expression changed from playful to pure lust. Oh God. What panties had I put on before bed? I couldn't even remember. I prayed to the god of girls who haven't been laid in months that it wasn't pink robots. "Backstreet Boys, hmm?"

"They were ahead of their time," I replied.

He stared at my lips for a long moment. I felt my mouth grow dry. "Solver," he whispered, placing his hand over mine. His long fingers splayed over my thigh.

"Y-yes?"

"I have a proposition for you."

I squinted in scrutiny as his thumb massaged my skin distractedly. "I have a big game tomorrow. I'll need my energy. I'll eat whatever you eat."

"That's ridiculous. You'll need lots of protein. Like at a minimum of thirty-five hundred calories," I sputtered, pulling away. My stomach growled at the mention of it.

"Exactly. I guess you'll have to eat something if you want me to have enough energy for tomorrow," he said with a smile.

"You're bluffing," I countered.

"I don't bluff."

My mind was racing, all thoughts of sexy time vanished. I did a quick round of math in my head. Burning one pound of fat was the equivalent of three-thousand five hundred calories. I typically ate around one thousand calories per day, which meant I would have to take in an extra twenty-five hundred calories. In. One. Day. I felt dizzy just at the thought of all that extra food. But I could fast for one day and then reduce my caloric intake by two hundred and fifty calories for the two days after that. That would undo the damage to my waistline, and since I was going home separately, Oakley would never know that I was fasting.

"Fine," I said with determination. "You're on." I grabbed the protein bar out of his hand and wolfed it down, not even stopping to savor the two hundred calories. I was one hella dedicated publicist. He smiled as I swallowed. "Delicious," I growled once my mouth was empty.

Oakley stared at my mouth and practically purred. "Yeah," he began, licking his lips. "Delicious."

12

I packed the wrong outfit for the game. I tried to go for a casually professional look. Sleek, long jeans clung to my legs, and the cream button-down shirt was in line with the university's school colors of orange and white.

But it was hotter than the devil's sweaty ass crack. I had lines of moisture trailing down my spine, and I stupidly left a hair tie at the hotel. I felt bloated from all the food I had to eat in order for Oakley to have enough energy for today's game, and the humidity in the air tasted like evaporated beer.

"Yaaaaaaas!!" a girl next to me screamed. She kept bumping into me every time she cheered, knocking her hard lemonade onto me. I was annoyed by her shrieks but envied her short outfit. Unlike me, she paired a cute orange sports bra with short cut-off shorts and flip-flops. If I didn't think it would ruin Oakley's reputation, I'd strip down to my panties and air out my pits.

How long were football games, anyway? There were four quarters that were fifteen minutes each, so like an hour? I could literally feel the makeup melting off my face. The one time I actually made an effort to look nice. Figured.

I had no idea what was happening on the field. They were passing, dribbling, or defending pretty fiercely though. I started thinking about things I could say that wouldn't make me sound like a complete asshat if someone asked me about the game. "They sure did a good job of moving the ball from one side of the field to the other!" and "They played with a lot of heart!" both sounded pretty lame. I started writing down some things that the announcer said so I could memorize them and sound like I knew what I was talking about.

Perky orange sports bra bumped into me again and slurred in my general direction, "Like, what are you even doing?" she asked while nodding at my notepad.

"I don't really know much about football, but I'm here to support one of the players," I replied.

"I can help!" she said enthusiastically. "I totally know about football!" I instantly felt a strong *Sisterhood of the Traveling Pants* connection with sports bra girl.

"So you see the dude with dreads peeking out of his helmet?" she asked while pointing toward the field. I vaguely recognized who she was indicating and nodded. "He's sleeping with my roommate and has an eight-inch dick."

I wasn't sure what this had to do with football, but call me intrigued.

"Oh really?" I asked.

"Yep. He's the quarterback. Basically when the ball goes there, we score."

I made a mental note. Score = Good.

"And do you see that dude right there?" she asked, waving her skinny index finger in Oakley's direction.

"Yep," I replied with a swallow.

"He eats ass like nobody's business." Sports bra held her dainty hand up to her mouth and giggled. "I mean, seriously. I didn't think I liked rim jobs, but—"

"So what position does he play?" I asked, derailing that train of thought. I did not want to hear how well my client ate ass. Nope. Not happening.

She looked at the sky with her pretty face twisted up in confusion. "I don't know. Running man? Run run run... Okay, so maybe I don't know much about football..."

You think? I wanted to say. I didn't know this chick, but for some reason I couldn't get the image of Oakley sticking his tongue up her asshole out of my head. I bet she bleached it. She probably had a pearly white speckled starfish of an ass. I didn't even know what mine looked like, nor did I want to.

"I just know he excels in *every* position," she giggled and then began jumping up and down.

"Every position?" I asked. Why I was goading her was beyond me. Color me curious.

She looked me dead in the eye and said, "He does this thing with his tongue that I had never even heard of. Like not even in porn!"

That was super descriptive. *What! What does he do with his tongue?!* I was dying to ask. But I also knew that I didn't want to be a part of this conversation anymore, especially if I ever wanted to be able to talk to Oakley again without picturing his tongue doing things to places that they don't even show on Pornhub. My mind wandered back to the hotel room and Oakley licking the melted chocolate off my neck.

I cleared my throat and stood up. "I, uh...I have to go to the bathroom. See ya!" I told her as I started walking away. I took one final look at her, then headed up the stairs and saw her flicking her tongue at me between her fingers. I felt a weird pang of jealousy, and my petty-ass self thought, "I bet she has fluffy pepperoni nipples," while I walked off.

Oh my lanta.

My first game was definitely interesting.

I WAS WAITING outside the locker room with the press and fangirls when the game ended. We won. Yada yada. I think Oakley scored the winning touchdown, or at least that's what I overheard from one of the reporters. I wasn't the type to pretend to like a sport for the sake of a guy or even my career. This wasn't in my vein of expertise.

The locker room door opened, and a guard stood at the door, checking press badges and his clipboard for letting people inside. I wasn't really wanting to go into a locker room that probably smelled like the seventh layer of body odor hell, but I also didn't want Oakley fucking up any interviews, and with the way the reporters were circling, I bet they had a few questions to ask.

"Name," the burly guard-dog-looking man asked. This dude looked like his spirit animal was a cross between a German shepherd and a sloth. His movements were slow, but his teeth looked impossibly sharp.

"Amanda Matthews, I'm Oakley Davis's publicist."

He didn't even look down at his clipboard. "Not on the list."

I knew for a fucking fact that Coach Howard put me on the list. "Check again," I said, annoyed, feeling my inner Karen dying to come out and ask for the manager.

He looked at me like my spirit animal was a shrew. "I don't have to. Oakley Davis doesn't *have* a publicist," he emphasized.

It took all of my self-control to not roll my eyes at Sid the Sloth, and I forced my face into a smile. I started to explain that I had been hired a few weeks earlier and that Coach Howard had asked me to come along to keep Oakley squeaky clean. Oakley's ears must have been burning or he just heard me trying not to screech, because he walked up and put his arm around my shoulders.

"It's okay, she's with me," he told Sid. He squeezed my shoulder and started to guide me into the locker room as Sid scowled at me.

I looked over my shoulder and smiled sweetly at the guard while calling out in a sing-song voice, "Thanks so much for your help!" Something told me I would not be seeing Sid pop up as a friend request later.

"Making friends?" Oakley asked with a grin.

"Winning games?" I replied with a wink. I absolutely refused to acknowledge the fact that he was shirtless and only wearing his football pants. I couldn't tell if it was the strategically placed padding beneath the spandex or just his overall physique that had his ass looking the way it did, but either way, it was distracting.

"I scored the winning touchdown!" he said, poking me in the side.

"Yay!" I replied enthusiastically. As his publicist, I was excited. As a girl that seriously needed to learn more about the game, I was barely enthusiastic.

Around the locker room, half-naked guys were chatting excitedly and talking to reporters. It smelled like sweaty socks and middle school body spray. "Oakley, can I ask you a few questions?" a reporter called. I turned to look at the man and the microphone he held in Oakley's face. Damn, dude. Personal space much?

Oakley smiled and nodded. "Sure, Mike. You know I always have time for the school newspaper."

Mike beamed at him. He was a tall dude with long black hair that curled at the ends.

"I haven't heard much about your extracurricular activities these days, Oakley," Mike said with an exaggerated wink. "What have you been up to?"

I rolled my eyes so hard I think I hurt myself. Oh good, Mike wasn't wasting any time getting into the things I really didn't want Oakley talking about or the media focusing on. I shot Oakley a stern look that I hoped said, *if you mention anything unsavory, I will fucking kill you in your sleep...in the bed we just so happen to be sharing for now.*

To Oakley's credit, he flashed Mike a winning smile and gave the most perfect answer I could have asked for. "I have been working extra hard at practices, squeezing in extra workouts, and picking Coach Howard's brain for feedback. I think it really paid off in my performance tonight."

Yes! I was mentally fist bumping myself. I am such an amazing publicist. I didn't even have to steal the microphone from Mike's boney fingers. "Really? So the rumors about you sleeping with the university president's daughter?"

Oakley smirked. "You mean Becky Smith? I would rather have my left nut slammed in a car door—that's off the record, of course. I'm sure she's a nice gal, but I'm too focused on my football and scholastic career to have time for anyone else. And she's too territorial for me."

I cringed. Not the best thing to say about the university president's daughter, but it was too late now. I spoke up. "Don't forget your volunteer hours."

Mike turned to me and pressed the microphone against my lips. Again, there was no concern for personal space. Disgusting. I pressed it away with the tips of my fingers. "And who are you?"

"I'm Oakley's publicist. And he doesn't have time to date because, when he's not studying or practicing, he's volunteering at a local nursing home. Oakley is extremely dedicated to giving back to the community."

Mike looked back at Oakley with an expression laced with surprise.

"I'm hurt that you look so shocked, Mike," Oakley said

playfully. "It just so happens that I got to know Cassandra Kitchen really well."

I cringed at his mention of that shit show but then reminded myself that absolutely nobody outside of the seven people who were there knew about us getting to know Mrs. Kitchen that day.

Mike followed up with, "One last question for you before I let you go. What is your favorite part about volunteering?"

"Aside from the great publicity and not being murdered by my publicist?" Oakley joked. "I really enjoyed just being able to connect with the residents. They all have such fantastic stories about their kids and grandkids. Getting to be a part of their family for even just an afternoon was actually really special."

He did it. Oakley had a good interview. "Thank you for your time, Oakley. I'll be sure to do a good write-up."

"You always do, buddy," Oakley replied, patting him on the back. The minute Mike was out of earshot, Oakley mumbled under his breath, "That guy annoys the hell out of me."

"You did good," I replied. Oakley was like a puppy; I just had to reward his good behavior.

"Well, you kind of terrify me…" he confessed, wiping his face with a towel. "I didn't want you to pinch my nipples if I said anything wrong."

"Pinch your nipples?"

"You look like the nipple-pinching type," Oakley teased while covering his pecs.

"I don't even know what that means, but if it's a punishment that keeps you in line, then yes, I'll pinch your nipples clear off."

A few other reporters wanted an interview, and Oakley navigated their questions with ease. Unlike Mike, most of them were professional and kept to questions about his skills on the field.

After the last interviewer finished up, Oakley told me he was going to hit the showers and sauntered off, taking a moment to call over his shoulder, "Don't think about me in the shower," and then blew me a kiss.

"Don't worry, I won't," I replied and stuck my tongue out. Just kidding, I was totally going to be thinking about him in the shower. I was already envisioning the water and soap running down his chiseled abs and further down to the happiest of trails.

I walked over to a set of benches in front of the lockers and used my foot to move a jock strap that was lying a little too close for comfort on the floor. I pulled out my phone to catch up on Oakley's social media, and I was pleased to find that there wasn't a single picture of a bleached blonde wearing eyeliner and a crop top with #iwokeuplikethis on his news stream. I heard the shower turn on, and Oakley started belting "Milkshake" by Kelis. I giggled and went back to my phone, secretly loving his confidence, not that I would ever admit that.

I was checking up on the dumpster fire of the internet—Twitter—when he stepped out of the showers with what was quite possibly the world's tiniest towel wrapped around his waist. There were a few other players casually loitering, but my eyes were stuck on him. "Get dressed," I ordered, dragging my reluctant eyes back to my phone.

"I packed my party clothes!" he hollered, making the other dweebs dancing around the locker room hoot in agreement. Party clothes? Uh. No.

I snapped my eyes back up just in time to see Oakley Davis drop his towel. Sweet mother of our lord and savior, Meryl Streep. Seeing Oakley's cock online versus seeing it in person was a completely different thing. It was a spiritual experience. It was like I left my body and was looking down upon the world with my lady garage open and ready for his bus of a dick to park itself right up in there.

I was so engrossed in thinking about how I was going to sleep next to Oakley that night, knowing exactly what he was packing on his side of the bed, that I practically jumped out of my skin when he came up beside me and put his hand on my shoulder. "Hey there, Solver. You looked pretty deep in thought. Everything ok?"

I nodded my head and stammered, willing my coochie to calm the fuck down. "Yeah, all good. How many parties are you going to make me follow you to tonight?" I asked, already dreading the answer. I was already hot and sweaty from the game, which by the way took three hours and thirteen minutes. Fifteen minute quarters, my ass. My makeup had melted into a swirling cakey mess, and I could smell myself. All I wanted to do was take a shower and change into pajamas.

He was already in boxers and was shrugging on his pants while staring at me, his head cocked to the side. "I was thinking we'd start off bar hopping at a couple of local hot spots," he began, crouching lower to look me in the eye from where I was sitting. I internally cringed. "Then, we could hit up a couple frat parties. They're all on the same block, so it's easy to get to."

I could already feel the blisters on my feet. I hadn't worn comfortable shoes today. "Sounds great," I forced out. I didn't want Oakley to go off partying, but we made a deal. I wouldn't cramp his style if he let me do my job. I was going to do my best to not annoy him.

"And then," Oakley continued, reaching out to tuck a strand of blonde hair behind my ear. "I can find some hot piece to bring home. Would you mind sleeping in the lobby? I shouldn't be more than a couple of hours."

Nope. I drew the line there. I opened my mouth to protest, but Oakley burst out laughing, interrupting me. "I'm kidding, Solver. Let's go back to the hotel and grab some take-out. I just want to eat and sleep. I'm fucking sore."

I let out a sigh of relief just as Dale exited the showers buck naked.

Oh. Em. Gee. I looked away quickly. Oakley threw Dale a towel. "Come on, man, Amanda's here. Cover up." Funny how Oakley suddenly cared about nudity.

"Did I just hear you say that you're not coming out tonight? After your big victory, you're not even going to celebrate? I *know* that's not what I just heard," Dale said as he wrapped the towel around himself loosely.

Damn, I was so close to being able to go back to the hotel and lie down. I hated Dale. I was busy cursing him for ever being born when Oakley replied, "Yeah man, I'm just going to go back to the hotel with a super hot girl. You're right, I'm totally not celebrating at all."

My first takeaway was that we were still going back to the hotel and I could take off these godforsaken shoes. That was followed very closely by the fact that Oakley said I was super hot. Did he really think that? Or was he just saying that to get Dale off his back? Fortunately, I had the entire walk back to the hotel to obsess about it.

13

Oakley ate like he was a man on death row enjoying his last meal. He devoured. He didn't care that he had spaghetti sauce all over his face and dripping down his chin. He didn't care that he chewed with his mouth open. He definitely didn't care that I was staring wide-eyed and terrified at his sloppy mouth opening and closing. It was nice to know his hotness wasn't limitless. He did have his faults; aside from being a huge partier, he was the world's messiest eater.

"You better eat up," he commanded while nodding at my salad plate. Now that the game was over, our agreement was off. He burned a lot of calories at the game and needed to refuel. It would be physically impossible for me to keep up.

"Just because I don't devour my meals like a rabid animal doesn't mean I won't eat…"

He took another messy bite with a snort. I nearly gagged. We were both sitting in our pajamas at the small two-person table in our hotel room. I was comfortable, and my face was makeup free. I'd showered as we waited for our food to arrive and was happy to wash the sweaty Oklahoma humidity out of my hair. I probably should have cared that I looked like a drowned rat right now, but I couldn't bring myself to care. I was too freaking tired.

"My sister used to say that," Oakley laughed. He then wiped his mouth with his napkin. Oakley had a distant look on his face. I realized just then that this was the first I'd heard of him ever speaking of his family. I wanted more information but didn't want to push him too far.

"Oh really?" I asked gingerly. I didn't want to have a repeat of what happened when I asked before. I definitely didn't want him to think I was trying to push for information and shut down. But I also wanted him to know that he could trust me and talk to me about his family. It got past the point of a normal pause in conversation, but Oakley still hadn't said anything. So I sat there silently, taking a little nibble of my salad. I wanted to let Oakley decide if he wanted to talk or change the subject.

He got a faraway look in his eye as if he was remembering something pleasant and painful at the same time. After an almost uncomfortable amount of time, he said quietly, "Yeah, she was always teasing me about how fast I ate and would say that I couldn't even be tasting it if I devoured it like a starving animal."

I decided to push it, just a little bit, and asked, "She *was* always teasing you?"

Oakley looked down for just a second but then looked directly at me. "I don't really talk about her much. She was an amazing big sister, and everything feels so empty without her. She died almost two years ago." He didn't break eye contact with me as he continued, "It happened on campus. She went up to the roof of the math building with a couple of her sorority sisters to see the moon. It was full that night, and they wanted to get pictures with it for Instagram. Daisy started walking on the ledge. She used to be a star gymnast and was trying to do some of her old tricks and she fell. There was nothing anybody could do, and they said she didn't feel anything."

I sat there in stunned silence. My heart panged for Oakley and his family. I tried to filter through my memory to see if I'd heard anything about this. Universities were quick to sweep deaths under the rug. No one wanted to send their kids away to schools with a bad reputation. It was Public Relations 101. No wonder Oakley could get away with anything. The school probably liked having him here and definitely wanted to show that they'd managed to support the Davis family.

"I was offered a full ride here, you know," he continued bitterly while staring at his plate. "I didn't take it though. My mom didn't want any of the university's blood money. They made my sister sound like some stupid party girl. And don't get me wrong, she had her fair share of fun, but I didn't like how the university was quick to drag her name through the mud to save their ass. She didn't even have that much alcohol in her system, according to the toxicology report."

My purpose for working with Oakley suddenly felt...wrong. "They want a redemption story," I mumbled. "Oakley, I'm so sorry."

"It's not your fault," he whispered. "But yeah. You working with me this season serves many purposes. You see, the building wasn't up to code. The door to the roof wasn't even locked. If we wanted to sue them, we could have."

The question escaped me before I could filter it. "So why didn't you?"

"No amount of money can make up for the fact that she's gone." He stood up and looked around the hotel room, avoiding my eyes. "I'm really worn out from the game today. I'm going to brush my teeth and go to bed."

I felt terrible for Oakley and disgusted with the university.

I couldn't imagine attending the same school where my sibling died. I had a lot of feelings to work through. A surge of angry energy flooded my system, and I needed to take it out on the treadmill. I told Oakley goodnight and let him know I was going down to the gym next to the lobby.

I cranked the treadmill up and let the pounding of my feet drown Oakley's voice telling me about his sister and the university's cover up. I ran until all I could think about was the screaming in my thighs and I just couldn't go anymore. I sat down on the floor next to the treadmill to cool off and stretch.

How could Oakley even stand to be around me, knowing that the university was just using me to try to paint a pretty picture with his family's tragedy and his skill on the football field? It explained a lot about his attitude toward me at the beginning. As I was working out the tension in my knees, I decided I would tell Oakley that I was going to step out of this internship as his publicist. I wouldn't be able to graduate early, but I would be able to live with myself.

I went back to the room to find it completely dark and Oakley in bed. I slipped into the bathroom to take another shower, trying to be quiet so that I wouldn't wake him. I scrubbed my hair free of the sweat while thinking about his sister. That could have easily been me. I was headed down a one-way street to self-destruction, and the only thing that saved me from that was a heavy dose of embarrassment.

I used to be so desperate for attention and validation that I'd do anything. Was that what she was doing? Showing off for the approval of her peers?

I shut off the water, slipped into my matching pale blue pajama set, then slid under the covers with a sigh. This job no longer felt right. What was I going to do? How was I going to graduate early?

Two strong arms wrapped around my stomach, and I was

pulled tightly against a warm, hard, *bare* chest. Was he shirtless? Oh my Post Malone, he was shirtless.

"Hey, Solver?" he whispered in my ear while nuzzling my neck. I allowed myself to indulge in this for a few seconds, then pushed him away.

"Yeah?" I croaked.

"For what it's worth, I'm glad you started working with me. At first I just wanted to be the mess they made her out to be. I wanted to make it hard on them. Now, I think I can prove them wrong."

Emotion crawled up my throat, and my eyes watered. My heart swelled three times its normal size with affection for this man. I wanted to tell him so many things in that moment. That he had potential. That the university was a steaming pile of shit. That he didn't have to prove anything to anyone.

But instead, I swatted his large hand and said, "Yeah, yeah. Get back to your side of the bed, Mr. Davis."

———

I RELUCTANTLY WOKE up the next morning to sunlight streaming in the window, hitting my face, instead of my usual alarm. *Huh, that's strange*, I thought before I even opened my eyes. I must have forgotten to set it, which never happened. It wasn't a big deal, though. My flight home wasn't until noon, so I had plenty of time. I squinted my eyes open, and the first thing I did was look over at Oakley's side of the bed, disappointment flooding my chest when I found it empty. I pushed the covers down and stretched my arms out, then slowly sat up.

There was a note on my nightstand, scrawled out in Oakley's almost illegible handwriting. Seeing the note reminded me that the team had left stupid early that morning. I picked it up and read:

Amanda - you looked so peaceful I didn't want to wake you. See you at home. I kind of promise to behave on the ride home, even without you babysitting.

P.S. Eat something *before* you get hangry

There was a protein bar sitting by the note. Ugh, did he really think I was going to eat that? If I were going to indulge in some calories, I sure as hell wasn't going to eat one of his nasty protein bars. I picked it up and tossed it.

My flight home was uneventful aside from the man I had to sit next to. He spent most of the flight staring at my boobs and coughing. I could practically feel myself breathing in his nasty-ass germs.

Shelby was home when I walked through the front door of our condo. She was also buck ass naked. She was *also* doing yoga. I also saw her lady garden. Thank fuck she was all natural, because I only saw a seventies-worthy bush, but it still made me drop my luggage and scream at her spread eagle pose.

"Fucking hell, Shelbs. I told you I was coming home today."

She didn't even stumble.

"What's wrong?" she asked on a breezy exhale.

"Couldn't you do that somewhere else? This is like a bad porno."

She rolled her eyes and stood up on her yoga mat and stretched her arms above her head. "I don't like to be restricted by my clothes, Amanda. Also, I tried one of your meditation videos. The one about harnessing your sexual power was truly enlightening."

I shook my head and sprinted to my bedroom, slamming the door with an angry thud and then plopping on my bed. I had two papers to write and needed to check my email for a follow-up review of Oakley's weekend. I still felt weird about my job. I knew that my future as a PR rep would have a lot of shady gray areas, but Oakley's reveal had me questioning what lines I should draw.

I was just about to type up an email to Dr. Haynes, asking for guidance, when my phone started ringing. Mom.

"Hey, Mom! I was just thinking about you. What's up?" I answered.

"Eleanor got a sports car! And it's RED! Can you believe that?" she blurted out. It sounded like she had been dying to talk about Eleanor's new sports car for days. Eleanor was my parents' neighbor and had been for the twenty-five years my parents had owned their house, although she had been there much longer. Eleanor was like an aunt to me; she used to color chalk on the sidewalk with me, sneak me M&M's, and when I was a teenager, she was a safe space for me to rage about how unfair my mom was being. I loved Eleanor. Her husband, Bob, had passed away unexpectedly right before I left for college. I had only seen her a handful of times since Bob passed, and I made a mental note to send her a letter.

"That's great?" I replied, not really sure how my mom wanted me to react to the news of Eleanor's choice of new car. "What kind is it?"

"What do you mean, what kind is it? It's red! And a convertible! At her age..." Ok, I guess we were feeling judgy about the car.

"Oh yeah. Well, when you put it like that!" I indulged my mom and rolled my eyes just a little. "What are you up to?" I tried to change the subject.

"I'm so happy you asked! We're coming to visit. Surprise!!" she said excitedly.

I internally cringed. Surprise, indeed. "Oh nice!" I lied. "Where are you staying?"

"Well, with you, of course."

I stared at my bedroom door, where on the other side, my naked roommate was ohmmmmming herself to sexual prowess. "Mom, my place isn't big enough," I sputtered. "Don't you think you'd be more comfortable at a hotel?"

"Nonsense!" she replied. "We can get an air mattress and relive the college glory days. I woke up on quite a few frat couches back in my prime. Can we get boxed wine? Gosh, it's been ages since I've slummed it with the cardboard Jesus juice."

I shook my head. "Sure, Mom. That sounds like fun."

"And I already checked the football schedule. There's a home game that weekend! It'll be so much fun."

She started rambling about plans and what she was going to wear to the game as I politely listened. After listening to her babble for a minute or two, I faked a meeting to be able to get off the phone.

"A meeting? Amanda, it's Sunday. Are you just trying to get me off the phone?" she asked, sounding hurt. Oh shit.

"No, Mom. It's a study group," I told her. "Text me your travel plans!" I said with as much fake excitement as I could produce. When we hung up the phone, I thought about talking to Shelby to see if she could be anywhere else while they were here, but then I remembered her au natural downward facing dog and winced. I'd just talk to her at dinner.

I sat on my bed and pulled up my calendar to look at what I had going during the time my parents were going to be here. Since they were just going to be here over the weekend, I wouldn't have any classes. The only thing on my calendar was the game. At least, with my parents there, I might actually know what was going on this time.

I started a list of other things I could take them to do, preferably that didn't include other people. I could take them on a tour of the campus, show them my favorite spots to study, and maybe I could even introduce them to Dr. Haynes? My mom would *love* his full head of gray hair. She had a thing for silver foxes. I didn't think there was that much damage that could be done meeting him. I felt strongly that my parents would behave around a man of Dr. Haynes's caliber. Oakley, on the other hand, could not happen.

I felt like I had a pretty solid plan to survive next weekend.

14

The library was my favorite place to hang out. It was a quiet space with open tables, with the smell of old books and pot permeating the air. It had been three days since my weekend with Oakley, and I was still reeling from what he had told me. As an only child, I'd always been mystified by the idea of having a sibling. I couldn't imagine the pain of losing one.

"This seat taken?"

I looked up from the paper I was writing and smiled. Oakley looked like he'd just gotten out of the shower. His hair was damp, and his face looked freshly shaven. And don't even get me started on the gray sweatpants he was rocking. If I were brave enough to stare, I could probably see the outline of his *team captain*.

I had checked his schedule this morning—not because I was a creepy stalker, but because it was my job to know what he was doing at all times—and remembered that practice was cut short this afternoon for some sort of annual team building ritual that happened prior to the first home game.

"Have a seat," I replied, gesturing to the chair across from me. Oakley dropped a Caesar salad in a plastic container in front of me, along with an apple, fork, and water bottle.

"I brought you dinner because I need your help tonight."

My stomach growled at the sight of the food, and my love button growled at the sight of Oakley's ass as he passed by me to sit down. I wanted to tear into the salad and hoover it into my mouth as fast as I possibly could. Instead, I politely thanked Oakley for bringing me something that I would actually eat and opened it with dainty ladylike manners.

I always forgot just how hungry I was until I saw food. Or smelled food. Or heard someone talking about food. After I had taken enough nibbles to be slightly satiated, I remembered that Oakley had just said he needed my help. What did he do now? Or what was he planning to do that he knew he needed my help in advance? I looked over at Oakley and asked with a slight panic in my voice, "What do you need my help with?"

Oakley flashed me a winning grin, complete with adorable dimples, and said, "It's too quiet in here. The library kind of gives me the creeps. When you're done eating, let's take a walk and talk about it."

"*Of course* places of knowledge and learning give you the creeps," I teased, then packed what was left of the salad in my bag and stood up. A walk outside sounded nice, actually.

"I'll have you know, I'm actually pretty good at school," Oakley retorted, grabbing the apple in front of me and stealing a bite with a loud crunch before I could pack it away. I watched his jaw work through his food and the steady bob of his Adam's apple as he swallowed.

"Your major is Business, right?" I asked once we were outside. The Texas sun was setting, but it was still warm, and I smiled at the buzzing city.

"Yep. I'm going to take over the family business."

"And what exactly is the family business? I still think it's weird you don't want to play professional football. Coach Howard mentioned that there are teams begging for meetings with you."

Oakley ignored my comment about the scouts and smiled at a pedestrian walking by. "My mom owns fifty flower shops across the country," he replied. My brows shot up in surprise. I wasn't expecting that answer. "Mom started her first store here in Austin and just kept growing. My sister loved working with the flowers. Daisy was making arrangements when she was five. She wanted to expand the franchise with more stores and was going to school for Marketing…"

Oakley's voice trailed off, and more puzzle pieces about this man started to click into place. Did he *want* to play ball? Was he self-sabotaging his career because he was trying to fulfill his sister's dreams? I tried to imagine him working in a flower shop and couldn't quite picture it. I wasn't the most knowledgeable about football, but he looked so natural on the field.

"Do *you* know anything about flowers?" I continued lightly. I didn't want to make it weird or ignore the fact that he was voluntarily talking about his sister. I also didn't want him to think he couldn't talk about his sister with me.

"Of course I do. I'm awesome at arranging flowers!" he said with that familiar cockiness I'd come to expect. "But I want to be on the business end of things," he finished.

"Well, I expect a huge bouquet of the most beautifully arranged flowers when the semester is over. You know, for putting up with your shit," I teased.

Just as Oakley was about to answer, a big black van pulled up next to us. At first, I thought it was just parking in front of the pizza place we were currently passing, but then the door flung open and three tall muscular guys dressed in all black jumped out. Before I could even react, there were hands covering my mouth and arms all over my body, pulling me into the van. My adrenaline spiked, and I instinctively looked to Oakley for help and to see if he was in trouble too. But no. That ass was laughing. Laughing! He thought it was funny that a group of guys were literally pulling me into a van and I was going to end up on an episode of Unsolved Mysteries. If I survived this, I was going to fucking murder him.

"Help!" I screamed. I started thrashing my body as hard as I could manage while two impossibly strong men lifted me off the sidewalk and put me in the van. I reached out for Oakley. Was he in on this? Did he arrange to have me fucking murdered because he was tired of working with me?

I kicked one of the dudes manhandling me in the groin, making him keel over on a groan. "She fucking kicked me in the dick!" His voice sounded oddly familiar.

"Dale?" I squealed.

The van door was locked shut, and I slammed my body against it, determined not to go down without a fight. I was going to end them. I would burn them alive and dance on their graves.

"Everything is fine," a voice said at my back.

I spun around to see three large dudes in their underwear. "What the fuck?" I cursed.

"It's the annual hazing. All freshman football guys have to do it," the largest of the bunch said with a groan. He had scratches all down his arm, like his captors struggled to grab him.

"I'm not a freshman football player!" I screamed. "I do not consent to this! Where are they taking us? What are they going to do?"

A shorter guy with a buzz cut and dark eyes spoke up. "Please stop screaming. We are literally in a metal cage, and your shrill voice is echoing everywhere." I was going to murder the entire team. Plain and simple. "It'll be over quick.

Oakley gave us strict instructions to watch over you," he added.

Oh, so that made this alright?

"I still don't get it. Why am I here? Where are we going?"

The van started moving, and I fell down on my ass with a thud. Oh my God, I had so much work to do, and I did not have time for this bullshit.

"It's a huge honor," the guy who hadn't spoken yet finally answered. He had curly blond hair and a black eye. "Most chicks would be excited. It's a big deal that Oakley wanted to include you. And my older brother told me about this. I know where they're taking us..." His voice sounded ominous.

"Where?" I demanded.

"Devil's Backbone."

THE VAN FINALLY STOPPED. I couldn't see where we were because the windows were covered in black construction paper. For some reason, I found this really funny and started giggling. I was in the back of a van against my will, supposedly at a place called The Devil's Backbone, and the windows were covered in a crafting supply from a preschool classroom. It must have been the combination of the adrenaline flowing through my body and my anxiety spiking. The guys looked at me like I was absolutely insane. Oh well, at least I wasn't in my underwear.

The back doors of the van flung open, and I could barely see past our kidnappers into the absolute darkness. The sun had fully disappeared in the time it took us to get here. There was no source of light. No street lamps, no buildings, not even the headlights from the van. Fun fact, I slept with a night light until I was twelve. I. Could. Not. Do. This. I didn't even know what *this* was, but I was out. I tried to panic quietly to keep at least a shred of dignity. The guys started to get out of the van as though this was just a super normal thing to do on a Wednesday night. My ass stayed firmly parked where it was.

"Come on, Amanda," one of the mostly naked freshmen said to me, gently. "It'll be okay, I promise."

Uh, no. No, it would not be okay. Hazing was illegal for a reason. I'd read enough dark romance books to know that a secluded place in the woods with three nearly naked men was a recipe for something I wasn't ready for.

"Hey, Solver. How was the ride?" a stupidly cheerful voice said from outside the van. There was only one emotion I felt stronger than fear, and that was blinding hatred for this massive pain in the ass of a man.

"You!" I screamed while scrambling out of the van. Some light chuckles could be heard as I tripped in the dirt and tried to lunge for him. Bright headlights from another van illuminated the varsity team, who were standing in a line with Oakley in the middle.

"What the hell is going on here? Hazing is hella against the law," I yelled.

Dale, who was standing next to Oakley, spoke up. "We don't like the term *hazing* here. This is a team building exercise."

"I'm not a part of the team!" I yelled.

A low whistle to my right drew my attention. "She's got the legs of a kicker though."

"Enough," Oakley interrupted with a stern look. "Tonight, you're the ball, Solver."

"Excuse me? Did you just compare me to inflated pig skin?"

"Ahh well, when you put it like that, no. No, I did not," Oakley stammered. He looked flustered for a moment but then recovered with, "You're the most important part of the game!"

"Game?! Hazing is a GAME to you? And on top of dragging me into this when I'm not even on the team, you are making me the ball. The ball that gets thrown, kicked, spiked, and bunted?" I screeched, only slightly resembling a banshee.

Oakley tried to stifle a laugh, but it managed to escape. Some of the other players tried to cover their laughter with coughs. Dead. They were all fucking dead.

"What?" I yelled at no one and everyone. My undone hair was hanging tangled, and my eyes were wide. The crazy was just spilling out of me.

"Uh," Oakley started, but even my dark silhouette must have looked deranged, because he stopped and looked like he didn't really want to continue talking.

"Spit it out," I hissed.

"Um. Bunting is baseball. Punting is football," he finished sheepishly. At least he had the decency to look ashamed of himself.

Dale, completely oblivious, interjected with, "And we don't like the word hazing!"

"Let's get this shit show over with," I finally said with a sigh. Based on how long we were in the car and the complete lack of civilization, I knew that the only way I'd get back to the safety of my apartment was if I agreed to this idiotic ritual.

Oakley cleared his throat and spread out his palms, like he was some Bible Belt preacher delivering a sermon. "Every year before the first home game, the freshmen are gathered here on this hallowed ground."

I looked around and scrunched my nose at the sight of a used condom tossed on the side of the path. Hallowed, indeed.

"Devil's Backbone is the most haunted road in Texas. Grown men have attempted to cross the five mile pass and have run home screaming for their mommies with piss dripping down their legs."

"That is a visual I could do without," I groaned.

"Your objective is to get the ball to the end of the road—the end zone—safely. She's the most important part of the game. You protect her at all costs."

"So I have to walk five miles in the dark with the three dudes in their underwear?" I asked while nodding toward said three dudes. I was ready to get this show on the road.

"Yes," Oakley replied dryly.

"I thought the ball was supposed to be the captain's girlfriend," another player interjected.

"Yeah, this ball is too chatty. Can we get another?"

"Enough!" Oakley yelled. "Amanda is the ball. Our captain is out with strep throat. I'm running this show, okay? Let's hurry up so we can go drink." At Oakley's declaration, everyone started cheering. Idiots. I was surrounded by idiots.

"One last thing," Oakley said while stepping up to me. I held my breath and clenched my fist to stop myself from nailing him in the jaw. "It's tradition for the captain to give the ball a kiss."

His words were smoky and dark. He lifted up his hand and ran it down my arm. I simply smirked. "Well, then I guess you'll have to catch me," I replied, walking over to my team.

Game on, motherfucker.

15

I turned and started walking in the opposite direction of the van. That was literally the only thing I had to orient myself. I sure as hell wasn't about to ask Oakley which way to go. I didn't hear the thudding of heavy feet behind me, so I turned and called out, "Are you assholes coming, or are you going to let the ball show you up?"

I guessed that did the trick, because I heard three sets of shoes crunching over rocks and leaves. It hadn't struck me as funny until just now that the players were stripped down to their underwear but were still wearing shoes. I giggled to myself thinking about these big tough guys in their boxers and tennis shoes.

Then reality set in. I was still scared shitless. Nobody knew where I was, and I wasn't sure that I could trust three fresh outta high school guys to keep me safe if shit went down.

I didn't believe in ghosts or the paranormal, but they still scared the hell out of me. I could feel all the hairs on my arms standing up. Oakley's little speech about this being the most haunted road got to me. All I wanted was to be back at home in a nice hot bath, making lists of the different ways I could kill Oakley and get away with it.

There was a worn path illuminated by the moonlight we vaguely followed. After aimlessly walking for fifteen minutes, I learned that the shorter dude was named Ryan, the tallest was a fuckboy named Heath, and the redhead was Kyle. They surrounded me as we walked, with fuckboy Heath at my back. I could feel his beady eyes on my ass as we traveled.

"This isn't so bad," I commented, mostly trying to reassure myself.

"That's because defense hasn't jumped out of the trees yet," Kyle whispered to my left.

Oh.

So the other players were going to jump out of the trees at us? Cool. Cool coolcoolcoolcoooooooool.

"About when should we expect creepy dudes jumping out at us?" I asked while looking up at the shadowy trees lining the path on both sides of us.

"Now," a deep voice said with a chuckle.

A man roughly the size of Chris Hemsworth fell from the trees like a motherfucking ninja. He looked all badass, roaring and shit as he surged forward and lunged for me.

I screamed, because that's a normal response to a big dude jumping out of the forest at you. Heath grabbed me around the middle while Ryan went to tackle our attacker. One second my feet were firmly planted on the ground, and the next I was slung over fuckboy's shoulder and had his massive hand resting on my clenched ass as he sprinted away. My boobs bounced against his back, and I demanded he put me down.

"Protect the ball at all cost!" he yelled.

What was it with dudes protecting their balls?

This ball wanted to go home.

A girlish scream that came from Ryan made me giggle. It

was loud and frantic, like a woman screeching. Kyle was running beside us, looking over his shoulder to see if we were being chased. "We lost Ryan!" he yelled.

"Leave him," Heath replied breathlessly.

Damn. All's fair in love and war *and hazing games* at the Devil's Backbone.

I was suddenly very happy to be the ball after all, mostly because I didn't have to run like hell. Kyle and Heath had been jogging for about a minute, and my boobs were starting to hurt from all the jiggling. I really wished that I had just stayed in my sports bra that morning. But no. I had to be an adult and put on a real bra with underwire and everything.

"Hey, guys, as fun as this is, I don't think we're being chased anymore. Can you put me down?" I directed toward Heath. He reached the hand that wasn't supporting my weight up to hold my back and lowered me down. He managed to brush my breast as I was sliding down off his shoulder. Before pulling away, he gave it a light squeeze. The feminist in me wanted to grab him by the balls and twist, but the survivalist in me didn't want to piss off one of the dudes whose entire focus was getting me to safety. I decided to let it slide. For now.

I smoothed out my clothes and started walking again. My heart was still racing from the chase. I took deep breaths and repeated the first mantra that came to mind: Allow me to accept the things I cannot change, the courage to change the things I can, and the wisdom to know the difference. Ok, it was the AA mantra, but I was currently under a lot of stress, and it was the only one that I could think of.

I had just about calmed down when a hand covered my mouth for the second time tonight. Strong arms pulled me backward. I couldn't make a sound, and Heath and Kyle didn't even notice that I was being kidnapped. So much for protecting the ball at all costs.

"Hey, Solver," a familiar voice whispered in my ear.

I gasped as a hard body dragged me toward the tree line. Oakley's hands pressing against my mouth stifled the scream that I wanted to release. These freshmen were useless.

"Where'd she go?" the fuckboy asked.

"Shit. Maybe she went back for Ryan. Let's go back."

Oakley pressed his body against mine, and I could feel him silently chuckling behind me. He was enjoying this way too much.

The moment both guys were out of sight, he spun me around and pushed me against the hard bark of a nearby tree. "Problem, you are in so much trouble," I said through clenched teeth.

"Solver, why are you so hot when you're mad?" he asked playfully.

I shifted on my feet as he invaded my space, his warm scent washing over me in waves. "Why are you so annoying when you tease me?"

Oakley laughed before biting his lip. I could only see the faint outline of his face in the dark night. I hated being out here, but somehow I felt safer now that I was with him. What the fuck was wrong with me?

"Do you know what I think?" he asked before leaning closer to whisper against the shell of my ear.

"Are you even capable of thinking?" I rasped. I desperately wanted to hide the heat in my voice, but it was proving to be impossible. He ignored my barb.

"I think you like being teased," he whispered, grabbing my hips. "I think you like it a whole fucking lot." He dug his fingers into the small slice of skin between my shirt and jeans, then pressed his pelvis against me. I turned my head away defiantly. I couldn't kiss my client. We couldn't cross the line. I needed to graduate. My hands braced against his chest, determined to push him away.

But instead, my fingers had a mind of their own, remaining on his chest and then roaming the expanse of his muscular torso with lingering, slow movements. When I dragged a sharp fingernail against his abs, Oakley gasped.

His hand cupped my chin, and he turned my face to his, inadvertently brushing our heated lips against one another. I whimpered at the short-lived contact. "You smell so fucking good," he whispered against my lips. "You feel fucking good, too."

He pushed his leg between mine, forcing my heat to brace against his thigh. Oh shit. Ohhhhh shit, this was bad.

But oh so good.

"We should probably go find the others," I stammered.

"We should."

"I have so much homework to do. And I need to check your schedule. We have a press release planned for your upcoming game."

"All very important things," he agreed.

"I should really..." I was running out of excuses.

"You should really let me taste you," Oakley insisted before diving in for a kiss.

His hot mouth against mine was devouring and harsh. His hands roamed my body without caution or restraint. I gasped against him, and the slight part of my lips allowed him access to deepen the kiss.

He tasted like Diet Coke and mint gum, an odd combination but still seductive all the same. Usually when I kissed someone, my mind wandered to all the insecure thoughts that plagued me when I was with someone. Did my breath stink? Was I bad at this? Did I shave my furburger?

But with Oakley, it was like the roaring perfectionist within me was quieted. I felt carefree and wanton, pawing at his muscular body with my fingers as he moaned into my mouth. We were loud. Frantic. Sloppy and passionate. He cupped my breast as I spread my legs wider to grind against his thigh.

My lady button was preening like a motherfucking peacock. She was used to attention of the vibrating variety, and it was nice to feel something alive and warm—and not battery operated.

"Wow, uh, you're really good at this," I sighed lamely as he moved to pepper kisses along my jaw and nip at my neck. "Like, so good." He pressed harder against my pussy.

"Stop talking, Solver," he said, chuckling. "Get out of your head for five minutes."

Get out of my head? I could get out of my head. I was cool as a cat.

A cat in heat.

A starving cat in heat that wouldn't stop meowing.

I trailed my fingers lower and rested them on the edge of his waistband. Oakley stiffened. He was stiff *everywhere*. Oh my God, was that a hammer in his pants? It felt lethal against my stomach. A weapon of mass destruction. One-eyed concrete member of fucking doom.

"Don't start something you can't finish," he moaned before devouring my lips once more. His warning was meant to taunt me, but it served as a stark reminder that this would never...*finish*.

Oh fuck, I was two seconds away from cupping my client's junk.

I pulled away breathlessly. "We should stop."

Oakley didn't pressure me. He pulled away after a lingering look and nodded. Just like that. I set a boundary, and he didn't argue, didn't protest or try to make me feel bad for ending our steamy make out session. It was something I'd never experienced.

I instantly missed the warm pressure of Oakley's body pressed against mine, but this was how it had to be. I couldn't fail. I couldn't fuck this up. I *also* couldn't stop thinking about the sensation of Oakley's fully erect cock against my thigh. I took a breath and smoothed out my clothes and hair, even though it was so dark nobody would be able to see the wrinkles in my shirt or the faint redness on my face from Oakley's stubble.

"Umm, after you, fearless leader," I tried to say confidently.

"Fearless leader. I like that," he chided playfully—not even a hint of frustration in his voice. He put his hand on the small of my back to guide me back onto the path. Such a simple gesture made me feel so fucking safe. I wasn't even scared of the ghosts. Just kidding, I was totally still scared of the ghosts. But, at least with Oakley here, they might go for him first.

As we made it back onto the path, we could hear Heath and Kyle still frantically looking for me, and it made us both laugh.

"What the fuck, man, where did she go?" Heath yelled.

"How am I supposed to know? You pussies left me back there!" I heard another voice that had to be Ryan's shout. Good. I'm glad they found Ryan. I felt kind of bad for him all by himself out there.

"So what happens now?" I asked Oakley. "I mean, is the game over? Did I win? Did they lose? Do the freshmen lose and have to dress up like Queen B and put on a show in the quad?"

"Whoa, slow down! For someone who didn't even want to be here, you suddenly care an awful lot," Oakley teased. "No, the game is not over yet. You cannot win, you're a ball. They haven't lost because the game isn't over yet. And why would they have to dress up like Beyoncé?"

Damn. I really wanted to win. I also really wanted my own private Beyoncé concert.

"Time out is over, and since you so easily lost the fucking ball," Oakley began while giving the guys a pointed stare, "you all get to carry her the rest of the way. And by my calculations, you have about four miles left. Don't lose the ball. Protect it at all costs. Always be looking to score."

That last line made me choke on a snicker. We almost scored in the woods just now.

I dared any of them to groan about carrying me. Now was not the time for fat jokes. "Yes, sir," Heath replied, quickly followed by the others, no complaint in sight. Damn. This team was a cult.

Oakley turned to me with a smirk barely visible in the night sky. "See you in the end zone, Solver."

16

It took the guys a little less than an hour to get to the finish line. Between the pitch black night and them having to carry me the whole time, they weren't super fast. Although they did try very hard. I found it really funny how much they wanted to impress Oakley. And to their credit, my feet never once touched the ground. Even when they passed me back and forth, they held me with one arm under my knees and one under my neck, kind of like a really big baby.

Ryan was the one who crossed the finish line with me over his shoulder, fireman style. He set me down gently, and managed to do it without fondling me. I started dancing wildly in place and yelled, "TOUCHDOWN!"

The guys all burst out laughing and looked at me fondly.

"I'm glad we didn't have a different ball," Kyle teased as he smiled at me.

The van was waiting to take the players back to their dorms, and my teammates started heading toward it. I followed, really looking forward to getting home. This turned out to be a lot more fun, and sexually awakening, than I had expected. But I did still have a lot to do.

Oakley reached out and grabbed my hand. "I'll give you a ride back to your place. Unless you want to ride back in a van full of dirty, sweaty, half-naked freshmen?" he asked with a smirk.

"As tempting as that sounds, I think I'll ride back with you." I laughed and let him lead me over to where his car was parked. I'd prefer awkward post make out session talks to sweaty man children any day of the week.

Even through the darkness, I could see the bright yellow paint of his Camaro. It had a soft convertible top, and when he started it, enough electronics lit up that it looked like a UFO.

"I didn't even know you had a car!" I exclaimed.

"It's easier to walk everywhere in the city," he explained with a humble shrug, though he arguably drove something that looked like sex on wheels. I didn't want to know how many girls had their kitty licked by Oakley in the back seat, and now that I knew just how skilled his mouth was, my own *purring tiger hidden dragon* was about ready to park somewhere and finish what we started.

Once we were both settled, he smoothly traveled down the winding back country road toward what I was hoping was the highway.

"So, uh, sorry for the kidnapping. I couldn't resist pranking you," Oakley said after a long moment of silence. He adjusted the collar of his shirt, as if he was nervous. Didn't he do this all the time? We didn't even fully hook up, but he was acting bashful.

"I could have done without the fake kidnapping. But it was still fun."

Oakley playfully grabbed his chest. "Did *the* Amanda Matthews just admit to having fun?"

I rolled my eyes. "Yes. I did…" I had the *most* fun while

we were in the woods, with his manly man thigh pressed right up against my—

"So about that kiss," Oakley interrupted my naughty train of thoughts. I took a deep breath. He was probably going to do that playboy dude thing where he reminded me it was nothing and that he didn't like to be tied down. It kind of stung to think about, but it was probably for the best. I needed him to be an asshole so I could continue my internship professionally.

"Can I take you on a date?"

I snapped my eyes to him. "What?" I asked.

He smirked and turned up the air conditioning. "You know. A *date*. It's this thing where a person takes another person out to dinner or something. They flirt. They hold hands. Maybe even end the night with a romantic kiss on someone's doorstep."

"I know what a date is," I mumbled. "I want to know why you think it's a good idea to take me out. You're my client, Oakley. What just happened was a one-time thing."

He gripped his steering wheel. "Why does it have to be a one-time thing?"

"Because you're my client, and I have already gotten in trouble for crossing ethical boundaries once." I reminded him of the little prank he pulled with Dr. Haynes at the beginning of the semester. "I almost lost this internship then. I absolutely will not survive any more scandal, and if I lose this internship, I don't graduate early," I finished. I couldn't believe I was actively talking this gorgeous man out of taking me on a date. Not even just being fuck buddies, but like an actual real date. The boyfriend experience.

Oakley surprised me by reaching over and squeezing my hand. "I'm really sorry about that. I was a complete ass and you didn't deserve that."

"Oh, um. Thank you," I said, a little shocked that he apologized. I was discovering every day that there was more to Oakley Davis than the "send an unsolicited dick pic" persona he hid behind.

"So, how's tomorrow night?"

"Uh, for what?" I asked, confused.

"Our first date," he said casually. This man either didn't listen or he was just so used to getting what he wanted that he didn't understand being told no.

I sighed, "Oakley…"

"Okay, how about lunch?" He tried again. "No flowers, nothing fancy. Let's just meet in the cafeteria, surrounded by people. How's noon?" He made it really hard to say no. But it was just lunch. In the cafeteria, of all places. Nobody could possibly misconstrue that as a romantic rendezvous. Just two friends grabbing lunch. So what if one of those friends had an enormous heat seeking moisture missile?

We pulled up outside my apartment, and I gave in. "Okay. Deal. Lunch at noon tomorrow. In the cafeteria. We can review your schedule!" I said brightly.

"Wow, you sure know how to get a guy hot. Schedules. Are you bringing a binder? How about color-coded tabs? You know that gets me going."

I clenched my thighs. I knew he was playing, but how on earth he managed to make that sound sexy was a mystery.

"And we can discuss your interview plans," I added. I was definitely stalling. Why didn't I want to get out of his car?

And I leaned closer. And then I practically sniffed him. Oh man, I was in way too deep.

"And maybe we can talk about other things…" he said suggestively, leaning over the center console to meet me in the middle. *Other things?* Maybe. Oh my lanta.

"I gotta go. This isn't happening. Friends, okay?"

"Sure thing, Solver," he said with a playful smile as I opened the door and stumbled outside.

Oakley was definitely living up to his nickname. And this was one problem I was ridiculously attracted to.

17

I woke up about five minutes before the alarm on my phone was set to go off. Despite being kidnapped and dragged five miles along a haunted road late last night, I felt strangely energized. It must have been because of *other* things that happened last night too. I smiled to myself and pulled up an empowerment mantra video. I pressed play and brushed my teeth while listening to the words: "I am a strong, intelligent, and empowered woman."

My eyes passed over my pathetically small stash of makeup. I had a progress meeting with Dr. Haynes this morning and then lunch with Oakley. I told myself that I was going to do my makeup because I just wanted to look nice today, but really I wanted to look pretty for lunch. I reached for my phone and stopped the mantra video, pulling up a YouTube tutorial on naturally sexy makeup looks instead. Even though I followed each of the five hundred and seven steps the makeup goddess on my screen walked me through, my makeup looked nothing like hers when we were done. Sighing, I washed my face and replaced my failed attempt at natural sexiness with some BB cream, mascara, and a quick swipe of blush.

My phone buzzed, and a message from mom appeared on my screen.

Mom: Can't wait to see you. Only two more days!

Oh my. I completely forgot my parents were coming. At least it was easier to fake excitement through text than it was on the phone.

Me: Me too - it's going to be so much fun!

I added a smiley face and hit send. Turning my attention back to the mirror, I decided that it was as good as it was going to get. I picked a white lace blouse from my closet, paired it with dark skinny jeans and black boots and headed for the door. I almost made it out when I heard a loud wolf whistle.

"Damn, girl. You clean up nice!" Shelby said as she eyed me up and down. "Got a hot date?"

Shit. Was it that obvious? Yes. Yes it was. Did I have time to change? No. No, I did not. "No hot dates for me," I insisted. This wasn't a date. Nope. Not even close. My palms were sweating just for shits and giggles.

"Well, I don't think I've seen you *not* wear yoga pants since you moved in," Shelby scolded. She was wearing a long skirt and tank top with no bra. I saw her nipples practically cutting through the shirt. It wasn't like I *wanted* to stare; I just couldn't stop. It was like they were pointing and accusing me of something.

"Are you yoga-pants shaming me?" I asked, acting offended.

"Ain't no shame in being comfortable," she replied with hands up in mock surrender. "I'm just saying the extra effort looks good on you."

I smiled politely. Dressing up felt like I was the try-hard girl of my past. I used to wear designer clothes to everything.

I couldn't leave the house without my hair done and my lash extensions expertly applied by Judy, my lash lady. My nails were always done. I was always polishing up my exterior to hide how fucking insecure I was—am.

"Well, I'll see you later. Also, we need to talk about my parents visiting. No naked photo shoots."

Shelby pretended not to hear me and walked over to her room, giggling mischievously as she shut the door. I debated hounding her about it, but the alarm on my phone alerted me to my meeting with Dr. Haynes.

I obsessed over my outfit the entire walk to Dr. Haynes's office. I didn't want Oakley to think that I had gotten all dolled up just for him. I mean, I had, I just didn't want him to think that. It was so weird to be obsessing over looking too nice and wishing I was in my comfiest leggings and oversized sweatshirt.

By the time I got to Dr. Haynes's office, I'd decided that comfortable clothes were preferable and that I'd never again subject my poor body to restricting clothes. The moment I entered his office, I sank in the chair with a sigh.

"Miss Matthews, I'm impressed with how you have been able to move on from your earlier indiscretion to be able to make Oakley shine and allow the university to showcase their star player," Dr. Haynes said, almost beaming. "I have also checked in with the coach, and he is equally happy with your performance."

Aw, shucks!

"We both feel confident that you are on track to graduate early like you have planned. I'm very proud of how you took a chance on this opportunity, even though I know it wasn't your first choice, and you figured out how to excel."

"Thank you, Dr. Haynes! I really couldn't have done it without your guidance," I gushed, trying to sound humble, but actually feeling myself.

"But if you really want to prepare for your desired career path, maybe I could speak to some connections about having you work with them on some projects. I'm representing a new company your father might actually be interested in. We professionals are always looking to wet our beak."

I swallowed. Dr. Haynes was going to let me work with some of his clients? This was the best news ever. I squirmed in my seat with excitement.

"Yes! I would actually really love that. Thank you!"

"Any time."

Dr. Haynes's glowing review gave me the courage to ask if I could bring my parents by on Friday and introduce them. He readily agreed, and we set a time before my phone alerted me to my next...meeting...with Oakley.

Let's do this thing.

THE LUNCH ROOM was buzzing with activity. I didn't have a meal plan and rarely came here during the school year. I preferred to plan my meals out for my food journal and avoided eating in front of others if I could manage it.

The room was smaller than I expected. It was set up like a food court, with various options lining the wall, and tables and chairs were crowded together in the center. I scanned the room for Oakley and smiled when I found him sitting at the edge of the room by the exit leading outside, giving us a view of the city street.

His eyes were on me as I walked over. The backpack I wore reminded me that this was strictly professional. I had typed up a list of speaking points for post-game interviews and also scheduled him a photo op with a famous alumni known for his nonprofit work.

"Hey there, Solver," he said with a smile. Oakley then

pulled out a lunch box. I'd expected us to have to buy a burger drowning in grease, but it appeared that he packed us both a modern bento box. When he took off the plastic lid, I took note of the smoked salmon, cucumber, boiled eggs, pita crackers, and what looked like some sort of dill cream cheese dip.

"Wow," I said before sitting down. "Thanks for making lunch."

"Oh, this is for me," he teased, yanking it closer. "You're going to have to enjoy that surprise meat pizza they're advertising."

"Oh, um, you know what? I'm really not even hungry," I said automatically.

Oakley laughed and said, "Calm down. I'm only kidding. What kind of a date do you think I am?" He pulled out a chair for me and motioned for me to sit. As I went to take a seat next to him, Oakley looked me over from head to toe. Slowly. His eyes lingered on my hips and then my breasts, which were high and perky thanks to a little help from Victoria.

"You look *nice*. Is all of that for me?" he asked with a devilish twinkle in his eye. He totally knew it was for him.

"No. Not that it matters, but I had an important meeting this morning. It was for him. I mean *that*. I mean I dressed up for that meeting." I stumbled over my words. Great. That was super convincing. I should have just gone back and changed this morning.

"Whatever you say," he said with a shrug, popping an entire boiled egg into his mouth. So. Gross. I stared at him in disgust as his cheeks puffed out, full of egg. How do you even eat that much boiled egg at once?

I was still puzzling over the egg when Oakley started waving. I looked over my shoulder to see who he was waving at. Oh great, Dale.

"Oh shit, now he's coming over," Oakley said, a little chunk of yolk escaping his mouth. Eew.

"If you didn't want him coming over, why did you wave?" I asked with a smirk. Oakley looked mad to have our lunch date crashed, and I was thanking the sweet gods of mystery meat pizza that we had someone to distract from Oakley's thoughtful lunch non-date.

"He saw me," Oakley said, scrubbing his hand down his face. "I didn't want to be rude... Our first date is ruined."

"Good thing it's not a date," I replied with a wink, then turned to greet Dale.

"Hey, guys," he said. "You look good, Ball. Get enough sleep after last night?" Dale pulled up a chair and sat down before grabbing a pita chip and loudly chomping on it.

If I was being honest, I didn't sleep hardly at all, but I wasn't going to answer truthfully. I evaded, instead. "I really hope this nickname doesn't stick for the rest of the season, because I don't like being called after something that shares a namesake with the two tiny marbles dangling between your thighs, Dale."

It was sassier than I intended, but both guys started chuckling loudly. "Her name is totally Balls now," Dale said loudly, slapping his knees. "I'm telling the group chat."

Oakley laughed, and I cracked a smile good-naturedly. Nicknames were signs of endearment, right?

"So what are y'all up to?" Dale asked.

Oakley opened his mouth to answer, but he looked far too mischievous for my liking.

"We're going over his schedule and press for the game this weekend," I said confidently, making Oakley frown.

"I hope you penciled in the kegger we're throwing after the game. You can't bail on us again!" Dale said, slapping Oakley on the back.

"A keg party?" a soft voice said. I tilted my eyes up to see a brunette with long wavy hair and impossibly long eyelashes. She looked like a Kardashian. While I was busy wondering how anybody could have such perfect brows, Oakley was appreciating her other assets.

"Hey, Kels," Oakley said with familiarity. "What do you think? Should we go to Dale's party?" Two more blondes had joined us at the table before Oakley had even finished asking *Kels* out. They were both gorgeous and looked like they belonged on the cover of magazines, half-naked and selling perfume. They were also both standing on either side of Oakley. Blonde Number One had her hand casually resting on his shoulder. What. Was. Happening?!

Kelseigh—I was just assuming that's what Kels was short for, while I was also being slightly petty and jealous—looked at Oakley through those damn beautiful lashes and purred, "Yes! I think we should go!"

In unison, the blondes pretended to pout. Knowing full well that they were invited, Blonde Number Two teased, "What about us? You know you would miss us."

"Ladies, ladies, ladies," Dale said Matthew McConaughey style. "There's plenty of Oakley, and *me*, to go around! You and all of your hot friends are invited. Spread the word! It'll be at my house."

I felt the jealousy raging through my veins and making my face hot. For someone who was adamantly declaring that she was not on a date less than five minutes ago, I was so uncomfortable I wanted to crawl out of my own skin.

I should have expected this. Oakley was a player. Just because he wanted in my pants didn't mean the rest of the world just magically stopped lusting after him. Not to mention, I had made it clear that we couldn't be much of anything. Someone like Oakley didn't play the long game, he was—as he so eloquently put it last night—always looking to score.

Oakley politely shrugged off one of the girls and scooted his seat over to me. "And what about you, Solver?" he purred in a low voice. The girls were leaning in close, trying to listen in to what he was saying. Out of the corner of my eye, I caught Dale smirking. *Smirk all you want, bro. I'm a stone cold fox.*

"I guess I'll have to go to keep your ass in line," I whispered back. Why did I sound like a cat in heat? And how could he turn me to a puddle of mush so easily? I didn't really do the whole party scene anymore. But this was part of my job. Was he inviting me for other reasons? Visions of us making out in a frat boy bathroom assaulted me. Not even nasty imaginary toilets filled with regurgitated Everclear could make the hope in my belly stop bubbling up. I'd kiss Oakley in a bathroom. I would kiss him in a spoon. I'd kiss Oakley Davis with green eggs and ham in the bottom of a lake, in a boat on a goat...

"I like how you keep my ass in line," he whispered against my neck, drawing me out of my thoughts. I flushed. My pink canoe was ready for a ride on the river, if you know what I mean.

"I'm sure there are plenty of others ready to ride your ass," I snarked. Yep. I sounded jealous. I might as well have lifted my leg and pissed on his patch of grass.

He smiled—the *nerve* of him. Smiling when I was here showing how pathetic I was. "I'd like you as close to my ass as possible for the duration of the evening, Solver."

That was such an odd statement that I didn't know which part to pick apart first. "Was that supposed to be sexy?" I asked.

Oakley burst out laughing. "I'm trying here, Amanda."

"Maybe try a balls joke?" Dale interjected.

"I, like, totally love your ass," Kelseigh piped in. "I'm an ass girl." The other two groupies nodded. This was officially awkward. We had an audience, and we were talking about Oakley's ass.

"I'll go," I said. "Not for your balls or ass," I then quickly added. "I will go because I'm your publicist, and I'm hella good at what I do."

I stared down Kelseigh and the blondes with a forced grin, then stood up quickly from the table and announced that I had somewhere to be. Really, I was fleeing before this could devolve into something worse than it already had.

"Aww, Amanda, don't go," Oakley pleaded. "You didn't even eat yet."

"I'm sorry, I wish I could stay. But I have a meeting that I, uh, really can't miss. Thanks for lunch," I said as I was gathering my things and getting ready to go. "Bye!" I called and ran out of there like my creepy Uncle Joe had just spotted me at the family reunion.

I was halfway back to the apartment when I realized that the kegger was after the game. This weekend. The same weekend my loving and adoring parents were coming to visit to see how much better I was doing here than in California. Fuck.

Now I had to figure out how to juggle my parents, the game, and keeping them from meeting Oakley. And to top it all off, a freaking kegger to consume my every waking thought instead of the way those girls were hanging all over Oakley. And how much Oakley was loving the attention. And how much I hated how much Oakley was loving it.

18

"This is so exciting!" Mom yelled. Their flight landed at seven this morning, and ever since they got off the plane and smothered me with hugs, she'd been saying that.

"You're not really wearing that to the game, are you, Tilly?" my dad asked, scrunching his brow. Mom looked like an older version of me, with faker boobs and bigger hair. Her tan looked flawless under the Texas sun, and the crop top she wore showed off her incredible physique. She wasn't necessarily dressing her age, but she was enjoying herself. That was all that mattered.

"It's hotter than a meth pipe on payday, Crosby. I worked hard for these abs, and I want to take enough photos for the Facebook. Lacey McGuire can eat my farts. This will get her to stop trying to sell me diet pills. Don't you ruin this for me."

Dad chuckled. Unlike Mom, he wore a *Proud University of Texas Dad* shirt tucked into dark jeans with a brown belt and black tennis shoes. I was so happy to see them, and other than a few comments about my weight loss and the large brunch I had to endure, I was surprisingly happy having them here.

"I got us really good seats, but I'm going to have to disappear after the game to make sure Oakley doesn't go rogue during his interviews," I said. The three of us were walking to the stadium. College students passed us by with beer cans in their fists and sloppy sways to their walks.

I had a very vague plan for keeping my parents busy tonight so I could keep an eye on Oakley. I had to find my old bangle flask in my closet and fill it with vodka—mom's favorite. She wanted to relive the glory days, so I was going to get her very, very, *very* drunk.

"Are we going to get to meet *the* Oakley Davis? I sure do like his Instagram posts," my mom said playfully as she gave me an overexaggerated wink. My dad chuckled and let out a dramatic sigh.

"I'll see what I can do," I straight up lied. "But Oakley is the star player, so after the game, he's going to be very busy giving interviews," I explained. It was better to let my mom think I was going to try than to tell her no. If I just told her no, she would never let it go. She'd already proven she couldn't be trusted.

I had arranged to introduce my parents to Dr. Haynes earlier since his office was conveniently on the way to the stadium. We stayed and chatted long enough for Dr. Haynes to tell my parents how well I had been doing, but not long enough for my mom to embarrass the shit out of me. Just kidding. While Dad and Dr. Haynes talked about the industry, Mom looked my mentor up and down, biting her lip.

We had barely made it into the hallway when my mom turned and said a little too loudly, "Amanda! You didn't tell me how cute he is, you've been holding out on me!" My mom had never really been aware of just how loud her voice was. I prayed to whoever was listening that Dr. Haynes hadn't heard my mom. Or if he did, that he would never bring it up.

"Oh, look at the time, we've really got to hurry if we're going to make it to the gift shop and get you guys all decked out before the kickoff!" I said while gesturing for my parents to walk faster.

"Look at you, Amanda! Using football lingo like it's nothing!" my dad gushed. It was actually really cute seeing how proud of me they were.

We quickly went to the gift shop, where my parents bought tee shirts, hats, and foam fingers for the game and still made it to our fantastic seats on time. "Mom, do you want something to drink?" I asked innocently.

"You know, I could go for a cocktail. Do you think I could get a martini delivered to our seat?"

"I figured you'd want to have some fun," I said. "Here." I slid my bangle flask off my wrist and handed it to her. Security patted everyone down before entering the stadium, so it was nearly impossible to bring in outside alcohol. But this little buddy of mine looked like an inconspicuous, oversized bracelet. I used to bring it with me to quite a few places back in the day.

"Oh!" Mom exclaimed, twisting off the small top and knocking some of the burning liquid back. "How fun! It's like 1994 all over again."

My dad's eyes went wide, and he shook his head, probably already mentally calculating how far my place was and if he'd need to order a car or carry her there.

The game started, and slowly Mom started to feel the buzz. I watched Oakley, this time with a bit more knowledge under my belt. He was so skilled. "SACK HIM!" Mom screamed. "Gosh, I love football," she added when a player bent over to stretch in front of us.

Being right next to the field meant I got a front row seat to how seriously Oakley took the game. His steel eyes were trained on the field. And when he wasn't watching the game...he was watching *me*.

"Is that Oakley?" Mom asked in a shout. "He's handsome, honey. Y'all would make beautiful babies. Oh my God. Do you think I'll be a hot grandmother? Like a GILF?"

I giggled, and Dad had to cover his mouth to keep the snort from escaping. "You'll always be totally fuckable, Mom," I assured her, deciding to graze over the conversation about Oakley and me making babies. Hell. No. I mean, I wouldn't mind practicing though.

"I just love you so much. You're doing really great out here. I'm glad you got away from it all. I just miss you all the time," Mom said while wrapping her slender arm around me. Dad stared at the scoreboard. It wasn't even half time and Mom was hella buzzed. I was beginning to wonder if my bangle flask held enough vodka to get us through the rest of the game, the way my mom was pounding it back.

"Crosby, look!" my mom said excitedly, pointing to a vendor carrying brightly colored frozen drinks in giant plastic cups shaped like footballs. "Look, look, looooook! They are just like the ones we had on our first date!" she said, booping my dad on the nose. Nobody could say that my parents weren't madly in love.

My dad waved over the guy selling the drinks and forked over an ungodly twenty dollars each for my mom, himself, *and me*. He probably didn't even realize what he'd done. I guess it was hard for them to understand that I couldn't have just one sip. One taste. One drink. Both my parents could easily handle a glass of wine at dinner or a bender once a month. But not me. I thanked my dad, took the drink and immediately set it down by my feet. I didn't even want to guess at how many calories were in it. I was also technically working, so I didn't think getting buzzed was the best idea.

My mom started cheering wildly and yelled, "GO OAKLEY!!! WOOOOO!" and then broke down into a fit of giggles. I giggled along with her.

The players cleared the field, and the cheerleaders came bouncing onto the field, yelling and waving their pom poms. They got into formation and started their first routine. To my horror, my mom was doing it right along with them, yelling the words and swinging her hips like she owned the place. She was bumping into everybody on all sides, but she was having the time of her life. I thought it was pretty funny until the whole stadium started going wild, and I saw my drunk, cheering, dancing mother on the jumbotron.

Nope.

This was not happening.

"Look, Crosby! I'm on TV!!"

I gave my father a look of pure pleading. "Fix this," I hissed in a low voice.

"Uh, babe. Sweet cake!" Dad yelled over the crowd, grabbing her arm. "You know what else happened on our first date?" Oh God. No. I needed to plug my ears, but my fingers weren't fast enough as he propositioned her, "Why don't I get us a hotel room so we can recreate it?"

"Oh, Crosby, you devil!!" Mom playfully patted him on the chest. "What about the game?"

I was trying not to vomit but managed to speak up. "I have to work the rest of the night anyway, Mom. We can catch up tomorrow."

She giggled and pinched my father's butt.

Yep. I saw that.

"Well, if you insist!" Both my parents gave me quick goodbyes and started fumbling up the stadium stairs and out the door.

I would have to scrub my mind with bleach after this. I loved that my parents were in love, but I hadn't expected the bangle flask to work *that* well.

The rest of the game went by quickly. We won the game, scoring in the last thirty seconds. Everyone was going fucking wild. I loved the adrenaline of it, and even screamed. Maybe I liked sports after all.

It took me a while to get to the locker rooms. I struggled through the crowd of drunk, happy coeds, and by the time I made it there, I had booze in my hair and a sweat-soaked shirt. When I walked in, the players all started shouting, "Ball!" I didn't even have to remind myself that it was a term of endearment. I was surprised by how happy it made me that *they* were all happy to see me.

Oakley ran up to me, practically giddy, and wrapped his thick arms around my waist. He easily lifted me and twirled me around. I briefly wondered if he could lift me over his head *Dirty Dancing* style, but he set me back down. I giggled at the look of pure happiness on Oakley's face.

"Hey there, Stud. Word around town is that you just won a football game. How does that make you feel?" I joked and held my fist up to his face like a microphone. The entire locker room went nuts when I mentioned the win. I didn't understand it before, but now it was easy to see why people celebrated for days.

Oakley leaned in close so that only I could hear him and asked in a low throaty voice, "So you think I'm a stud?" His hot breath on my neck sent an instant wave of heat up my entire body.

"Uh, no. I mean yes, on the field. You're a stud on the field," I said lamely. "Have you done your interviews yet? How about that party? We don't want to leave Kelseigh hanging!"

"I like the way you think, Solver. Interviews went great. I

answered a couple of questions, but since Hanley broke a school record, they're more interested in him tonight." I frowned. My PR brain was already working to think up ways to make the media interested in Oakley. "Let me grab a quick shower, and Coach wants to chat for a minute, then we can go!" he added.

I was already hot and bothered. Picturing Oakley and his vagina miner in the shower was not going to help. I needed a distraction. Most of the other guys were already in the showers, so I pulled out my phone to keep me occupied. I texted Dad to make sure they got to a hotel okay and then looked at my calendar for tomorrow. All I had was a late breakfast with my parents and then seeing them off to the airport. I opened YouTube and saw that there were a few new mantra videos in my favorite channels. Huh. I hadn't watched one in days.

I had done such a good job of distracting myself that I didn't even notice when Oakley walked over to me. He cleared his throat and bowed deeply, extending his hand to me. "M'lady, are you ready to go?" Weirdo.

I didn't take his hand. I was too busy staring at him now. Oakley looked good. His hair was effortlessly styled. His shirt was way too tight. His jeans hugged his long legs. I felt tiny standing next to him. "I'm taking you to dinner first," he said matter-of-factly.

"Huh?"

"I'm hungry," Oakley explained with a smile. "I'm always starving after a game. And since our date that wasn't really a date was interrupted by Dale, I figured we could grab a bite to eat."

I opened my mouth to argue, but Oakley cupped my cheeks.

Oh yeah, this would definitely get some curious stares. The locker room was still a flutter of activity. Some players were getting prepped for ice baths. Some were getting cuts and bruises tended to. One was having his groin stretched. And I wish that were a euphemism, because the way the middle-aged trainer was up in his no-no zone just looked wrong.

"I'm taking you out, Solver. I'll even go over the interview with you so you can pretend it's work." He pulled me out of the main area of the lockers and toward the outside hallway. All of the coeds and press had filtered out, so we were alone.

I bit my lip, and his dark eyes zeroed in on the movement. Fuck. Was it hot in here or just me? "Oakley," I said with a sigh. "Are you gonna have dinner with me, then disappear with one of those girls? The client thing is a big problem for me, but also…" I debated for a moment how to tell him my issues with the party scene without revealing my deepest shame. "We are very different. I feel like a short-lived challenge to you, and once the novelty wears off, you'll find something else to occupy your time. Why cross that boundary if we both know it can't work?"

I felt embarrassed admitting that, but it was worth talking about. "I like you," Oakley replied simply. "I really like you. I don't do the whole girlfriend thing, yeah. And if we're being honest, this will probably blow up in our faces."

His palm landed on my neck, and his index finger tested my pulse. We were in a compromising position, in a very public space, but I felt trapped in his orbit. I couldn't push him away, and I didn't want to. Oakley leaned over to kiss me, and I let him.

It was soft and sweet. His lips had a waxy layer of ChapStick on them, and his tongue tasted like mint. When he pulled away, I practically *melted*. "But I think about you all the time—and not just because you set five million alarms on my phone. I think about if there's anyone to take care of you.

I wonder if you're eating. I wonder what you look like naked..."

I snorted, but he continued. "I think about kissing you. *Everywhere*. I bet you taste so fucking sweet." I was squirming at his words. "I think about what you're going to do after college. And for the first time in a long time, I think about how my actions affect someone else. I'm just a boy, standing in front of a girl, asking her to go have dinner with me, then hold my hand at a party—and maybe kiss me a few more times. Can we just give this a chance?"

I braced my hands against his chest. "Let's go eat, Problem."

19

The dimly lit Italian restaurant Oakley took me to was kind of a dive, and that was being generous. I looked around at the yellowing counters and torn, outdated booths and grimaced. There were only two other occupied tables. I tried to muster up some enthusiasm, but Oakley could read my face like a book.

"I promise, this is the best lasagna you will ever eat," he said with gusto.

The only waitress on staff that night led us to a booth and handed us menus that looked like they had been printed twenty years ago. Well, at least it was clean, I told myself. Oakley was so excited to bring me here I decided to let my initial judgements go and have an open mind.

I perused the menu and realized that I was looking at entrees I actually wanted to eat instead of what had the least amount of calories. I still wasn't going to order the lasagna, because come on, carb city, but the chicken piccata sounded pretty good.

As we were waiting for our food to come, Oakley reached his hand across the table and took mine. I could still smell the soap on his skin; it was clean, refreshing, and slightly intoxicating. He looked at me slyly and said, "You know, I seem to remember a certain promise to fuck you so good that all of Austin was going to hear you moan."

"Oakley!" I yanked my hand back and laughed. It was definitely a tempting offer. But I was so impressed that he even remembered that night at all, let alone actually saying that to me, that my hooha forgot to be turned on.

Our food came and we ate, talked and laughed. I couldn't even remember the last time I felt this comfortable with anyone, let alone a man. I didn't want this dinner to end. And to top it off, my chicken was so fucking good I thought I might actually come right there at the table. I even tried a nibble of Oakley's lasagna.

We skipped dessert, and by the time the check came, we had been there for almost two hours. Everybody was going to start wondering where Oakley was if we didn't get to the party soon. After a little back and forth on who was going to pay, I let Oakley take care of it.

We walked to the party hand-in-hand. But a couple of blocks before we got there, I pulled my hand away. "I'm not sure I'm ready for everyone to see whatever this is. I'm your publicist. I don't want to *be* the story. Business as usual?" I stuck out my hand to shake on it.

Oakley ignored my hand and pulled me in tight against his hard chest. He threaded his fingers through my hair and brought my mouth to meet his. And then he pulled away. It was a short, sweet kiss that left me wanting more.

"Business as usual," he said with an impish grin. Holy hell, he was so hot. I followed him wordlessly to the party.

———

"OAKLEY! MY MAN!" Dale yelled over the music. The party

was in full swing, and there were at least three couples going at it in various spots in the trashed living room.

Dale gave me a heated once over that had me rolling my eyes so hard I think I hurt myself. It felt so practiced that I was certain he'd used it on lots of girls. Dale was cute, don't get me wrong, but he seemed to poach Oakley's appeal for himself. "Let me get you a drink," he said with a wink.

"Just water for me," I replied. I needed to keep my sobriety if I was going to keep Oakley out of trouble. The moment he walked through the door, he seemed to buzz with excitement. He was a true extrovert, shining in the adrenaline of others' attention. It wasn't bad, it was like staring at someone meant to be in the spotlight. Once again, I couldn't help but feel like his dreams of working at the flower shop were a lie.

"Water? You're no fun," Dale whined. "Oh shit, there's Kaydence. Fuck, I swear she's the hottest girl I've ever seen. Be right back." Dale disappeared without getting me a drink, and I couldn't help but laugh at how he fumbled across the room to see a girl with long blonde hair, alluring eyes, and bright red lipstick.

"I'll get you a drink. Would you like sparkling or flat?" Oakley asked while spinning my hair on his finger.

"Only the finest water from Fiji for me," I teased back. "Tap is fine."

Oakley disappeared through the crowd, and I leaned against the wall, people watching as I waited.

"Hey there, Balls," a familiar voice called out. Ahh, Heath. Fuckboy freshman extraordinaire.

"Hey. Did you enjoy the game?" I asked politely.

"Yeah. It was good. I would have preferred to watch it with you, though," he said, standing alarmingly close to me. I had not forgotten the full-on boob squeeze. He smelled sickly sweet, I'm guessing from whatever the red liquid in his cup was.

"Yeah, too bad players have to, you know, watch the game with the team and all," I snarked.

"I know, baby. If they let us, I would've brought you down to the sidelines and let you watch as my special VIP," Heath told me, trying to be smooth, my sarcasm having gone right over his head.

He shot a hand up surprisingly fast for a drunk dude and started stroking my face. "You're so soft. And pretty," he said with all the charm of a teenager trying to ask out a girl for the first time. He dipped his head like he was going in for a kiss.

"What the fuck, man?" Oakley yelled, standing in front of us. His rage was palpable.

Heath lifted his head to look at Oakley. "Hey, man!" Heath babbled, absolutely oblivious to Oakley's anger. Alcohol was a powerful thing. I mean, I didn't think Heath was all that bright to begin with, but this was next level.

Oakley shoved Heath off of me and stood over him aggressively. Heath was a big dude, being a football player and all, but Oakley made him look so small. It dawned on me that these guys were going to get into a fight over me. Huh, cool. No, not cool. Bad. Very bad.

"Oakley, it's okay," I said, resting my head on his arm.

"Back the fuck off," Oakley said to Heath, ignoring me. "Find somewhere else to be annoying, or I'll have you cleaning equipment all day."

"You can't do that," he argued. "But I wouldn't mind scrubbing some balls," he then added in a slur.

His joke was lame at best. I honestly doubted he scrubbed his balls at all. Heath didn't look like the type to take hygiene seriously. Oakley, however, wasn't amused. "Out," he said, pulling me closer.

"I was just playing, man," Heath replied.

"I don't really give a fuck. You disrespect Amanda, you disrespect me. Out."

Heath rolled his eyes and mumbled something under his breath. The macho display of protectiveness was cliche and...well...hot.

Oakley followed Heath with his eyes until the annoying fuckboy was out of the house. "That dumbass," he growled.

"Down, tiger. As your publicist, I have to say getting into a fight with your teammate would probably look bad," I said. He curled me even closer. Any more and I'd have my legs wrapped around his waist. "Did you get me any water?" I asked. All of that manly protectiveness had me hankering for a drink.

"Ah shit," Oakley sighed. "No. I saw Heath talking to you, and I just…"

"Got adorably jealous and came to my rescue?" I offered.

"Got ferociously protective and planned to beat his ass in your honor."

I chuckled. "Come on. Let's get me some water."

We made our way into the crowded kitchen, where the music was less loud but the chatter was just as intimidating. I'd been to plenty of parties like this. I knew the score. A sense of *ick* traveled up my spine, and I was hit in the gut with the embarrassment of what I'd done at my old school. Being here was like digging up the remains of my old life. I went to grab a drink, then frowned when I saw Kelseigh and her two buddies lock their laser eyes on Oakley and me.

"Do you want me to fight them off?" I joked as they started to walk over.

"Only if you're naked and in a mud pit." I looked at him wide-eyed, a challenge in my raised brows. "I mean, no. I can handle it," he quickly added.

"Oooooakley!" Kelseigh whined in that all too familiar

high-pitched, nasally, drunk girl song. "Where have you beeeeen?" She dragged out that last word and flung her arms around Oakley's neck. "I missed you." She giggled.

I wasn't so much annoyed with Kelseigh as I was self-aware. Okay, I was both. But I used to be exactly like her. In fact, I probably would have been best friends forever with her if I had lived in Austin this time last year.

"Hey, Kels!" I teased. She looked over at me as though she had just realized I was there.

"Oh, hi, Lauren," she replied, turning her attention back to Oakley.

Bitch didn't even remember my name, and she had her fingers all up in *my* man's hair. I let the jealousy flare. It only took a moment to get control of myself again, but damn, where did that even come from? I liked Oakley and all, but did seeing him like that with another woman really trigger me that much? Yep, I guess it did.

"Sorry, Kelseigh. But I gotta steal Oakley." I reached out and physically grabbed him, separating him from her grip.

Oakley looked at me, amused, and I looked at him like if he even thought of accusing me of being jealous, I would shave off his eyebrows in his sleep. "Do you want to go somewhere quieter?" I asked.

"Solver, you read my mind. How come when I'm with you, I suddenly don't feel like partying, hmm?"

"I *am* the party," I joked with what I hoped was a flirty wink. I was crossing all sorts of boundaries tonight.

"Oh really now?"

"Really."

"How about this," Oakley began. "One dance, then we can go somewhere quiet. I want to see your moves."

I chewed on the inside of my cheek for a moment. "You just want an excuse to feel me up." One glance in the living room gave me an idea of *just* the kind of "dancing" Oakley wanted to do. I wasn't complaining, but I also didn't want to end up on any Instagram stories, either. I already felt like the center of attention standing beside Oakley. I didn't bother looking around, but I could feel everyone's eyes on us. The entire fucking world was drawn to him, and I wanted to avoid that attention like the plague it was.

"I would *love* to feel you up, Solver. I've been thinking about how soft your skin feels." Oakley was rumbling in my ear, and it was like my panties were doused in sriracha. "I've been thinking about how you taste. I've been thinking about those cute little moans that escape your lips when I touch you."

Oh my Sushi. I needed a drink. Ice. Someone call an ambulance. Oakley continued, "I think about prying your pretty thighs open and—"

"Oh myyy godddd. If you don't dance with him, I'll fuck him on the dance floor," Kelseigh interrupted. Oh. Could they hear us?

"One. Dance," I conceded.

I let Oakley lead me into the living room. He turned toward me and slid his hands low around my waist, pulling me impossibly close. He started gyrating his hips to the rhythm. When I didn't immediately follow along, he repositioned his hands so that one was holding me firmly at the base of my back, almost on my ass. He used this hand to keep my already roaring kitty glued to where I could feel his dick stiffen in his jeans.

Oakley lowered his mouth to my neck, his breath sending shivers down my entire body. He started slowly kissing me, starting by my ear and working his way down with featherlight touches. I was going to lose my ever-loving shit in the middle of this kegger, surrounded by practically the whole university. I was going to have to move. Again.

Just when I thought I couldn't take the motion of his hips

combined with his wet tongue on my skin, he spun me around. I bent over slightly so that my ass was nestled right into his cock and moved my hips in fast circles, in time to the music. I heard a small moan escape his lips, and it made me smile. It seemed to go on forever. His hot hands roamed my body as we moved. Whistles could be heard as I lost myself to the sensations of it all. My heart was pounding, and heat traveled up and down my spine at his nearness. I spun around and wrapped my hands around his neck. "I think it's been two songs."

"I think you're going to ruin me," he replied.

I leaned up and pressed a faint kiss to his mouth. Soft. Warm. Needy. He nipped at my bottom lip playfully while rubbing my sides. The edge of his thumbs brushed my breasts. His hips jolted against me. "Mmm, I think we should go back to my place," he murmured.

I knew I should have said no. But I couldn't.

When the song ended, Oakley was slow to let me go and whispered in my ear, "Ready to get out of here?"

I knew the unspoken question. *Do you want this? Do you want me?*

"Let's go," I rasped.

We made our way through the crowd, and he ordered us an Uber, though it was just a short walk. I guess neither of us wanted to waste any time.

The entire car ride, I was choking on the tension and squeezing my thighs shut. We didn't banter or talk. The only communication between us was the subtle brushes of his skin on mine. Every little touch had me panting. It was like I was under a spell, and both of us weren't sure if speaking would ruin the moment.

At his apartment, I got out of the car and stood on the sidewalk. I knew I had a decision in all of this. I knew that if I marched myself up to his room, there was no escaping where this was headed. Oakley was used to one-night stands. I needed to mentally prepare myself for this to be a one-time thing—a dive into the passion that had been building between us.

"You don't have to come up. We don't have to do anything," he whispered, grabbing my hand and pulling me close. "We can sit on the couch and watch a movie. I just want to be with you."

I hooked my fingers through his belt loops, pulling him closer. "Let's go upstairs, Problem," I whispered, taking charge of this. I didn't have the excuse of being caught up in the moment, but still I wanted Oakley Davis. If just for one night.

His apartment was clean and smelled like his cologne. I briefly wondered if he'd tidied up. Did he know it would come to this? It was a small space with a leather couch and flat screen TV. The apartment was minimalistic in design and had various details sprinkled in that felt like Oakley. A picture of him in his uniform on the side table. A gaming console on the entertainment center.

"Do you want anything to drink? I never got you that water…"

I nodded and made my way over to the large window in his living room to look out over the city. His place didn't have a spectacular view, but I needed the distraction. I heard him grab some ice and pour me a drink, then walk back over to me. He pressed the cool glass against my neck, making me flinch. "Oops, sorry, was that cold?" he teasingly asked. Oakley then leaned over and licked the chill away with his hot tongue.

I took the glass from his hand and took a steady gulp, with his dark eyes focused on me. My hands were trembling. "You cold?" he asked, noticing the slight tremor in my movements.

"I'm actually kind of hot," I choked out. Oakley smiled and grabbed the glass from me, setting it on the black coffee table nearby.

"You could always take off your clothes?" Oakley offered, helping me out of my white silk tank top. I immediately wanted to cover my body with my arms. It was an instinctual insecurity. "You are so fucking beautiful," he groaned, kissing my neck. The chill in the air traveled over my skin, making my nipples pebble through the thin lace bra I was wearing.

"I'm, uh, still a little hot," I said, staring up at the ceiling with him poised in front of me. Oakley chuckled, pulling away from me. I'd expected him to start working at the buttons of my skinny jeans, but instead he went over to the glass of water and took a cube of ice out of it with his fingers before plopping it in his mouth.

I opened my mouth to ask what he was doing when he started kissing my neck again. I gasped at the cold ice mixed with his hot tongue trailing over my skin. He trailed lower, licking at my collarbone and cleavage. Reaching behind my back, Oakley then unclasped my bra, letting the thin material fall to the ground.

"Still hot, Solver?" he asked.

"N-nope," I stammered. He wrapped his lips around my nipple and sucked. Oh holy mother of trash television.

His hands moved lower and lower, unbuttoning my pants as he moaned against my skin. I writhed against him as he worked my jeans over my thighs and off my body. The only thing I was wearing were my pink hip huggers.

"Why are you still wearing clothes?" I asked as he peppered kisses on my thighs.

"Because I'm in charge," he replied. My breath hitched when he sucked on a tender sliver of skin on my inner thigh. My legs started to shake. "Put your hands on the window, Solver."

I did as he told me, turning around and leaning forward on the glass where anyone could see us. It was still dark in his apartment, but it wouldn't be difficult for someone to see me. Oakley was on his knees at my back, and I looked over my shoulder just in time to see him grab the fabric of my panties with his sharp teeth and drag them down my legs.

"Oh my Pornhub, you're, like, really good at that," I said. I pushed thoughts of *practice makes perfect* far from my mind.

"You always like to be in control, Amanda," he said before dragging his teeth along the cheek of my ass. "I think it's time for you to let go. Spin around."

I did as he asked and looked down at him. Seeing Oakley on his knees in front of me was a powerful feeling. Also, from this angle, I could tell that he had ridiculously long lashes. Why did guys always get pretty lashes? It seriously wasn't fair—

"Get out of your head, Amanda Matthews," he ordered, lifting my left leg up and placing my thigh over his shoulder. He was eye level with my cave of wonders, and a flash of insecurity spiked through me. Did he like shaved girls? Did I have any razor bumps? Oh my God, I should have eaten some pineapple this morning. Wasn't that supposed to make you taste good? Please kiss me. Holy son of a motherfucking—

He leaned forward and tenderly kissed me. I leaned my head back and gasped. "I could taste you forever," he moaned while diving in. Now, Oakley was a messy eater, but he devoured pussy like a skilled target master. His tongue flicked my clit with precision and in rhythm to my bliss. His strong hands wrapped around me as he lapped me up.

I was shaking so hard he had to hold me in place. The whimpers escaping my lips were harsh and needy. I felt so close to that peak of pleasure I couldn't handle it.

I didn't even have time to feel embarrassed about how I

arched to follow his movements. And when he pinched my clit between his demanding lips, an orgasm tore through me. It was hard and fast, bursting through every nerve ending in my body.

"Oh-oh. Oakley!" I cried out as the shocks rocked through me.

He stood up and wiped his mouth with the back of his hand. There was no mistaking the slickness coating his lips. I reached for his shirt and practically tore it off of his body. He quickly moved for his jeans and shrugged them off like a frantic man on a mission. "I can't wait to hear you say my name when my cock is buried inside of you," he said.

The moment his perfect body was free of clothes, I wrapped my legs around his waist. He carried me to his bedroom, kissing my neck. It felt good, to feel light and small against him. He picked me up like it was effortless.

My back hit the mattress, and he quickly pulled a condom from his nightstand. Then, he did that hot guy move where he tore open the foil with his teeth. I greedily watched as he slid it on his monster cock.

Once it was on, he pried my thighs open and stared at my cunt like it was the best damn thing he'd ever seen. "Amanda, you're going to ruin me."

I reached for him as he positioned himself between my legs. I looked him in the eye, grabbing his ass, guiding him inside of me. "Oh, fuckkkk," he groaned.

Oh fuck, indeed. Oakley was fucking huge. My lips parted on a moan as I adjusted to him. "You're so freaking big," I choked out.

"You okay? Need me to go slow?"

"No! Hard. I want you h-hard." I'd never been the type to demand things in bed. I was always too nervous to stumble through the motions with lackluster frat daddies to demand much of anything. But I felt safe with Oakley. I felt cherished. I felt...sexy.

Oakley didn't waste a second. He started thrusting, pounding power in his movements. I squirmed as filthy, wet slapping sounds filled his room. We clawed at each other's bodies, kissing, biting, crying out as our hips rolled with each hard intrusion.

"You're so tight," he groaned. "I'm not going to last."

I squeezed him while dragging my nails down his back. I could feel another orgasm rolling through me. Building, building, building.

We both came together. His body went rigid, and my back arched off the bed. If it was possible to see stars, I did. I wasn't thinking about calories, consequences, and college. It was just us. It was just Oakley.

Fuck. There was no way this could only happen once. I was addicted.

20

I woke up in Oakley's bedroom for the second time this semester, only this time, I woke up in the bed, snuggled under the covers, with his arms wrapped around me. And for the second time, I was up before he was. I lay in bed with my eyes closed, savoring the moment for just a minute longer. I knew it was wrong, but it just felt too damn good.

I forced my eyes to open and gently extracted myself from the tangle of limbs and sheets. My parents' flight was later this morning, and they liked to get there at least an hour and half early, just like the airlines recommended. I mentally calculated what time they needed to get to the airport and what time they would be leaving their hotel, factoring in breakfast. Light was already filtering in through Oakley's window—holy shit, that window. I had to hustle to get to the hotel.

I got out of the bed as gingerly as I could, trying not to wake Oakley. I got to work collecting all of my clothes from the floor and got dressed in record time, only pausing to give the armchair a nostalgic glance. I decided to go commando since my panties were still completely soaked from last night.

I draped them strategically over the chair so that Oakley would see them when he woke up.

I grabbed my purse and looked over at Oakley one last time. He was still dead to the world, snoring softly. Damn, I really envied his ability to sleep that well. Although, now that I was thinking about it, I didn't wake up once during the night. Must have been all that extra cardio.

I snuck out of the apartment like a walk of shame ninja, closing the door with a soft click. I texted my mom to let her know I was on my way, and to be honest, to gauge whether she was already awake or if I was going to be pounding on the hotel room door, trying to get her up. While I was waiting for her to respond, I called an Uber. My mom replied with a simple thumbs up as I got into the car and started the twenty-minute drive over. Good enough.

I couldn't bring myself to look at Instagram; who knew what was going to show up there after the party last night? As good as last night felt, I couldn't deny that I was feeling nervous about the consequences. To try and calm down the ball of anxiety growing in the pit of my stomach, I passed the time in the car by popping in my headphones and watching a manifestation video.

By the time we pulled up to the five-star hotel my parents used as their drunken love nest last night, I was feeling slightly more composed. I hopped out of the car, smiled at the valet as I passed by, and made my way into the lobby.

This hotel was stunning. The floors were the first thing to catch my eye. They were a cool white and gray marble that complimented the gray textured wallpaper perfectly. The front desk was black and had a beautiful bright pink orchid sitting on top, and a man dressed in a black suit stood behind it. He looked me over and was clearly not impressed with my wrinkled clothes and last night's makeup. I gave him a small wave and let him know that I was meeting my parents in their room.

When I found their room, I knocked lightly, not wanting to wake other guests. My mom flung the door open and gave me the same look the front desk clerk did. "Is that what you were wearing yesterday?" my mom said, her voice carrying down the hall. I looked down at my white tank and jeans.

"Uh, yeah," I said as I pushed past her into the room and shut the door. "I was just so exhausted from all the fun we had at the game, I fell asleep in my clothes and slept straight through my alarm," I said weakly.

"If you say so!" my mom said, still looking at me suspiciously. She looked surprisingly good for as drunk as she got last night. I knew her well enough to know that it was expertly applied makeup and sheer determination not to admit that she couldn't party like she was twenty anymore.

"Hi, pumpkin," my dad said, sticking his head out of the bathroom door. "Can you help your mom finish packing while I finish shaving? Then we can go get some breakfast."

My mom was busy shoving everything into her bags, trying to make them fit. I stopped her, took everything out, and folded it meticulously. Since they were only here for a couple of days, it only took me a few minutes to have my mom's bags perfectly packed and ready to go.

"So you just stayed in your clothes," Mom prodded while Dad was out of earshot.

"Yep," I answered, popping the *p* for emphasis.

"Are you sure? Because that looks like a hickey on your neck," she said, preening like a detective that just solved a case.

"Mother. Let's not discuss this right now."

My phone started ringing, and I absently answered it, not bothering to check the caller ID. I was just thankful for the interruption. "Hello?"

"Where are you?" Oakley rasped. His voice was heavy and sleepy, like a low purr.

"I'm busy, what's up?"

"What's up?" he snapped. "What's up is I woke up and you were gone." Wasn't he used to that? I eyed my mother and excused myself into the hallway. I knew she'd probably press her ear to the door, but I didn't want to make eavesdropping easy on her.

"I had plans," I said in a low voice. "I didn't want to wake you up."

"Plans? Plans with who?" he growled. Was that possessiveness in his tone?

I scoffed. "None of your business. I didn't think you'd care." Wasn't this what one-night stands were supposed to be? You fuck, then sneak out the next morning. Usually I was hella hungover when it happened.

"Of course I care. I was going to fuck you in the shower," he replied. I imagined him pouting on the other end of the line.

"Shower sex never works. The space is small, and it just turns into a game of human Jenga with us flailing around."

"I'm a pro at shower sex. You just need someone strong enough to pick you up and hold you against the wall, Solver." I swallowed. My mouth suddenly felt very dry. All the moisture had gone to my lady flower. "Where are you? I wanted to have breakfast."

"I told you. I have plans, Oakley. I'm too busy. And what happened last night can't happen again."

He chuckled. "Oh, it's happening again, babe. And again...and again...multiple orgasms is my forte."

"Oakley Davis, you are incorrigible. Look, I got to go…"

The door behind me opened up, and I nearly fell when the support holding me up had vanished. My mother, in all her glory, appeared with a grin on her face. "Oh honey!" she said loudly. "I'm so excited we're having breakfast at the HILTON HOTEL IN DOWNTOWN AUSTIN OFF THE CORNER OF MAIN AND FIFTH STREET IN TWENTY MINUTES."

I couldn't hang up in time. Yep, that bitch was definitely listening in and was loudly letting Oakley know where we were. "I'll be there in fifteen," he chuckled before hanging up.

TWENTY-FIVE MINUTES LATER, we were sitting in the Hilton's dining room, surrounded by my parents' luggage. The tables were all covered in white linens with sunshine yellow daffodils in the center. I was beginning to think that maybe Oakley wasn't going to come after all, and I relaxed a little bit, but then my mother started waving frantically, and all hopes of keeping her from meeting Oakley Davis vanished.

He headed straight for our table and very politely introduced himself to my parents, as though he hadn't had his tongue all up in my lady business not even twelve hours ago. I could tell that my mom was immediately smitten with him. He was charming, I had to give him that. But my parents liking Oakley was not what I was actually worried about.

"Oakley, it's so nice to meet you!" my mother said while hugging him in greeting. I noticed how she felt up his muscular back and nearly swatted her away. Down, Momma.

"It's nice to meet you too," Oakley said, his voice like honey. "Thanks for the invite to brunch. I'm glad I could make it." He poked me in the side, then moved to shake my father's hand. Naturally, Dad did the macho display of power, squeezing Oakley's palm a little harder than necessary to mark his superiority. I think everyone at the table knew Oakley could take him in a thumb war any day of the week.

"It's nice to meet you, son," Dad said through clenched teeth. "You play a nice game of ball."

Oakley grinned. "Did you play?"

"I was more of a mathlete in school. Made some money on calculated bets, though." Dad winked, and I forced myself not to roll my eyes.

"Sit, sit!" Mom said, gesturing to the chair between her and me.

Oakley waited until I was in my chair, then made sure to settle right next to me, pressing his leg against mine under the table suggestively. I kicked him away, but he didn't move. Instead, he slipped something into my hand. I opened my hand under the table and saw the pink fabric from my panties I had left on his chair. Oh. My. Loki.

"What are you going to school for?" Dad asked.

"Business. My mother owns a few flower shops across the country. Gonna help her out once I've graduated."

"Oh, I love flowers," Mom interrupted. "Roses are my favorite. It's the ultimate gesture of love," she added suggestively, waggling her eyebrows. Way to go for overkill, Mom.

"I'll be sure to have my mother send you a bouquet." Oakley winked, and just like that, my mother was putty in his hand. Damn, he was good.

"We are just so glad we got to meet you. I follow you on Instagram, you know," Mom said.

Oh shit. Stop talking, Mom. Oakley grabbed my knee under the table. "Oh?" he replied.

"That photo of you shirtless with the puppy on the beach was really inspiring," Mom purred, making Dad laugh.

"That was from three years ago..." Oakley looked confused, and I wanted to hide.

"Okay! I'm hungry. Ravenous," I said with a choked cough. "I want pancakes. Who wants pancakes?"

"I'm pretty hungry too," Oakley added. "Worked up quite an appetite yesterday." He let a long suggestive pause fill the space before adding, "At the game, of course."

After a few minutes of more awkward chitchat, my mom went in for the kill. "So what did the two of you get up to last night?"

"Oh, nothing," I started to say.

"We went to an after-party to celebrate the win," Oakley told my mom at the exact same time.

Both of my parents went quiet and looked at me nervously. The tension was thick enough that Oakley looked genuinely concerned and asked, "Did I do something wrong?"

"Amanda, are you partying again?" my dad asked sternly, completely ignoring Oakley's question.

"No, Dad," I said. "I mean, yes, I went to a party, but I wasn't *partying*." I tried to clarify.

"Oh honey, after everything we did to give you a fresh start after that unfortunate streaking incident," my mom said, looking distressed. "Oh Crosby, I knew I shouldn't have drank last night. Did it make you spiral? I feel so selfish."

Oakley's eyes practically bulged out of his head. He looked at me like he was dying to hear more. He was the fucking worst. I really just needed this breakfast to be over, and I did not feel like getting into my past with anybody, let alone Oakley.

"Mom!" I said firmly, my eyes wild. "I'm fine. I went to an after-party to keep an eye on Oakley; it's my job. I did not drink. I did not do anything stupid." At least, not anything that anybody other than Oakley knew about.

"We didn't even stay that long," Oakley quickly added in a

half-hearted attempt to help me out. "We were barely there for an hour."

"Then why were you out so late?" Dad asked, and my cheeks flamed red. I was not about to tell my parents I left early to fuck my client.

"Pancakes," Oakley spat out awkwardly. "Where are those damn pancakes?"

We finished our breakfast in an uncomfortable silence, with Oakley staring at me intently the entire time. I was so relieved when the check was paid and it was time to leave. I gave both my mom and dad quick hugs and reassurances that I was doing really well. They then left in a taxi for the airport. Now, I just had to deal with Oakley.

"Streaking incident?" Oakley asked the first moment we had alone. I knew this was coming. I could only escape my past for so long. I turned to face Oakley with a sheepish grin, though there was a heavy sense of remorse tugging at my stomach.

"I got very drunk one night and went streaking on our campus president's lawn," I said as fast as I could get the words out.

His eyes widened, but he didn't say a word. I took his silence as encouragement to continue. "It was sloppy. I fell down. And when he went outside, I puked on his slippers."

"That's...bad," Oakley replied with a sympathetic wince.

"What's worse was that it was all caught on video. I was about forty pounds heavier. The fat shaming was really intense," I admitted. The act of what I'd done was enough to scare me. My whole career was built around developing reputations, and that single act ruined mine. But the comments. The snickers. The hashtags. It was a lot.

"Is that why you're...picky about food."

"It's why I'm picky about my entire life. It's why I moved

here. It's why I stopped partying and started dieting and took a fuck ton of hours to graduate early."

Oakley seemed to chew on my words for a bit. He stared at me intently, his eyes penetrating my soul. His prolonged silence let my insecurities run wild. He was probably thinking that he was an idiot to trust his image and career with someone who fucked up her own so badly. Oh God, he probably didn't want to be with me anymore either, because how could he risk having someone find out about my past and have that reflect poorly on him? Not that it mattered, we couldn't be together anyway, but maybe this was what was going to actually convince Oakley of that.

"I'm sorry," he apologized.

This was it, this was where he was going to tell me that he's sorry, but he can no longer work with me. Running all the way to Texas didn't erase my past; I was never going to be able to leave it behind.

"I understand," I said solemnly. "I'll work with Dr. Haynes to get you a new publicist as soon as possible."

"What?" Oakley asked, bewildered. "I don't want a new publicist. I'm sorry that I was such an ass."

"Huh?" I not-so-elegantly mumbled. Now it was my turn to be confused.

"You worked so hard, completely turning your life around. And then you got stuck with me. I almost got you fired from your internship, and then I have been dragging you to bars and after-parties," he said genuinely. "I'm sorry," he repeated. "And I'm done partying."

I blanched. "You're done?"

"Done. If I had known how uncomfortable they made you, I would have never suggested it to you. It all makes sense now." He wrapped his arms around me, pulling me in for a hug, and I let him. It felt good to be comforted in his arms. It was a relief to stare the thing that had been haunting me for the last few months and feel...grace.

"Is it too soon to ask to see the video?" he asked with a chuckle.

"Too soon, Problem."

I pulled out of Oakley's arms and looked up at him. I wasn't sure what we were supposed to do next. Was this the part where we had the awkward conversation about last night? "Listen, Coach wants us watching tape this afternoon, but I'd like to see you again this week."

I swallowed. "I'd like to see you too."

Oakley beamed as if he'd never been happier. "A real date?"

"A real date," I conceded. There was no going back now. Last night, Oakley stole my body. Today, he stole my heart.

21

Oakley and I walked back in the direction of the university together, hand-in-hand until we came to the point where we had to go different ways. He pulled me into a quick hug and planted a soft kiss on the top of my head. I inhaled the clean scent of his soap mixed with his spicy cologne; it was exhilarating. Oakley was the one to release his arms first so that he could tilt my face up to his. He kissed me greedily, and I fully lost myself in it. When he ran his tongue over my bottom lip, I parted my mouth, allowing him to completely take over.

I brought my hand to his chest and gently pushed while also taking a step back to put a little bit of distance between us. He groaned his disapproval at the sudden absence of my mouth on his. If I didn't stop him, we were going to end up getting down and dirty right here in the middle of the sidewalk. As much as I didn't want it to end, Oakley had to get to the stadium, and I was still his kickass publicist after all.

"Go watch footage and strategize or whatever you do when you watch tapes," I teased.

"I'll text you later, and we can talk about where we should go on that date."

He planted one last quick kiss on my lips and then turned to head toward practice. I watched him walk away for just a moment, taking the time to appreciate how good his ass looked in his jeans. Plus, staring at Oakley's butt gave my legs time to recover from being turned to total mush.

I was on cloud fucking nine. I had the best orgasm of my life last night, I had come clean and told Oakley everything, and he still wanted to date me and let me be his publicist. Which meant I was going to graduate early with killer recommendations and a hot boyfriend. I practically floated the rest of the way home, thinking about how awesome I was and how great my life was going.

And then my cell phone rang. "Hello?"

"Miss Matthews, I know it's a Sunday, but this call couldn't wait." I grabbed my chest. My mentor sounded angry, and I wasn't ready to hear why. "There are photos of you and Oakley at a party."

I squeezed my eyes shut. Holy hell. Last night hit me like a sledgehammer. We were practically grinding on one another. I didn't even have to see the photos to know that it probably looked really bad. "The lack of professionalism is really concerning, Miss Matthews. I can't in good conscience give any sort of recommendations if you consistently cross boundaries with your clients."

Shame crept up my neck. It was almost worse than disappointing my parents. Dr. Haynes was a huge deal in our industry. "You're supposed to be learning right now. This could be a massive stepping stone for your future, and you're blowing it. Either you hold yourself to a higher standard or give up. We can't keep working this way. It is starting to reflect badly on me, and unlike you, I actually care what people think about me."

"I'm so sorry," I sputtered.

"Me too. We'll have a formal meeting tomorrow. I suggest you manage the social media portion before then."

He hung up, cutting me off, though I wasn't sure what I could possibly say. My thumbs moved lightning fast to check the damage, and the moment I saw the photos and accompanying speculation, it felt just like the streaking incident all over again.

The photo was hot. We were lost in one another, his hands were cupping my ass, and my lips were pressed against his neck. Every muscle in his arms was flexed. His eyes were locked on me. I knew better. It felt so fucking good at the time, but I knew better, and I let it happen anyway.

I started frantically swiping through the photos, not that it could really get worse than that. But I had to know what was out there so I could get in front of it. Oakley was tagged in picture after picture with me in various compromising positions. I landed on one picture, and it took me about three seconds to process the fact that the girl draped all over Oakley wasn't me. What the actual fuck? When did he even have time to take this?

I didn't even care.

I felt like I was going to puke. My entire world was falling apart, again. And it was all my fault. Again. I was going to get fired tomorrow from the best opportunity I ever had. I wasn't going to graduate early, possibly not even at all. There's no way I would get another PR internship at this school. Probably not at any other school either. My boyfriend? I didn't know, was he even my boyfriend? Whatever he was, there was photographic evidence of another girl with her tits pressed tightly into his chest while she kissed his cheek. After that picture, he sure as shit wasn't my anything. I quickly screenshotted the post in case it disappeared. I've watched enough episodes of *Cheaters* to know to save the evidence.

I had to sit down. I took a few steps, looking for anywhere to sit. I couldn't find anything, so I sat right in the middle of the sidewalk and brought my hands to my temples, using my thumbs to rub out the tension. Coeds went around me like I wasn't even there. I was trying so hard not to cry or vomit right there on the sidewalk. Is this what a panic attack felt like?

I tried to breathe in and out. I was gasping for air, but it was like my lungs couldn't fully expand. I was just panting without relief. Oh gosh. This was why I couldn't get distracted. This was why I couldn't relax for even a second. I was toxic. I was fucked up.

"Amanda?" A soft voice broke through my panic. Slender arms wrapped around me, and I was yanked up off the ground. My roommate stared at me. Her red hair was a wild mess of curls, and her eyes were full of concern. She decided what to do in a split second. "Let's get you inside, okay? Let's go home."

I wordlessly let her guide me up to our apartment. She didn't ask me questions; she was just there. It wasn't until I was sitting at our kitchen island with a cup of tea in my palm that she spoke up. "Panic attacks are such a bitch. Do you feel the warmth of the heat from the cup on your palm?" she asked. I drew what little energy I had to my sense of touch.

"Y-yes," I croaked.

"Do you see my crazy ass outfit?" she then asked, her voice growing more and more animated with every syllable. On the street, she treated me like a wild animal, approaching cautiously. That caution was fading now. My eyes took in her purple jumpsuit, and I smiled.

"What are you wearing?" I asked, my voice hoarse.

"We aren't talking about me. Can you hear the cars outside?" she asked.

I listened to the traffic on the street outside our building, various honks and purring engines could be faintly heard. "Yes," I replied, this time my voice stronger.

"Great. What happened down there?"

I let everything spill. I told Shelby everything. About why I was in Texas. About my fears about food.

About Oakley.

"So what if you fucked him? You're an intern. It's not that big of a deal."

"It is if I want a good letter of recommendation."

"You and I both know that your father is going to hire you. You honestly don't even need to finish your degree. He's got that privileged nepotism process," she assured me, snorting.

"But I want to earn it," I stammered.

"Do you? Because it seems like you really just want to prove you're perfect. I don't think it was ever about this internship."

I cradled my head in my hands. Was she right? Was that what all of this was about? I really needed to call my psychic for a tarot reading.

My phone buzzed, and I saw Oakley's name. Without thinking, I picked up my phone and threw it across the room, not caring if it was completely destroyed. I didn't need it, and I didn't need Oakley either. Shelby looked at me, a little surprised, but mostly calm.

"Amanda?" she asked, going back to her more cautious approach. "It's okay. You are going to be okay." She came and sat on the floor right in front of me in what I now knew was the lotus pose, her legs crossed with her toes on her thighs.

"Take a deep breath with me," she said when I didn't

respond. "Breathe in through your nose and breathe out slowly through your mouth."

I followed along with her breathing exercises, and she led me through some basic stretching poses until I did actually start to feel better. Or at least more grounded. I couldn't change what I did in California, and I couldn't change what happened last night. The only thing I could change is how I react to it. I learned that from my favorite manifestation video.

"Thank you for being there for me, Shelby," I said, my heart absolutely overflowing with love for her. One minute I was raging, the next I was giggling, and now I was about to start ugly crying over how much I loved my roommate. Emotional trauma is weird. Thank Zeus Shelby was so understanding, and also the only one who was seeing me like this.

Just as I was getting a handle on myself enough to go check the damage I did to my phone, there was a knock on the door. It started off slowly, but became louder and more insistent. Then I heard Oakley's voice.

"Amanda! Amanda are you home?" he shouted.

Shelby went to the door to tell him that I didn't want to see him and to leave. I heard them go back and forth before I stood up and went to the door.

"It's fine, Shelby. He can come in."

Oakley pushed past her and wrapped me up in a hug. I was surprised by the gesture. "I came over as soon as I could. Why didn't you answer your phone?"

I turned away from him to stare at the cracked device on my floor. Okay, so maybe throwing it was a tad melodramatic, but I'm allowed to have my moments. "Fuck," he cursed. "Dr. Haynes emailed me, and I saw the photos."

I pulled fully out of his hold and looked up at him. I didn't even want to know what I looked like. I was a sobbing, sweaty mess and hadn't showered since last night. I just wanted a warm bubble bath to wash away the mistakes of the last day. "I told Dr. Haynes that I absolutely refuse to work with anyone else. I made Coach write a letter stating how well you're doing. I also"—he paused to pull out his phone—"had every guy on the team reach out to accounts with the photos of us, and they offered signed merchandise to anyone willing to delete them. I think Dale has a date with a stage five clinger as a result of it."

My mouth dropped open in shock. "Wh-what?" I couldn't even process it all. "Why? How?"

"You cleaned up my image; I want to protect yours," he said softly. He stepped closer, and I breathed in his scent. My heart was melting for this guy. I had him all wrong.

"I don't even know what to say..."

"I'm sorry. I really like you, okay? Let someone else be the solver for once."

I reached up, planning to kiss him, when something else crossed my mind. "Who was the girl hanging all over you last night?" I asked. The timing was bad, and I sounded like a jealous idiot, but considering I had a panic attack in the middle of a busy sidewalk, this was the least of my concerns.

"Uh, that would be you," Oakley replied with a confused chuckle.

"No. There was a photo last night. Some girl was pressed all up against you."

Oakley looked confused, so I instinctively went to whip out my phone with the evidence. My hands searched my pockets, then remembered that I had thrown it. Shit. That was stupid for so many reasons. I bent over to pick up my phone and found that it still worked, the screen was just cracked. At least something was going my way tonight.

I navigated to the photo and held my phone up to his face. "This girl. Who is she? Why is she kissing you?" Why did I sound so damn jealous? I was going to blame the shrillness in my voice on my roller coaster of a night.

Oakley looked at the picture and laughed. Was this man trying to get murdered tonight?

"What the hell is so funny?" I snapped.

"One, you're insanely cute when you are jealous. Two, she was just a random drunk girl. Her friends dared her to come get a picture with me. I overheard them telling her to pinch my butt, so I made sure to keep it out of grabbing range. I thought she was just going to give me a hug, but she went in to kiss my cheek at the last second."

Oh. Okay. I felt really dumb.

I folded myself back into his chest. "Oakley? Can you stay with me tonight?"

"Anything for you, Solver," he said as he easily scooped me up and carried me to bed.

22

I could count off the top of my head three conversations that made me cringe.

The first conversation was when my mother told me about sex. I was eleven years old and had gotten my first period during a math test. I was wearing white jeans like the badass middle schooler I was. The entire class knew, and when I got home, my mother threw me a period party.

Yep, a period party.

She made us eat tomato soup. She also had a vagina piñata and filled it with pads. It was seriously traumatizing to beat it with a baseball bat. Then, she dragged me kicking and screaming up the stairs so she could tell me about the birds and the bees. I'd already known the mechanics of sex thanks to health class, but after four Bloody Marys, my mother felt like she needed to give me the nitty gritty.

"Anal is painful, Amanda," she'd said. "Even if he begs, don't do it. You'll never be the same, and the pain isn't worth it."

I'd scrubbed the conversation from my mind while keeled over with cramps. It was terrible.

The second worst conversation was when I had to explain to President Gentry why I was buck naked on his lawn. Listing the amount of Four Lokos I'd had seemed appropriate at the time, but I still felt a twinge of secondhand embarrassment every time I thought of it.

But the third worst conversation? It was happening right now. "So what is this?" I asked with my heart pounding. Defining the relationship was like getting an annual pap smear: No one really wanted to do it, but it was necessary. If I had to compare this conversation to having Dr. Johari's hands up my tunnel of doom, I'd say her tender touch and the feet stirrups were preferable.

We were lying in my bed, my head nuzzled into the crook of his arm that was holding me tight. It was the darkness of the room that gave me the courage to even ask in the first place. Not being able to see Oakley's intense eyes, especially when I looked a hot mess, was definitely a plus.

Oakley shifted onto his side. He turned to look at me as he adjusted his arm so that he could rest his head on it. I closed my eyes and breathed in slowly as I waited for him to answer. Now that everybody knew just how *close* we had gotten, I felt like I could finally admit to myself how much I wanted this. Wanted him.

"I like you a lot, Amanda." He paused, and I waited for the *but* that always seemed to follow that statement. "I know I said that I'm not a relationship guy and I don't have girlfriends. But..."

Ah. There was the *but*. I didn't want to get my hopes up too high, but this seemed like it was going in a good direction. A good *but*. Like a superhero's ass in spandex kind of but. I gave in to the flood of excitement, and my whole body started to tingle.

"I can't stop thinking about you. When I'm not with you, I want to be. I feel like I can talk to you about anything, and

I've never felt this comfortable with anyone. Plus, you're hot as hell and fuck like a goddess. I can't stand the thought of you being with anybody else. I want you to be mine."

Well, put me in spandex and let's save the world.

"That was quite the romantic speech," I replied. "I'm just not sure if I'm sold yet. I need some convincing." I wiggled. I knew he was packing some impressive morning wood under these sheets, and I wasn't against telling Oakley junior gooooood morning.

Oakley chuckled and grabbed my wrist. "You're mine," he growled playfully. "But let's not do any labels."

Ah, and in the words of Tag Team, *Whoomp, there it is*.

Red flag. Bright red fuckboy flag of surrendering shame.

"No labels, huh?" I asked, scooting away. His grip on my wrist tightened.

"This is new. I finally convinced you to go on a date with me. And yeah, I'd like to pretty much stab anyone in the eye that looks at you for too long, and the idea of anyone touching you sends me into a fucking rage."

"But no labels," I repeated dryly, distancing myself even more. No labels was the hallmark of man whores. I'd had my fair share of commitment phobes, and I knew that was code for, *if I don't call you my girlfriend, there's no accountability if I find something better.*

"Stop pulling away from me," he growled as he pulled me back. One minute I was ready to run to the bathroom and to kick myself for risking my career for this dude, and the next he had me pinned to the mattress with his hard body. The feminist in me didn't like being manhandled, but also that simple move had me wetter than a slip and slide. Maybe I did like being manhandled?

"You wanna know why I don't like labels, Solver?" he asked, pressing into me. "It becomes a game."

"It's not a game. It's a way for us to know the clear

boundaries of our dynamic. What the fuck are you talking about?" I asked, squirming.

"I've been with a lot of girls—" My groan of annoyance cut him off. "And all of them wanted to know what we were so they could hashtag boyfriend me on Instagram. I like trophies, but I don't want to be anyone's participation badge."

I thrust my hips up in annoyance. The move simply added more heat to the moment. "And you think I'm just some girl looking to brag about my football star fuck buddy?" I asked. "I didn't want this."

"And I know that," Oakley purred, kissing my neck. I don't know how he knew where every sensitive little spot on my neck was, but he teased them expertly. "It's a hang up I have. I'm working on it, okay? I'm trying to navigate a lot of change right now. My party life. My image. My...my future."

I wanted to ask him what he meant. I really fucking did. But he looked like he was about to run from the room. I recognized how vulnerable he looked and didn't want to pressure him.

But I didn't want to compromise my own sanity, either.

"We can take things slow," I replied. "I don't want you dipping in any infected ponds while we're sharing a lily pad, though."

Oakley grinned. "How could I possibly want another pond when this one is so perfect?" His lips found my collarbones, and that skilled tongue of his swiped out to taste me.

Then he was gone. I was just about ready to spread-eagle for him when he jumped off the bed and started searching for something. Once he found his cell phone on the dresser, he came back. "Take a photo with me," he pleaded.

"I'm naked," I argued. Oakley rolled his eyes and grabbed my hand, making sure to thread our fingers together. Within an instant, he snapped a photo—making sure to crop out my freeballing titties. After what felt like two seconds of filtering, it was posted to Instagram and already had four hundred likes.

"What did you say?" I asked as he tossed it on the mattress beside me.

"See for yourself. I'm about to take a shower."

I watched him disappear, then greedily picked up his phone. The photo was slightly blurry and sweet, but it was the caption that made me smile.

#mine

I supposed I was okay with being his. For now.

AFTER SOME SEXY time in the shower, because *oh yeah*, Oakley got some after that Instagram post, I had to get ready to face the music. And it was a slow haunting death march that was leading me like the pied piper to Dr. Haynes's office for that formal discussion he promised me on the phone last night.

What did one wear to be humiliated in front of a legend and then fired? Black? I went with all black. This was a funeral for my future, after all. And no makeup. I was just going to cry it off two seconds after leaving his office anyway. No need to have stinging eyes and mascara streaks to add to my shame.

Oakley offered to walk over with me, but I put my big girl panties on, sucked it up, and walked over by myself. My feet felt like they were encased in lead, and the hot ball of anxiety in my stomach was radiating nervous energy. Before knocking on death's door, I did a few of the breathing exercises Shelby taught me and repeated my favorite mantra. When I felt ready, I turned solemnly to face the door and knocked, fully aware of my own melodrama.

"Come in, Miss Matthews," Dr. Haynes called. His voice was cold and disappointed. I almost couldn't make my body move into his office. This was going to fucking suck.

I walked into his office and took my usual chair, not daring to say anything. When I finally got the courage to look up at him instead of looking at my shoes, there was none of the usual warmth in his face.

"When we first met, I was surprised that my newest PR student was being accused of crossing ethical boundaries. Your professors have raved about your coursework. It was hard to believe that anyone could accuse you of acting anything less than professional," he started. "Mr. Davis recently told me the truth about that night, which made far more sense than the version of things that were spun to me in that first meeting."

I listened intently, still not willing to speak.

"I am very disappointed to find myself in this position again. If it were solely up to me, I would not keep you in this program. However, it is not entirely up to me. Coach Howard has made a convincing argument for you to stay. It also seems that you have charmed the entire football team. It has come to my attention that every single photo has been removed. That is incredibly impressive.

"By the skin of your teeth, you will remain in your internship. But I think maybe we need to come to a better arrangement to ensure your success moving forward," Dr. Haynes said, peering at me.

"I'm willing to do anything, Dr. Haynes," I stammered. "I have learned so much from you. I hate that I've disappointed you, but my work ethic is spotless."

Dr. Haynes got up from his desk and sauntered over to me. It was the first time since meeting him that my mentor seemed predatory. My eyes went wide when he leaned on his desk next to me. "Miss Matthews," he purred, every syllable of my name dripping with sex. This was starting to feel like a cheap porno, but I wasn't sure if that was just my imagination or what.

"I think I have a way that we could work through this," he rasped, leaning forward. I wanted to scoot my chair back but also didn't want to show any weakness.

"And what way is that?" I spat, crossing my arms across my chest.

"You know I do some freelance representation, right?" he then asked.

"Of course. It's one of the reasons I wanted to work with you. You have such a track record of success, and I really see the value in your mentorship," I insisted. I couldn't figure out where this conversation was going.

"I'm working with a company that wants a partnership with your father's company. Plotify is taking the music industry by storm, and we'd like in on the pot."

It suddenly made sense. Doctor Haynes didn't want to mentor me, and by the looks of it, he didn't even care about my...image. He wanted an in with my father.

"You have his number," I began with a sneer. "I'm sure the great Zachary Haynes doesn't need an intern's help to get the job." I didn't like how I was being used.

"We both know you don't need this internship. We both know you'll have your dream job after college. You didn't have to work for it. Hell, you went streaking at your old school, and Daddy covered it up for you. I just figured…"

"You just figured what?" I asked, emotion clogging my throat.

"I just figured you'd like the opportunity to pretend that you deserve this. Half of this job is about who you know, the other half is who you can bribe. We spend years teaching you ethics and best practices, but at the end of the day, we all do whatever is necessary for our clients. And I'm willing to work closely with you for a phone call with your Dad."

As he spoke, he grew closer and closer, invading my space with a sinister grin.

My mind raced. Despite how little Dr. Haynes clearly thought of me, I did actually want to earn my degree and position in the industry. I didn't want to have this just handed to me because of who my dad was. I had worked really hard all semester, and I had done a damn good job.

"Well, Amanda?" Something about the way he said my name instead of the usual Miss Matthews made my skin crawl, and I made up my mind.

"No," I told him.

"You're really not going to make one simple phone call to secure your future?" he continued to pressure me.

Without warning, Oakley burst through the door.

"What the hell do you think you're doing?" he snapped at Dr. Haynes.

"Mr. Davis, I'm not sure what you are referring to, but this is a private meeting with Miss Matthews to discuss the consequences of her actions," he said calmly, as if he hadn't just been attempting to blackmail me.

"The hell it is. I heard everything that you just said," Oakley accused.

Dr. Haynes's face went pale, but he remained composed. He was clearly thinking about his words very carefully, but Oakley didn't give him a chance to respond.

"Let me tell you how this is going to work. Amanda is my publicist, she basically pulled off a miracle by turning my image around. If you don't pass her AND give her a glowing recommendation, I'm going to go to the Dean and tell them exactly how you 'mentor' your students," he finished as he stared Dr. Haynes down.

Dr. Haynes started chuckling. That's right, this asshole

thought being exposed for blackmail was funny.

"And what makes you think that the university is going to side with a womanizing frat boy?"

I watched the scene unfold in front of me in horror. I couldn't get off this emotional rollercoaster, nor could I process what was happening fast enough to even react. And while I wasn't totally digging the whole damsel in distress thing, I did really appreciate that I wasn't alone.

Oakley turned pale for a moment. "I think we both know that the university can't handle any more bad press where my family is concerned," he replied in a low voice. My heart sank. I didn't want this.

Dr. Haynes seemed to chew over his thoughts for a moment, then finally decided what to do. "Fine. I'll be following your progress, Miss Matthews. You have an away game this weekend, so I suggest you do your job. At the first sign of trouble, you can bet I'll bring it up with the university president." I swallowed his threat like the bitter pill it was and nodded.

"Come on," Oakley said, gently grabbing my hand and guiding me out of there. The moment we were away, I clutched Oakley's arm tightly and let out a whimper.

"Thank you. What were you even doing here?"

He gave me a sheepish grin. "I just wanted to make sure you weren't punished. I'm glad I was here."

"Me too."

"He is a total dick. I don't like how close he was standing to you either," Oakley growled. I let out a sigh and nodded. The entire meeting wasn't anything like what I'd expected. Dr. Haynes was supposed to be professional, the epitome of industry standards. Now everything I'd learned from him felt tainted by his blatant ambition.

Oakley held me in the hallway for a moment, stroking my back and peppering light kisses on top of my head. "You really are good at your job. Don't let him get to you," he added. "I really want to stay, but the coach arranged a meeting for me that I can't miss."

"What kind of meeting?" I asked, pulling away.

"Nothing to worry about. Are you okay to get home? I'll stop by as soon as I'm done."

"I'll be fine. Go," I urged, shaking my head free of the hurt. "I need to call my dad."

Oakley kissed my forehead again before pulling away. "Okay. Text me when you get home. I'll see you tonight."

Even though the apartment was a short walk, I was exhausted from everything that had happened in the last two days. I ordered an Uber and let Bill with a red Subaru take me home. When we got to my building, I decided for the first time since the day I moved in to take the elevator instead of the stairs.

Thankfully, Shelby wasn't home. She was like a goddess sent from above to save my ass in my moment of total weakness last night. But today, I just wanted to be alone. I ran a hot bath and tossed in a rose-scented bath bomb that made the water turn pink and smell like the bushes that grew outside of my childhood home.

I played thunderstorm sounds on my phone and eased myself into the steaming water. All of my muscles let go of the tension they had been holding on to so tightly. I couldn't fight the tears anymore, so I let them fall, mixing into the pretty pink water. I sobbed until my eyes stung and turned red and puffy.

I cried in the bathtub until the water turned cold. Shaking from a mixture of emotion and the temperature, I stood up and dried myself off. I didn't bother draining the tub before I walked back into my bedroom, slipped on a tee shirt, and crawled into bed. Even though it was barely lunch time, I fell asleep immediately.

23

"That motherfucking asshole. I'm going to make sure no one works with him," my dad shouted. I had to pull the phone receiver away from my ear. I pictured my father pacing the floor of his office in our San Francisco home. I'd called him after I had time to process everything. "The nerve of him. To blackmail my own daughter."

I didn't like explaining everything to him. It was embarrassing to once again be caught up in a scandal. Luckily, my parents liked Oakley and didn't understand the issue of us dating, and now that I was clear of Dr. Haynes's ethics lectures, I didn't see the problem either. I did my job. I hadn't done anything wrong.

"You don't need his recommendation, sweetheart. You know you have a job here whenever you're ready. You were practically raised at Plotify. You were born for this."

I sucked in a deep breath. This would be the hard part. "I'm not sure that's what I want to do anymore, Dad." He went quiet. The sounds of his pacing footsteps completely stopped. I took a deep breath and continued. "Dr. Haynes is an asshole, but something he said really hit me. I don't want to be handed this job. And I'm actually really enjoying sports representation. I really want to succeed on my own merits."

Dad sighed. "I'm so proud of you. I support whatever you want to do. I'm going to chat with some connections I have. There's a football player in New York that likes to randomly release rap albums. Maybe I could—"

"Dad. I think it's time you stop cleaning up my messes. I think I need to...I need to do this on my own." I ran away to Texas because I needed to escape the bullying, but a lot had happened since that night. I wasn't the same girl anymore. I was a hard worker. I knew my shit. I needed to find my own road, wherever it led.

"Can we talk about it when we see you this weekend?" Dad asked.

"What? Y'all were just here."

"Oh my...did you just say y'all? You need to get out of Texas pronto, my dear." I smiled. I hadn't even noticed that it had slipped. "And no, you're coming here. UT has a game at USC. Your mother and I got tickets."

My stomach sank. My alma mater? I was destined to run into someone I knew. And since I was still Oakley's publicist, there was no getting out of it. Shit. Shit. Shit. I told my dad I loved him and hung up the phone so that I could start obsessing, I mean, *planning* for the weekend.

I couldn't believe I forgot about the game. I had it in my calendar. Hell, I had the entire practice and game schedule in my calendar, but I guess it just didn't register that this game was *the* game.

I was definitely slipping. Normally, I would have had a countdown widget with annoying blinking numbers reminding me how many days left until the big game. I would also have events on every day in the calendar with a daily alarm to remind me. I decided to blame not being prepared on Oakley. It just seemed easier than taking responsibility.

I jumped on my travel app and booked a flight, car, and hotel within minutes. My parents had wanted me to stay with them, but I decided I would be happier in the hotel. This time, it wasn't to make sure Oakley stayed in line, it was so that I could have a safe space to hide if I needed it.

The next thing I did was research the university media presence. I knew they were going to want to interview Oakley, because quite frankly, everybody did. After a lot of deliberate online stalking, I found three news outlets wanting exclusives. My hope was that they wouldn't know who I was since Dad expertly buried the footage from when I decided to publicly, and nakedly, humiliate myself. Threatening to sue was apparently good enough to keep it out of the news.

I was starting to feel semi-confident that this weekend wouldn't be a complete shit show. I could handle this. It was time to stop feeling sorry for myself and ignoring my feelings. Someone knocked on the door, and I got up to open it, half expecting to find Shelby on the other side. She was always forgetting her keys. But to my surprise, it wasn't Shelby. No, it was Oakley, dressed in a fucking killer suit with a bouquet clutched in his palm.

"What's all this?" I asked.

"We have some celebrating to do. My mother sends these," he explained, holding out the fist full of flowers. "Not to brag, but I arranged them. Also, she wants to meet you."

Just this morning, he didn't want to label us, now I was meeting his mother? Talk about emotional whiplash. "Wait, what are we celebrating?"

Oakley walked inside and started shuffling around my kitchen. "Where do you keep the vases? We need to put these in water."

"Oakley...what are we celebrating?"

He spun around to look at me. "I've been turning down scouts for years. But today, I told Coach I wanted to work hard this season and that I'd be open to meetings. I don't know if they'll even want me—"

"Of course they'll want you," I reassured. I'd seen the evidence of it in his email. Plenty of agents, coaches, and scouts had reached out, but he strictly instructed me to ignore them. "What changed?"

"I don't want to work in a flower shop," he replied. "That was always my sister's dream, and my mother has her empire handled. She just opened another shop in New York, actually."

"So what are you saying?" I was excited for him. So much had changed so quickly.

"I'm saying I just want to do things differently. A few big wigs are going to the USC game and want to chat afterward. This could be it." I let out the breath I was holding. Wow. I didn't even know what to say. "Now don't get a big head about this," he teased.

"Oh, I'm totally taking credit for this."

"Get dressed, I'm taking you out, Solver."

I TOOK a few extra minutes getting ready. I had to at least try to look hot; Oakley was in a suit, after all. While I was applying the best smoky eye I could, I thought about the injustice that was men getting ready versus women. It's really not fair how fucking good men look in a well tailored suit. All they had to do was get dressed and smell nice, and they're sex gods.

I chose the sexiest dress I owned. Out of habit, I started looking for my Spanx. It took me a good three minutes of searching to remember that I didn't own them anymore. It was so weird. I used them like a shield of armor. I shimmied into my favorite little black dress. The dress hugged my hips and stopped mid-thigh. The plunging neckline was held up by straps that crossed in the back, and it had just enough sequins to be sexy but not enough to cross the line into trashy. This dress made me feel powerful and confident.

I slipped on some black heels and small diamond stud earrings and headed out to the living room. Oakley was watching the enormous sixty inch TV when I came in. I waited patiently for him to turn around and drink in the sight of me, but his eyes were glued to the screen. He must not have heard me. Seriously? Didn't he know I was making an entrance here? I cleared my throat dramatically and waited for his reaction.

He stood up and drank me in. His eyes worked their way up from my heels to the soft curls I had put in my hair. He lingered on the spot where my hemline stopped on my thigh and again at my breasts where the neckline dipped.

"You look fucking incredible," he told me in a low raspy voice. "Maybe we can just stay in tonight. I'm not sure I want to share you with the rest of the world, after all."

"Not a chance, cowboy. I got all dolled up, you're taking me out," I said and then stuck my tongue out at him, playfully.

"Alright, Solver, let's go. But I have a few ideas for what you can do with that tongue later," he teased.

The restaurant that Oakley took me to was considerably nicer than the first one. It was still dimly lit, but this time it was for the atmosphere instead of trying to hide dinginess. It was a Japanese restaurant with dark floors and walls with pops of bright color. It smelled so good I was basically drooling. Bonus, sushi was relatively low in calories.

The hostess sat us at a small quiet table away from the chaos and noise of the main section. I ordered salmon rolls, and Oakley ordered what felt like the entire menu. Damn, this man could eat.

"So tell me all about what Coach said when you told him you were open to being recruited," I said, excited to hear the details.

"Coach was pumped. He's been trying to get me to take my career more seriously for years. I don't know, something about it just feels so right."

"I'm really excited for you, Oakley. You've worked hard this semester both on and off the field."

"Yes, well, there's this girl I met," Oakley murmured playfully.

"Oh? What's she like?"

"She's kind of crazy. Definitely doesn't put up with my shit. She likes to set alarms on my phone that go off all hours of the day and distracts me with her feisty personality. I'm pretty much hard every second we're together."

"She sounds pretty high maintenance," I replied with a smile.

"She's perfect." Oakley locked his eyes on mine. "You came into my life like a whirlwind and changed everything up. For the better," he said. Aww shucks! Despite the verbal lashing I had gotten from my mentor, I was pretty damn good at my job. And it was paying off for my client.

We went quiet for a minute. I pushed around my sushi rolls, debating on indulging in another one. "Can I ask you something?" Oakley asked, nodding toward my plate.

"Sure, what's up?" I asked.

"Let me preface this with something: I'm not even going to begin to pretend to understand your eating habits. I'm not a therapist, and I definitely am not entitled to an explanation. We've discussed it a little, and I'm not trying to be insensitive at all. I just...notice things."

I chewed on my lip. "Spit it out," I encouraged him.

"After every meal, you pick up your phone and calculate your calories," Oakley said.

"There's nothing wrong with keeping a food diary," I argued.

"Absolutely, I mean, I track my own macros," Oakley replied with his hands tossed up in surrender. "But I just want to make sure you're being healthy…"

"This isn't exactly the best conversation for a date," I said dryly.

"Fuck. I know. I just… Have you always been picky about your food?" he asked, trying to be delicate.

I let out a sigh. "No. Not always. I don't really know how to explain it."

"Try. I won't judge."

"I was—am—really insecure. I spent most of my college experience overcompensating by making people laugh. Everyone loves the life of the party, until they don't anymore. I drank a lot. I ate a lot. I fucked shitty guys because I didn't think I deserved any better."

"That's so fucking crazy to me. I mean, look at you," Oakley said while nodding at me. "You're the most confident woman I know. And if we're being honest, the way you boss me around is kind of hot. I can't picture you as anything different."

I smiled at Oakley, but that bubbling pit of insecurity traveled up my throat. I couldn't help but wonder if he would have found me as attractive just a few months ago. "When my streaking video went viral on campus, it just highlighted all the things I'd become. I was drunk off my ass and doing anything for a laugh. I couldn't handle being her anymore. People were cruel."

"What did they say?" Oakley asked.

"What didn't they say?" I scoffed. "I was body shamed by everyone. It was then that I realized I was nothing but a joke to these people. I'd created a persona that wasn't truly me."

I picked up a bite of sushi with my chopsticks and placed

it on my tongue, slowly chewing it before swallowing. It really was delicious.

"I'm so sorry that happened to you," Oakley said in a low voice.

"I did it to myself. And yes, I developed an unhealthy relationship with food, but I've been slowly finding a middle ground. I like being aware of what I'm putting into my body. I'm getting to a point where I'm researching and learning what is good for me and what isn't. This started as a toxic crash diet, but it's evolved. Hell, eliminating alcohol was most of the battle with my weight."

I paused and took a sip of my water before continuing. "Every time I took a bite, all I could hear was the cruel things they had said to me. But right now, with you, I'm just enjoying my meal."

Oakley smiled. "I want you to enjoy things with me. I'm sorry I brought it up."

"It's okay. I'm glad I could tell you."

"For the record," Oakley began, leaning forward. "I think you're beautiful. But it's that feisty attitude of yours that turns me on most. I want every single version of you, Amanda Matthews. I'm sorry it happened, but I'm not sorry you found your confidence."

I smiled. "Me too."

We finished our dinner while Oakley talked excitedly about different scouts and what teams he would like to play for. He was really adorable when he talked about playing pro ball. He was downright sexy when he was passionate. And somehow, by the time the server brought the check, I found myself thinking about future dates. Future #mine moments.

"I want to take you somewhere else," Oakley said with a grin, and I had to force myself not to pout. After our dinner, I wanted nothing more than to go back to my place and lick those delicious abs of his.

"Oh? Okay," I replied lamely.

"You don't sound excited," he teased, signing the bill.

"I just, um, was looking forward to going home with you."

"It's the suit, isn't it?" he asked, lifting his arm and flexing. I laughed at his joke and waited for him to explain where we were going. "I promise to let you have your way with my irresistible body, Solver. I just want to show you something, first."

I grinned. "Okay."

24

The building had a bright yellow door, and the windows were filled with beautiful arrangements. The Tilted Tulip sat in the heart of Austin. "Is this your mom's flower shop?" I asked excitedly.

"Her flagship store. It all started here," Oakley explained while holding my hand and guiding me toward an alley with a side entrance. "Every day after school, Daisy and I would help Mom with arrangements."

"Daisy and Oakley," I mused as he unlocked the door.

"My mom was a bit cliche with the names," he agreed.

"And your Dad?" I asked.

"Left a few months after I was born. Mom took everything she had and bought this shop." As he spoke, he flicked on the lights, illuminating the room. I looked around greedily, excited to have a glimpse into his life.

The shop was warm and cheerful, flowers filling every space. The walls were the same yellow as the front door, and there were refrigerators full of elaborate arrangements and beautiful single stems. The countertops were a cozy teal, giving the shop a bold, cheerful feeling. I spun around, taking it all in. I could almost envision Oakley's mother from the way the shop was decorated and cared for.

"Pick some out, anything you like!" Oakley said, gesturing to the black bins full of loose flowers. He handed me a flat wicker basket with a handle to collect the stems in. It was so cute how excited he was getting over flowers.

I walked around, bending over to pick up brightly colored flowers and put them in my basket as he took off his suit jacket and rolled up his sleeves. The slow, methodical movement that revealed his muscular forearms made me pant. What was it about a good pair of forearms that made me go crazy? I could feel Oakley's eyes on my ass, so I picked up a flower and pretended to drop it on the floor.

"Oops," I said innocently. I bent over slowly to pick it up and gave my ass a little shake. He walked past me and gave it a playful smack on his way to the next row of bins.

He picked up a pretty yellow flower.

"This is a golden columbine," he started. "It's a flower that's native to Texas and was the inspiration for the yellow doors on all of Mom's shops." He looked really proud of himself, teaching me about the flowers.

"And this," he said, picking up what looked like a sunflower, "this is an Indian Blanket. It's an annual bloom in the sunflower family." He put the flower in between his teeth and wiggled his eyebrows at me.

I giggled and showed him my full basket of flowers.

"I'm officially impressed with your floral knowledge. But can you put your money where your mouth is and turn *this* into one of those amazing bouquets?" I asked, hefting my basket into the air and nodding toward the expertly arranged vases.

"Of course I can. Follow me," he said with an air of cockiness. I followed after him and set up at a nearby table. "Wedding season is my favorite," Oakley explained, grabbing some scissors and twine. "The brides can be crazy, but spring is always all hands on deck. My mother has been featured in so many bridal magazines it's insane. She has a waitlist of thousands wanting her to do their arrangements."

I never thought flowers could be the foundation of such an empire, but the success of their company explained Oakley's expensive clothes and nice car. It was nice to see him roll up his sleeves and get his hands dirty, though. Most kids would have just mooched off their parent's success. "The trick is to have a sense of variety in length. You're going to want to trim the stems cohesively, while still allowing differences."

I followed his lead, trimming as I saw fit and trying to match his process.

"Then, after you have your stems cut, put a foundation of greens and leaves in the vase first," he said confidently. "Next, you can find the natural gaps and fill them in with the flowers. Most people will try to alternate between the different types of flowers and then add the filler, but this is the best way to get a really pretty and full bouquet."

Oakley Davis: football star, playboy, and expert flower arranger. Who knew?

I got to work on my flowers, focusing on following the guidelines Oakley had given me. I fluffed out my greenery and carefully placed the different colored flowers to fill in the openings. After a few minutes, I had a gorgeous vase of flowers. I was super impressed with myself. I looked up to tell Oakley that he should be impressed with me too only to see that he was already staring at me.

He came over and pretended to grade my work.

"This is an excellent first attempt, Miss Matthews," he said smartly and moved to position himself behind me. "However, I think you will find with just a few small adjustments, it could be perfect."

Oakley slid his arms under mine and pressed his chest tightly into my back. I let out a small laugh because it felt like he was about to teach me how to play mini golf. He picked up a few more stems and placed them into the vase, grazing my breasts as he did. His pelvis nudged into my ass every time he leaned forward, and I could feel his excitement. I started grinding into him when he moved, and I heard his breath hitch.

He spun me around to face him and effortlessly picked me up and sat me on the table top. I parted my legs, making Oakley's eyes dart to where my dress was riding up. "You're so fucking tempting," he growled, grabbing a nearby pink flower. Gripping the stem, he started dragging it up my thigh. The touch made goosebumps break out over my skin. "So sensitive. You respond to the lightest touch," he added before dragging it higher and higher, removing the flower once it was close to my slick heat.

I licked my lips as he dragged the flower across my arms, my chest, my cheeks. It was so teasing and slow. Oakley Davis was taking his time with me, and every pass of the potent petals had me dripping with need. "Kiss me," I demanded. I wanted to feel his lips on mine.

"So impatient. I thought we were going to make an arrangement, hmm?" he teased as he put the flower down.

"Oakley," I pleaded, my voice a whimper. He was enjoying the neediness in my tone. I watched as he grabbed some velvet ribbon nearby. Taking it in his hands, he pressed my wrists together, tying them with an expert bow. The soft material rubbed against my skin.

"I've fantasized about doing this for ages," he rasped before lifting my arms up and wrapping them around his neck. I scooted forward on the table, aligning our sexes as he tempted me with a kiss.

"I'm all tied up. All yours," I whispered. It was like speaking loudly would ruin the tension-filled moment.

"All. Mine," Oakley growled while lunging for my lips. The force of his kiss made me arch my back. His tongue fought with mine. We tasted one another. We moved like ocean waves, our bodies giving in to the pleasure. I struggled against the velvet restraints, wanting nothing more than to run my hands along his hard torso.

"No moving," he demanded between kisses. I bucked on the table as his lips edged the line of my jaw. He sunk lower and lower, stealing pieces of me as he went. The trail of his sharp teeth made my creamy skin turn red.

"Oakley, *please*," I begged. I was squirming from his relentless teasing. My dress kept rolling up until the little thong I was wearing was the only thing covering my sex. His mouth continued to wander. He pushed down the straps of my dress and exposed my breasts.

"Look at you, Solver. Seriously. You have me hard as a rock every second of the fucking day." He then cupped my heavy breasts and pinched my nipples. "Pretty pink little nipples. I love touching them. You make the cutest sounds when I..." His voice trailed off as he lowered to kiss them. I moaned. "Yep. That sound right there. Fuckkk," he added.

I pulled my bound wrists against his neck, pressing him harder against me. I wanted to drive him lower and lower until his hot breath was on the building ache between my thighs. He straightened and stared at me head on. "Amanda Matthews, I want to fuck you until all I can feel is that sweet little pussy clenching around my cock," he rasped, grabbing a condom from his pocket and unfastening the button on his suit pants. Within moments, his hard cock was nudging at my entrance. "These are in the way," he whispered, threading his fingers through the straps of my thong and shimmying them down my legs. Slowly. Teasingly. A shudder traveled up my spine as I became overwhelmed with need.

"I need..." I began, not even sure how to articulate what I craved. I wanted him hard and fast. Demanding. Punishing. The silky feel of his light touches made me heady.

"What do you need, Solver?" he asked, the question like a taunt.

"You. I need you."

Oakley surged inside of me, making my head roll back and my toes curl. The moment he was fully inside of me, he bit his lip and let out a grunt. "Fuck, Amanda. You feel so good," he murmured.

Oakley started pumping harder. I felt ravaged by his movements. The silky restraints binding my wrists added a sense of excitement to it all. I was flooded with sensations. We were electric. Erotic. I sunk into the feeling of his large cock piercing me. I glided across the table. Hell, I could have been flying for all I knew.

He didn't ease. We were spiraling. Climbing. The smell of sex mixed in the air with the fragrant flowers. "So fucking close," I croaked. My voice was a broken mess of bliss.

Oakley shuddered, and soon both of us were exploding on the table. I cried out, not caring how loud I was. Oakley was nothing but a mess of moans and curses. "Fuck, fuck, fuck," he said while grabbing my hips. He dug his fingers into my skin, and I rode out my bliss along with him.

"Fuck, Oakley," I said once the last bit of pleasure had passed. "That was..." I couldn't even articulate what that was.

He pressed his forehead to mine. "You're mine, Amanda Matthews," Oakley said.

"Ditto, Problem."

25

The California sunshine beat down on my shoulders as we waited for the charter bus that would take us to our hotel. The three hour flight was okay. The entire team sat together, so it smelled like I was breathing in filtered farts the entire time. Oakley held my hand, and I ended up falling asleep on his shoulder, earning us various curious stares and winks from Dale and his other teammates. We might not have been officially dating by conventional standards, but it was pretty well-known where we stood.

"Are you ready for your meetings?" Coach asked. He'd been standing nearby, eyeing Oakley's hand laced with mind with scrutiny.

"I prepped him on possible questions. I also arranged for some journalists to be there to catch them going into a meeting to get some buzz," I answered, looking up at the approaching charter bus. Our hotel was close to the stadium, and I was freaking out about possibly running into someone I knew.

"I'm ready," Oakley added.

We got on the bus, and the moment I sat down, I started

checking Oakley's social media and articles featuring commentary about the upcoming game. Nearly everyone was mentioning how Oakley seemed to be taking this season seriously.

"I've emailed all of you the schedules for the weekend. I want each of you to go to your hotel rooms and lock yourselves inside for the duration of the evening. No partying. No canoodling. Nothing. I'll have eyes all over the hotel. You can leave your room to eat. That's it. Be smart, or I'll make you run until you puke. This is a big game. Lots of important people are watching," Coach Howard said while staring at me. "I'm putting Miss Matthews on watchdog duty. Since she's done such a good job keeping Oakley in line, I'm promoting her to babysitter of all your sorry asses for the night. Her room is at the end of the hall, and I have it on good authority that she'll kick you in the balls if you break the rules."

What? That was news to me. The entire bus started whistling.

"Coach?" I whispered. "We didn't discuss this. If I'm managing the image of the entire team, I need to be prepped. How do you expect me to keep them out of trouble if I don't have advanced notice?"

Coach leaned over to look at me. "I have complete faith in your ability to wrangle them. It's one night. Keep my team out of trouble. Sit in the hallway if you have to. I'll have a very positive letter of recommendation if you do."

I gritted my teeth. "Got it."

Oakley squeezed my hand and smiled. I supposed I would be spending my evening in the hallway tonight.

―――

THE CARPET in the hallway was so gross. I mean, it looked

fine, but it had a faint smell of dog piss and spray deodorizer. For the last hour, I had been sitting on the floor, leaning up against the door to my room, trying not to think about the last time it was actually shampooed. Since my room was at the end of the hall, anyone trying to leave would have to go past me.

So far, all of the guys were behaving. I could see all of their doors from my spot, and every now and again, one of them would pop their head out to see if I was still playing watchdog.

"I see you, Liam. Don't even think about it!" I shouted as one of the players opened his door and peeked out. The escape attempts had died down since they figured out I really was going to sit in the damn hallway on the disgusting floor.

Oakley slowly opened the door from the inside of our room and gave me the chance to sit up before opening it all the way. He was holding a Styrofoam cup of the terrible complimentary coffee brewed inside the nineteen-ninety-something coffee maker in our room.

"I thought you could use this," he said, handing me the coffee. "You've been out here forever. How about I text the guys and tell them that we need some *alone* time and to keep their asses in their rooms? Then we can go inside, and I can do that thing you like with my tongue," he teased.

"No," I said firmly. "I need the recommendation. I can't fuck up. Again." At this moment, I really hated Coach. That recommendation had better fucking sing.

Oakley crouched beside me and started slowly kissing my neck, sending shivers down my spine. He made his way up to my mouth, and his skilled tongue started to weaken my resolve.

"Are you sure you can't come back inside? Just twenty minutes..." Oakley said in a throaty voice between kisses. "In fact, I bet I could make you come in five..."

Oh hell. I started to squirm. I was about two seconds from humping his leg. I could use a good orgasm. Five minutes couldn't hurt. "You have to threaten them," I began, slowly standing up.

"What would you prefer?" he asked, pressing me against the wall.

"Tell them I'll cut their dicks off."

"I love it when you talk dirty to me," he replied with a chuckle. "Anything else?"

"Tell them if they leave, I'll have the school newspaper publish an article about a chlamydia outbreak in the athletic department."

"Oh, that sounds so hot," Oakley teased again. He then pressed me against the wall and whispered in my ear, "Anything else?"

"Tell them—"

"For fuck's sake! We get it!" I snapped my head down the hall in time to see a lineman poking his head out the door. "You'll maim, embarrass, and shame us if we leave. Just please stop with the creepy foreplay. I'm hard as a rock listening to the two of you, and I don't really want to explain to my therapist that I got off to this. It's bad enough I'm trapped in here, don't make me listen to you guys fuck in the hallway, too."

Oakley and I started cracking up, and our intruder disappeared. Grabbing my wrist, Oakley pulled me inside his room and started frantically unbuttoning my pants. I clawed at his shirt, neither of us able to get our clothes off fast enough.

This felt different. This was pure animalistic lust. Fast, hard, and powerful.

Oakley deepened his kiss, his tongue moving with mine furiously. His need for me was so fucking hot that I didn't know if I would last even five minutes like this.

He tore my shirt over my head and pushed my bra up, exposing my breasts.

Oakley shoved me against the wall, knocking over a lamp from the nightstand. He held my hands over my head with one of his big hands while the other hand feverishly roamed my body, stopping only long enough to pinch my nipples. Moans escaped my lips every time his fingers teased me.

"Oakley...I need you inside of me," I begged.

Without hesitation, he let go of my hands long enough to let me attack the button on his jeans. When I couldn't get them undone fast enough, he reached down, thrusting them just past his thick muscular thighs. His rock hard member was barely contained by his boxers. I grabbed the waistband and yanked them down over his flexed thighs.

A loud pounding on the door snapped both of us out of our shared frenzy.

"Amanda! Amanda! Amanda, we need you!" a loud voice accompanied the now crazed knocking.

"I am going to kill whoever is on the other side of that door," Oakley growled.

"Do we have to answer?" I asked with a pout. "Let's ignore them," I added before kissing him deeper.

"Dale snuck out to a USC party," the voice yelled.

Fuckity fuck fuck FUCK. I swung open the door, forgetting that I was currently naked and Oakley had his pants around his ankles.

"Oh shit," Kyle said with wide eyes as he stared. Oakley stepped in front of me, his hard cock pointing like an arrow at the asshole interrupting us. I quickly found Oakley's shirt and put it on.

"What?" he asked. "And you better scrub the memory of my naked girlfriend from your brain, or I'll make you run until you puke, freshman."

Oh my God, he called me his girlfriend. Nope. Not important right now.

But like, oh my God!!

Kyle stammered, staring at the ceiling. "Uh. Dale snuck out, like, an hour ago? He found the fire escape and took the stairs."

"That slippery bastard. I'm going to end him. I'm going to deflate his balls," I growled.

Kyle let out a chuckle, then swallowed his amusement when he saw my furious expression peeking from around Oakley.

"Where is he?" Oakley asked.

"USC's Pike house? I don't know where it is."

"Shit," I began. "I know where that is." I started looking around the hotel room for my pants and shoes. I was literally going to have to march myself into the lions' den. This was exactly what I wanted to avoid. It would be one thing to see the people who tormented me from across the field, and another thing entirely to march into their home.

"Is he in trouble?" I asked absentmindedly, shrugging on my yoga pants.

"Someone posted on Instagram that a University of Texas player was seen kissing a girl outside the party," Kyle explained, his voice quivering from fear. "I told him not to go. I'm going to get in so much trouble."

"Yeah, you are," I grumbled. "I'll be back. And please, for the love of ice cream, make sure no one else does something stupid. I will personally end anyone who so much as thinks about leaving this hotel." I stepped forward and slammed the door shut.

Oakley let out a sigh and started looking for his clothes. "How far of a drive is it?"

"I'll order an Uber. It'll probably take thirty minutes," I replied.

"Great. Let's go."

My brows shot up in surprise. "You're not going," I insisted. "You can't be seen at a USC party, Oakley."

"And you can't waltz into that party alone. Dale is probably drunk off his ass, and I don't trust anyone not to fuck with you. I know you're nervous to be back here. You don't have to do this alone, Amanda."

"I—"

"Stop arguing. The longer we wait, the more opportunities Dale has to fuck up. Let's bring him back before the coach finds out, okay?"

I let out a sigh. As a publicist, I knew that Oakley needed to keep his fine ass in this hotel room. But as a girl about to face the horrors of her past...I just needed his support.

"Please don't let anyone take photos of you," I relented.

Oakley wrapped me up in a quick hug. "We got this, Darlin'."

"Oh, we're doing cute pet names now, huh?" I replied with a sniffle. The anxiety coursing through me was intense. I couldn't stop shaking.

"Just testing it out," Oakley answered with a sly smile. "Let's do this thing, Sweetie. Schnookums. Dear. Sweet Pea. Love."

That last nickname made me preen.

"Let's go, Mr. Snuggles."

26

The atmosphere screamed frat house. It was packed with guys wearing USC shirts and girls wearing as little as they could get away with. Sweaty bodies were pressed against each other, dancing to music that was far too loud. Cheap beer flowed freely, and bad decisions were being fueled by it. I didn't think I would ever set foot in here again.

I was going to eviscerate Dale when I found him.

Thankfully, nobody had noticed the steamy hunk of perfection that was my boyfriend yet. Even just thinking the word *boyfriend* made me feel giddy, like a thirteen-year-old girl practicing writing her name with her crush's last name.

I laced my fingers through Oakley's for some much needed support and gave his hand a squeeze. It was too loud to hear myself think, let alone hear each other, so we searched without talking. I relied on Oakley's height to see above the crowd, and I shoved through people to make room to get by them.

As I was working my way toward the other side of the house, where the music wasn't as loud, someone turned around and ran into me, spilling beer all down the front of my shirt. Ugh, great. I was going to spend the next few hours smelling like lite beer.

"Amanda? Amanda Matthews?" the person I had bumped into squealed in my direction.

Oh God. Oh God Oh God Oh God. I had been so focused on finding Dale that I had momentarily forgotten where I was and who I was surrounded by. I had just run into Legacy Small, former sorority sister and best-friend-forever-turned-mean-girl.

Legacy was a perfect ten. She had the figure of a model, flawlessly applied makeup, and tan skin she achieved from hours of sunbathing on the beach. Her dark brown hair was always shiny and perfectly styled. She had been my roommate in the sorority house and spent Christmas with my family sophomore year. Legacy had also been the one to film me streaking on the Dean's lawn, and then she texted it to everyone she knew.

"Legacy," I said coolly.

She not so subtly checked Oakley out, giving him lingering sex eyes. She tore her gaze away long enough to shout to a gaggle of my former sorority sisters that I was here. Fuck. Everybody heard her. Legacy had one of those voices that just carried, even over loud ass music.

"Chuck!" she screamed over the music. "Come here! Look who it is!"

Oh fuck. I squeezed Oakley's arm harder. "Sorry, we don't have time. We're looking for someone," I stammered as Chuck made the crowd part like Moses and headed over to us. I used to have a crush on Chuck. He'd let me shamelessly dance on him at parties, and it wasn't until the video of me leaked that I learned I was the butt of his jokes the entire time I'd known him. He wrapped his arm around Legacy and looked me up and down like a predator, smacking his lips as if I was a tasty treat. Oakley stiffened at my side.

"Who are you?" he asked in a sultry tone. Did he seriously not recognize me? Figured.

"It's Amanda Matthews, silly! I almost didn't recognize her myself," Legacy replied, playfully slapping his chest.

Chuck's eyes widened as recognition flashed across his features. I wanted nothing more than to run away and pretend I'd never been here. Oakley looked like he wasn't sure what I wanted to do.

"No shit? Amanda Matthews! You look good!" He laughed, eyeing me up and down.

"We really need to leave," Oakley interrupted while tugging on my hand. Legacy reached out and grabbed my other hand, stopping me from leaving.

"I can't believe it's really you. I mean, last time we saw you, you were—"

"Fat and running across the president's lawn," Chuck interrupted with a booming laugh.

Ice filled my veins. It was insane how easily he insulted me. "What did you just say about my girlfriend?" Oakley growled.

Chuck glanced at Oakley, then did a double take. "You're Oakley Davis. You play for UT, right?"

"We really need to go," I said again before jerking out of Legacy's grip.

"You're dating this guy now?" Chuck asked before tipping his head back and laughing. "Here, let me airplay it to the flat screen. I'm pretty sure I have it saved."

Before I could stop him, Oakley lunged after Chuck. He was fast, but not fast enough to get the phone before Chuck had cast the video to the biggest screen in the frat house. I watched in horror as my lumpy and dimpled ass filled the screen. Everyone had gone silent, even the DJ stopped the music to watch.

I couldn't actually remember that night, but I had seen

this video hundreds of times. I had watched it obsessively when it was circulating around USC a few months ago. I knew the whole fucking video by heart, but seeing Oakley watch it made me feel the same way as the very first time I saw it.

My stomach dropped as naked Amanda happily ran through the grass singing USC's fight song. Legacy was laughing, both in the video and standing right next to me. I started tossing my cookies right onto the president's slippers, tits heaving with each retch, and Legacy's voice filled the room: "Oh my God, she's such a sloppy mess. So fucking pathetic," followed by more giggling. "Look at her ass jiggle."

"See? That's why I didn't recognize you, I was looking for that fat ass." Chuck sneered at me when the video cut off. Chuck moved forward and pinched my stomach. Hard. I gasped and swatted him away, but he refused to move.

"Leave her alone," Oakley yelled.

"What? She likes it," Chuck said with a hard laugh before grabbing my throat and squeezing hard. "She likes being pushed around and teased. She's desperate. Or at least she was. Doesn't matter how much weight she loses, Amanda Matthews will always be nothing more than a fat, pathetic bitch."

This time, I couldn't stop Oakley. His fist connected with Chuck's jaw, and Chuck fell backward, yanking him off of me. He was back up again before Oakley could land the next punch, and he started swinging wildly in an attempt to defend himself.

The whole frat house went wild with coeds chanting, "Fight! Fight! Fight!" Phones were being whipped out faster than dicks on Tinder.

"Oakley!" I yelled. "Stop, he isn't worth it!"

Oakley threw one last punch, blackening Chuck's eye before we heard the police sirens.

Fuck. Fuckity Fuck Fuck.

I grabbed Oakley's arm, hoping to pull him out of the room so we could escape, but the crowd grew thicker. The video of me was on loop, and I felt the familiar vise of a panic attack closing my throat. "We...we have to l-leave," I croaked out as Oakley wiped the blood on his knuckles off on Chuck's shirt.

"Breathe, baby," he said over the loud shouts as uniformed officers ran inside the frat house. A pair of cops took one look at Chuck, who was out cold, and started putting Oakley in cuffs.

My lungs felt like they were filling with sand. My eyes watered as I willed my voice to work. "Please don't take him," I choked out, but it sounded like more of a whisper.

"Oh my God, she looks like she's going to puke again," Legacy shouted.

Strong arms wrapped around me, and I was guided outside by a female officer. "Someone call the paramedics," she said into her radio. No. I didn't need paramedics. I needed to get to Oakley. "Sit down on the concrete and put your hands over her head."

I helplessly did what she said as she spoke into her radio again. Outside, blue and red lights flashed across the pavement. My throat kept closing up. My vision was speckled with anxiety. "I think it's a panic attack," another officer said.

I squeezed my eyes shut and opened them again only to see Oakley thrashing against the cops holding him so he could get to me. Tears streamed down my cheeks as they forced him into the car. And when the door was slammed shut, locking him inside, my chest constricted.

"Fuck," I croaked.

"Hey, girl," the female officer said, sounding impatient. "Who do I need to call for you?"

I tilted my head back and let the events of the night swallow me whole. "Call Coach Howard."

I WAS SITTING on a bench outside the police station when Coach Howard emerged from his car. He refused to acknowledge me, though we had locked eyes. It was four in the morning. The remnants of my panic attack still rocked me to my core, and I couldn't shake the impending sense of doom traveling up my spine. Everything was ruined. Everything.

I continued to sit outside, waiting for word. The police officers got my statement, and I made sure to tell them about Chuck grabbing me. They asked if I wanted to press charges for assault, and I told them yes. I was tired of letting people from my past run all over me. I wasn't the same girl that left a crying mess. And I certainly wasn't going to let him get away with tormenting me any longer. Besides, it would help Oakley's case if a judge knew he was defending me. I didn't even have to be a good publicist to know that.

Coach Howard stayed in the police station for five hours. Given that it was the weekend, I doubted a judge was able to release Oakley until Monday, but surprisingly, they both emerged from the station a little after nine.

I immediately stood up when I saw them, and Oakley ran to my outstretched arms. "I was so fucking worried about you," he whispered against my neck before pulling away to look me over.

"Both of you get in my car right now. It's a miracle the press isn't swarming this place already," Coach Howard grunted. I lowered my head and clutched Oakley's hand as we made it to Coach's rental sedan.

"What in the hell happened here tonight?" Coach

seethed. He was so angry he was barely able to get the words out.

"That asshole grabbed her, and I just saw red—" Oakley started to defend himself.

"Not you. I'm talking to Amanda. I just spent the last five hours listening to your side," Coach cut him off. Directing the conversation back to me, Coach said, "You were supposed to keep the players in the hotel. Nobody in, nobody out. So I will ask you again. What the hell happened?" Coach was on a warpath. He spat his words through gritted teeth, and his knuckles turned white from how tightly he was gripping the steering wheel.

"I'm sorry, Coach." I started to try to explain the night's events. "I, um, stepped inside my room for a moment."

I tiptoed around referring to Oakley and my room as "our room," and I did not want to volunteer the details of what exactly was going on inside the room that distracted me from playing warden. Although, the entire team knew what was up, so I was sure it was only a matter of time before Coach found out that Oakley and I were well on our way to bumping bellies instead of babysitting.

"There was a knock on the door and someone was yelling."

"Kyle, it was Kyle at the door," Oakley interjected.

"Yes, Kyle was at the door to let us know that Dale had snuck out by taking the back stairs. I honestly don't even know how long he was gone, because I stayed at my spot near the elevators for most of the night," I explained.

"Except for when you *stepped inside for a minute*," Coach growled.

I sighed and kept explaining. "Kyle told us where Dale went, and well, you know the rest."

"Yeah, I know that my star player got into a damn fist fight the night before a huge game. Over his publicist. Who was supposed to be keeping the team from getting into any fucking trouble," he yelled.

We rode in relative silence the rest of the way back to the hotel, the tension-filled quiet only broken by Coach occasionally cursing or mumbling about how his team was full of idiots.

We walked into the hotel lobby all together, and I tried to apologize to the coach one more time.

He turned to look at me and spat, "Pack up and go home. You're fired."

I knew this was coming, but it still hurt all the same. "She did nothing wrong. Dale snuck out the fire escape. You can't hold her responsible for this."

"I can and I will," Coach Howard yelled. "She should have called me the exact moment she learned of Dale's behavior. She absolutely shouldn't have brought you along. You had scouts today that were going to see you play. And now, according to league rules, I have to bench you for the most important game of the year—fuck—the most important game of your life, Mr. Davis."

Moisture collected in my eyes. He was right. I handled everything wrong, and now all the progress we'd made with Oakley was ruined. I slowly averted my eyes, staring at the concrete in slumped shame. "Go home. If I have to repeat myself, it won't be pretty," Coach said.

I ran inside the hotel room with Oakley hot on my heels, choking back sobs as I went. Coach Howard was screaming at Oakley to stay put, but he ignored him. I guess things couldn't get much worse, so it didn't matter.

I let my tears fall freely as I frantically shoved all of my clothes into my suitcase. Oakley grabbed my hand in an attempt to get me to stop, but I shrugged him off. I had to just get out of here. Like, now. I was mad at myself for not thinking to call Coach, I was mad at Oakley for getting into that fight, and I was mad at Dale for sneaking out in the first place. Fucking Dale.

But, mostly, I was embarrassed. Oakley had seen the most shameful moment of my life, and I was forced to relive it with the people who made my life hell. I was embarrassed that I managed to fuck everything up for about the millionth time, and I brought Oakley down with me. I just couldn't take it.

I headed for the door, and Oakley followed, this time reaching up for my shoulders and gently spinning me toward him.

"I'll come home with you," he said gently, not a trace of judgement in his eyes.

"No. Absolutely not. You need to stay here and support your team," I replied firmly, wiggling out of his grasp.

"Amanda, if this is about the video, I don't care."

"But I do. It was embarrassing. I can't escape it," I cried out. "And now it's affecting you. I can't believe you saw that." I shook my head.

"You know what I saw?" Oakley asked, and I didn't want to hear the answer. He stepped closer, locking me in with his body and hard stare. "I saw my beautiful girlfriend struggling. I saw people taking advantage of you. I saw people shaming a body and a person that's very precious to me. I would stand by your side and defend you every time if given the chance."

More tears streamed down my cheeks. "Oakley, can't you see? Somehow in this dynamic, I've become the problem. I've got to go. What you did was very sweet, but I might have already ruined both of our futures. I just need space." I opened the door, took one last look at Oakley, and walked out. I just needed to be alone.

27

The condo my parents rented out for the weekend was in the heart of Southern California. When I called them this morning to say that I was fired and being sent home, Mom insisted that I just meet them there.

I showed up with red eyes and wrinkled clothes, clutching the handle of my suitcase. "Oh baby, it's okay," Mom said, flinging open the door and rushing to hug me. "Come in. I made pancakes."

I could barely eat. My stomach was in knots, and it was embarrassing to tell my parents what had happened. I told them about Dale escaping, and my reunion with Chuck and Legacy. I expected disappointment or frustration from them. This was the second time I'd fucked up, but surprisingly, their reaction was the opposite. "Oakley defended you?" Dad asked.

"He punched Chuck. The dude was out cold when paramedics arrived."

"Good," Mom sneered. "What hospital is he at? I'm going to skin him alive. Did he hurt you when he grabbed you?"

"I already filed a police report," I said. "I'm fine."

"I knew I liked Oakley," Dad grumbled. "Is he okay? Does he need anything?"

"He needs to stay far away from me," I said in a low voice while stabbing my plate. My phone started buzzing, and texts from Oakley started coming in rapid fire succession. His ears must have been burning.

Oakley: Did you get a flight?
Oakley: What flight are you on?
Oakley: Call me when you get home.
Oakley: I just want to make sure you are safe.

Not that I was planning on answering, but if I was, he was barely giving me a chance to read his texts, let alone send a response. I looked at my phone for a minute and then did something that I never did. I turned it off. I didn't put it on silent or do not disturb, I turned it completely off.

"I'm exhausted. I didn't get any sleep last night," I announced to my parents as I stood up from the table. "I think I'm going to try to take a nap before the game."

"Ok, honeybunch," my mom said. "I love you, and we'll talk more when you're up for it." I loved that my mom got me. She just knew that I was going to want to talk about this later, but I wasn't able to right now.

I made my way to the spare bedroom and crawled under the covers, not even bothering to take off my clothes. I snuggled way down, pulled the comforter over my head and cried. I cried for my pride. I cried for the girl of my past. My future. Oakley's future. I choked on sobs as exhaustion took over. I was so wrapped up in my own sadness that I didn't hear the bedroom door open. It wasn't until the mattress dipped beside me and Mom snuggled under the covers that I realized I wasn't alone.

"Baby, talk to me," she said, wiping at my face. "You can't keep beating yourself up for one mistake. At some point, you've got to forgive yourself."

"I just am so embarrassed."

"Have I ever told you my most embarrassing story?" Mom asked, nuzzling deeper into the mattress.

"The time your dress fell completely off in a public park?" I asked dryly.

"No."

"The time your phone started going off during a parent teacher meeting and your ringtone was 'My Neck, My Back' by Khia?" I offered again.

"No. But that one is up there," Mom replied with a laugh.

"The time you bought a stripper pole for your bedroom to spice things up with Dad, and you broke your arm and knocked yourself out while practicing alone, and the paramedics found you in your neon stripper gear?" I rushed out on a single breath. This was a more recent story.

"No—can you please stop guessing so I can spit some wisdom?"

I cracked a smile. "Sure."

Mom let out a sigh before responding. "When I was in high school, I got dared to flash the hot soccer coach. He was Brazilian, baby. Brazilian men are just a different league of sexy," she said dreamily.

I blanched. "Did you do it?"

"Yes. But I didn't realize we had an audience. Half the soccer team saw me, and I got expelled. It completely derailed my graduation plans. I ended up taking an extra semester. It was so incredibly stupid, and not only did I get in trouble, he was fired. It was a different time. People thought he was encouraging the attention of his students. I ruined his career."

Wow. That was awful. I couldn't imagine doing that. "What did you do?" I asked.

"I did what I had to. I moved on. I felt guilty. But at the end of the day, we all make mistakes. And I have it on good authority that he's now a successful coach for the International Soccer League. Sometimes, things have a way of working out. We can't give our mistakes all our energy forever. I'll always regret what happened, but I'm not the same stupid seventeen-year-old I was. And you aren't the same girl anymore, either."

Knowing that my mom had done something shockingly similar actually did make me feel better. My mom was one badass human being, and if I turned out to be anything like her, I would be proud. "Thanks for sharing that, Mom. I love you."

"Learn from your mistakes and have grace for yourself. You will be unstoppable," she finished.

After a hug and a kiss on the forehead, my mom asked, "Do you feel up to watching the game? Your dad has prepared a feast."

I actually did feel like watching the game, so I followed my mom to the living room. In light of recent activities—i.e., their daughter showing up in tears—my parents decided to watch the game on TV instead of going. I loved the hell out of them.

My dad had made enough potato skins and Frito pie to feed the entire football team. We grazed lightly on cheese and crackers in the shape of footballs and tiny meatballs as we watched the pregame show. I hadn't eaten all day, so I wasn't too concerned with the calories, but I still picked around the most carb-laden snacks.

The host started talking stats and highlighting some of the players. Oakley's photo flashed on the screen, and the host greedily started spilling why he wouldn't be there, like a sorority sister with juicy gossip.

"Oakley Davis, star running back for the University of Texas, was arrested last night by Los Angeles police—" I groaned, and my mom quickly flipped to another channel.

Once the game started, my mom was in her element. She was cheering and yelling at the ref like she had her life savings bet on UT, which was totally for my benefit, because she was a hard-core California girl.

My guys lost, and I felt a pang of disappointment at the score. More guilt laced through me when I realized they probably would have played better if Oakley were there. I also noticed that Dale was benched for the game. I'm glad he at least was punished too.

"There's always next time. Oakley won't be benched forever," Dad said, turning off the game and patting me on the shoulder.

"Yeah. Next time." I chewed on my nails. Guilt was eating me up. No longer feeling social, I kissed my parents on the cheek, then made my way to my guest room. Giving in to the exhaustion, I finally fell asleep.

"BABY, WAKE UP," my mother said while shoving me. "Baby. You gotta see this." My room was pitch black aside from the faint glow of my mother's cell phone illuminating her tired face.

"What?" I replied, my voice deep with sleep.

"I was just casually checking Oakley's Instagram..." she began.

I checked the clock. "At two in the morning?"

"Don't judge me. That boy is fine. And I had purely innocent motivations. Honey, he's at a bar and is getting tagged in sloppy posts. I know you care about him—"

I grabbed the phone and stared at the screen, groaning when I saw Oakley slumped over a bartop and swaying on his seat. Two girls wearing jerseys were posing with him, pressing against his body like he wasn't drunk as hell and out of his mind.

"Shit," I croaked before shuffling out of bed and grabbing my phone. I quickly turned it on and immediately got a slew of messages and missed phone calls.

Oakley: We lost the game.
Oakley: Where are you?
Oakley: R you breaking up with me?
Oakley: solvr what are u doing
Oakley: call me backkmmm

"Oh shit. I have to go get him," I said, looking at my mom.

"He was tagged at a bar near here. Want me to drive?" she asked.

"Yes." I probably would need her help to get his drunk ass in the car.

WE PULLED up to the bar within ten minutes of my mom getting me up. I hadn't even bothered to change out of my flannel pajama pants and tank top. My hair was piled into a messy bun on top of my head, and I had thrown on flip-flops as I left the rental. I looked a hot mess.

I asked my mom to wait in the car and headed in solo. It didn't take long to find Oakley; he wasn't exactly trying to hide. He was sitting at a table, surrounded by women, making a complete ass out of himself. He was definitely drunk. I didn't see any of the other players. After everything that happened, Coach must have threatened them with their lives if they stepped out tonight.

The girls at Oakley's table were leaning in as close to him as they could get from across the table, their low cut tops putting everything on display. They were laughing like

Oakley was saying the funniest thing they had ever heard. There were a couple of women standing behind him, and one was even perched in his lap. I was too tired and emotionally drained for it to even register that I should be upset about that.

I headed directly for Oakley, prepared to drag him out by his ears if I had to. As I got a little closer, I realized that there was something familiar about the girl with perfect shiny brown hair sitting on his lap. Fucking Legacy.

She ran her hand through his hair, and I saw red. I couldn't even hear the over-the-top comment she flirtatiously tossed his way over the roaring in my ears.

"Problem," I said loudly while pushing through the crowd. Some looked at my pajamas and messy hair with disgust. Legacy looked me over and smiled coolly, moving her hand from Oakley's hair to his chest.

Oakley turned to face me, his expression twisting from confusion, shock, and then finally excitement. "Solbeeeeer," he replied.

Legacy was massaging his chest, starting at his glorious pecs and working her way up to his shoulders. She clearly thought she had already won a non-existent competition. I wanted to tear her off of him.

"Come on, Baby. Let's go home," I cooed. Drunk Oakley was like an excited toddler, coddled and enticed with the temptation of candy.

I was the candy in this scenario, despite how ridiculous I looked.

"He doesn't need a babysitter, Amanda." Legacy laughed at my attempt to lure Oakley out of the bar. She was drawing lazy circles on his chest with her long nails. If it wouldn't have looked ridiculous, I bet she would have straddled him right there in the middle of the bar. I mentally rolled my eyes at what she thought was a display of dominance.

"Oakley? Come on. Come home with me," I said softly.

He quickly pushed everyone away, as if he'd just realized we had an audience. His movements were slow and forced, each choppy extension of his limbs was like wading through syrup.

"I didn't kiss thennnn," he slurred, swaying toward me. "Why didn't you fall—call?"

"I'll explain when we get back. Come on, I'm going to fix this."

Seeing Oakley drunk broke me. He was struggling today, and I wasn't there for him. This wasn't about me being his publicist. This was about being his friend—his person.

"You've always been an attention whore, Amanda. Can't even let the poor man drink. He's had a hard day, and you're making it about yourself. You always fucking make it about yourself," Legacy spat. She realized she had lost, and insulting me was a last ditch effort, trying to regain her control.

Oakley's face twisted up in rage, but this was one battle I wanted to fight for myself. "That's rich coming from you," I snarled. "You humiliated me to make yourself look better."

"You humiliated yourself. I was just along for the ride," she sneered.

"We were supposed to be friends. I'm responsible for my actions, yes, but when you care about someone, you protect them. You don't show the world their indiscretions while you laugh on the sidelines. That is what I'm doing for Oakley right now, protecting him."

I took a step closer to Legacy, seeing her with clear eyes for the first time. She was trying just as hard to fit a role as I had been; the only difference was I escaped it. All the anger fled my body, and a surprising emotion overcame me: pity.

"I wish I could hate you, but you probably saved my life that night, Legacy." Her eyes widened in shock, as if she wasn't expecting that. "You forced me to change—to be better. And I hope one day you learn that you are beautiful and capable of better things, too. I'm not letting you walk all over me with your knock off Louis Vuitton heels anymore. You are nothing. No one. I don't want or need your validation anymore. And when my boyfriend isn't drunk—"

"I'm still your boyfriend?" Oakley interjected, his voice sloppy and full of awe. I ignored him but felt a burst of affection.

"He's not going to want you. He wants something real—something you're not capable of being right now because you're too busy tearing others apart and using their mistakes to make yourself look superior."

"Yep. What she said," Oakley added, making the growing crowd watching us laugh. Legacy's face soured as she realized they were laughing at *her*. It was probably something she wasn't used to, considering she was usually the one pointing the finger.

I took Oakley's hand and led him out of the bar. I didn't look back at Legacy as we left; I wasn't about to give her another second of my time. My mom helped me get Oakley settled into the backseat of the car, and she started the drive home.

"Thank you fer coming to get me, Solbeer," Oakley slurred as he fell asleep with his head in my lap.

28

Oakley slept like the dead. I, however, was up before the sun, because apparently being drunk made snoring about a billion times worse. It was a cycle, his soft gentle purr escalating into a burst of roaring snores, finishing with one final explosive snore. A snorgasm.

I sat up in the bed, all protective feelings from earlier gone. I was now thinking about whether or not I could get away with smothering him with my pillow. I finally gave up on the idea of getting any more sleep and opened up my laptop. I was briefly concerned about the bright screen waking Oakley up, but he snorgasmed again, and my moment of concern passed.

I wanted to face my demons head on, so I pulled up Instagram to see what the damage was. I didn't even bother looking at the tagged posts, I went straight to the last photo he'd shared. I knew the first step would be to delete any unsavory comments or maybe turn off commenting altogether. The photo was of him on the airplane that brought us here, with his award winning smile and bright, hopeful eyes. He looked hot as hell. With a deep breath, I started reading.

LickMyKitty69: Omg did you get arrested for defending your gf?

Mrs.Hemsworth20: I want to sit on your face.

Comefeelme: Amanda Matthews is one lucky gurl.

ItWasntMe: #PutOakleyBackInTheGame #NoFatShaming

ILikeToBeChoked91: I would have punched that dude, too.

ClevelandHotWaffle: Oakley! I have a great opportunity for you. If you'd like to make extra income while working on your phone, join my #Bossbabe empire.

TheKentuckyKlondikeBar: #TeamOakley #TeamAmanda #FuckBodyShamers

Smashturbating: I got pregnant just looking at this photo.

What? How did they know about… I quickly started searching, and it didn't take me long to find what had everyone buzzing. A full video of what happened last night was uploaded by a girl I didn't recognize. Based on her Instagram feed, she obviously attended USC, but I had never seen her before. I clicked on it and watched with a frown, shame filling me up as the embarrassing debacle played like a movie before me.

It hurt to watch, but it also angered me. And apparently, it angered others, too. The hashtag #FuckChuck was trending across various platforms. A quick check of my email showed that a few news sources wanted an exclusive with Oakley. I reached for Oakley's phone and saw hundreds of missed calls, the latest one from Dale.

On a whim, I called him back. "Dude, where are you? Our flight leaves in an hour," he answered in a rush.

"Hello, Dale," I scolded like a sinister villain about to feed her opponent to sharks. "I'm so glad we could talk."

"Fuck, Balls. I'm so sorry. I just wanted to see a girl I went to high school with. A man has needs."

Yep. I was going to kill Dale. "That is the most bullshit excuse I've ever heard in my life. You got a right hand, Dale?" I asked.

"Yes, ma'am."

"How about a left hand. You got one of those?"

I could feel his shame through the phone. "Yes, ma'am."

"Next time you think about ruining somebody's future for some pussy, I want you to wrap one of those hands around your tiny little cock and do the two bump chump into a tissue like normal horny assholes."

"I'm more than a two bump chump—"

"I highly doubt it," I snarled.

"But I fixed it! Didn't you see the video?" he sputtered.

"You uploaded that?" I asked incredulously. "How?"

"The girl I was with. She caught it on camera, and we bailed when the cops showed up. You probably didn't see us. I figured if everyone knew the truth, it would help."

I let out a slow exhale. "And you didn't think that I wouldn't want my naked video to go viral?" It was mostly blurred out so people couldn't see the actual footage, but I bet it was only a matter of time until it resurfaced.

"Well..." he replied, dumbfounded. "No. No, I didn't. Want her to take it down?"

"It's too late, Dale," I shouted, making Oakley stir. Good. I was ready for a nice long chat with him. "It's out there, and you're lucky my hooha isn't clearly visible, or I would have filled your sinuses with urine and boiled your teeth."

"Fuck, Balls. That's terrifying. Who even says shit like that?"

"Oh, you have no idea. Looking forward to chatting again. Try not to do anything stupid during your flight home," I said as I clicked the little red button to disconnect the call.

I turned to look at Oakley, who snapped his eyes closed the moment I saw him. "If you think pretending to sleep is going to help, I still have some good threats left in me," I growled.

"Fuck. How bad is it? Where are we? What did I do last night?" he asked in a groggy voice that had no business sounding as sexy as it did.

"Well, you're not in jail, so it could be worse," I started. Oakley winced when I mentioned jail. "You went out to the bars last night. Do you remember anything?"

"Uhhh, yeah. I do," Oakley said as he sat up and rubbed the sleep out of his eyes. I waited for him to elaborate.

"Well?" I prodded when he didn't volunteer anything on his own.

"I'm so sorry, Amanda. I know I promised I wouldn't party anymore," he began. He paused and looked like he was trying to find the right words to say. I gave him what I hoped was an encouraging look, but I was tired and still kind of raw. I probably looked about as reassuring as a grizzly bear.

"I thought that I lost you and ruined my career all on the same day. It's not an excuse, but I was so mad at myself. I was devastated and didn't want to feel anything anymore," Oakley finished.

His vulnerability completely melted my heart, and I wrapped my arms around Oakley, squeezing him tight. My *penis fly trap* started to tingle, excited to be this close to Oakley again. I willed it to settle down, as it clearly had no concept of timing.

"I'm sorry too. I was so focused on myself that I completely shut you out, and I wasn't there for you," I told him. "I just didn't know what to do."

"You don't have to shut me out," he whispered. "I'm here for you, babe."

"Do you remember Legacy?" I asked. "Or the other girls

hanging all over you? That stung." I had empathy for needing to forget, but it still hurt to see him so drunk he didn't realize that a bunch of women were circling him like hawks.

"I remember the girl of my dreams waltzing into that bar, wearing the cutest—no—sexiest pajamas I've ever seen. I remember her taking charge. Being there for me. I remember seeing you tell that girl off while still being the better person."

"Your memory is impeccable for someone who drank an entire bottle of vodka," I spat.

Oakley reached out and pulled me on top of him, bringing his mouth to mine for a makeup kiss that was laced with stale alcohol and morning breath. I didn't even care, I just wanted more.

I let my hands wander over Oakley's delicious muscles as I deepened our kiss. I let out a small gasp as his hand slipped under my shirt and found the contour of my breast, teasing my nipple with his thumb.

I was still kind of mad. Still kind of hurt. But mostly, I was still kind of falling for this man.

He pulled away from my mouth and started kissing my stomach, slowly working his way down. He reached the line of fabric where my panties met my skin and took them in his teeth—right as my mom came through the bedroom door, saying something about breakfast.

"Oh! Oh my. So, uh, good to see you both have worked things out," Mom said, giggling nervously. She lingered as Oakley practically flung his body off the bed. "I can see why she likes you."

Oakley hit the floor and gathered the thick comforter up at his waist, likely to hide his monster erection from my mother. She stared at his hands before realizing how inappropriate she was being. "Breakfast is ready!"

She spun around and was about to leave when she paused

to whisper. "I'm not like regular moms, I'm a cool mom. But my husband will skin you alive if you have sex with our daughter while he's flipping pancakes in the next room for you."

"Copy that," Oakley replied nervously. I could see him blushing from here and had to stifle a giggle.

"Toodles!" Mom waved, leaving the guest room. The moment the door closed, Oakley let out a sigh.

"Fuck. You could have told me your parents were here!"

"You distracted me," I argued with a smile. "With pissing me off, then kissing me, and that thing you do with your lips..."

"I need a cold shower."

"Yeah you do," I joked while wrinkling my nose. "You smell like cheap perfume and the beer sweats. Besides, we have a lot of work to do this morning if we want to fix this."

"Oh?" Oakley asked.

"Get ready, Problem. You've got interviews today."

He grinned. "She's back."

"Who's back? Is my mom..." I stared at the door.

"No," Oakley replied. "You. Damn, you're feisty. Confident. Take charge. My girlfriend is back."

He took a step over to me, and I playfully rolled my eyes. "I thought we didn't do labels. You've called me that at least four times over the last two days."

"Damn," Oakley said. "My epic plan to play hard-to-get has backfired." His sarcastic tone made me giggle.

"Hop in the shower, superstar. We can awkwardly define the relationship *after* I've saved your career."

OAKLEY WAS in hair and makeup, getting ready for an interview on the local news channel. Dale's video of Oakley punching out Chuck, defending my honor, had gone viral. The social media buzz had gotten the attention of several media outlets, and my phone was blowing up with interview requests. We had to stay in California an extra two days to accommodate all of the interviews.

I stood next to Oakley as the makeup artist was doing her thing. I didn't see the point of the makeup; Oakley was basically a god. I practiced some questions with him, but he already knew what to say. This was his chance at redemption, and he knew it.

An assistant came back and got Oakley. It was time to start. I reached up and gave him a quick kiss for luck.

"You've got this, Problem," I told him confidently.

I watched the interview from behind the camera. Oakley was navigating the questions with ease. I am one hella good publicist.

"Oakley, tell me what was going through your mind when you saw Chuck grab your girlfriend's throat." The interviewer, Mia Mitchell, looked at Oakley intently.

Oh. Em. Gee. Mia just called me Oakley's girlfriend on TV.

"Honestly, I wasn't really thinking. I saw his hands wrapped around her throat, and my instinct to protect her just took over. Everything in my body reacted to stop Chuck from hurting her," Oakley answered.

Oh my lanta. My feminine sensibilities were all atwitter.

"And it was your friend, Dale, that released the video. Given the sensitive nature of the video, are you upset with Dale for doing that?" Mia followed up.

"No," Oakley said immediately. "I feel like he did the right thing. Amanda and I took a lot of heat, and we were affected both personally and professionally. By releasing the video, Dale was able to show the whole truth of what happened. Amanda had a few choice words for him, though," Oakley added with a chuckle.

The news reporter laughed with him. "This entire ordeal has sparked conversations about body shaming and bullying. What is your take on the response, and how do you feel collegiate football could benefit from this?"

I chewed on my inner cheek as Oakley thought over his response. "I think it's important to call out injustices as we see them. I also think it's important to stand up for people and speak up when we see something wrong. I didn't know Amanda back when this original video was shared, but I would have absolutely stepped in and rejected the bullying, and I'm just thankful I was able to do so now. I do not stand for body shaming. My beautiful, intelligent, confident, and—forgive me for saying this—freaking sexy girlfriend did not deserve the backlash from her peers. She had to transfer schools and decided to graduate early just so she could escape the cruel things they said. She's so strong. It absolutely infuriates me that this happened to her."

The journalist nodded. "You yourself have been on the receiving end of scrutiny. Your social media has been the talk of college football for quite a while."

"I won't deny that I've been liberal with my online presence. The University of Texas is not only one of the most academically prestigious colleges in the country, but we know how to have fun."

I rolled my eyes. That was not on the agenda today, Oakley Davis.

"But I think social media has made bullying more accessible. Things can go viral at the click of a button. It's why my mother and I have decided to start a foundation called Daisy's Promise. We are in the process of setting up a team to support victims of social media bullying. We've hired a group of experts to assist those who have had their embarrassing moments streamed online—from revenge pornography shared by angry exes to harmful memes created to bully classmates. Our lawyers, therapists, and internet watch dogs are here to help."

Tears filled my eyes.

Oakley finished the interview flawlessly. After the way he talked so passionately about me and then finished with his new anti-bullying foundation, Mia was eating out of the palm of his hand.

Oakley Davis, former womanizing playboy football god who made my life hell, just gave the perfect interview. I wouldn't be surprised at all if Oakley got offers because of the way this interview showcased his strong character, loyalty to his teammates, and because of how likeable he was on screen.

I met him backstage where he was scrubbing the stage makeup off of his face. I stared at his back adoringly for about two seconds too long. Long enough to be considered creeper territory.

"Solver, were you just checking out my ass?" he asked as he spun to face me. I could tell he was totally feeling himself, and after that interview, he should be.

"No," I said casually. "I was just waiting for you to hurry up and finish washing your face so we can go. I have a ton to do now that you're hot shit," I teased.

Mmm, that ass though.

29

The moment we landed back in Austin, Texas, Oakley had to get to practice. After missing two days and a game, I pretty much assumed the coach would make him run until he puked. Gross. Shelby greeted me wearing clothes—thankfully—and I finally worked up the courage to give Dr. Haynes a call after a long shower and a pep talk in the mirror.

You are a divine goddess.

You fucking rocked this press circus.

Your ass looks great in those overpriced yoga pants.

Dr. Haynes answered on the second ring. "Miss Matthews. Surprised you're calling."

"What, did you think I was going to hide? I saw a problem, and I fixed it." I decided to be confident right off the bat. I was totes rocking this. Dr. Haynes went silent, as if waiting for me to continue. "Although we got lucky with the video going viral, I managed the crisis accordingly. I spun the narrative to best project my client in a positive light. I used my resources to get him interviews with reputable sources and even managed to secure some inquiries about Oakley being the face of a few anti-bullying campaigns."

"So why are you calling me, Miss Matthews?" Dr. Haynes asked.

I let out a sigh. "Because regardless of your recommendation, I know that I am damn good at this. I had really hoped to learn a lot from you this semester. I still think you're a god in our industry, despite your shady tactics. But I don't care if I have to start over with my internship. This is my dream job. I might have messed up, but I cleaned that mess up pretty damn well. I'm like the Hoover vac of publicists."

Did I seriously just compare myself to a Hoover vac? Fuck.

Dr. Haynes replied. "That's a very odd analogy, but I'd be inclined to agree."

"Wh-what?" I asked. I wasn't expecting him to agree with me.

"I got a call from the university president today, congratulating me on my work with you. They've also decided to donate funds to Daisy's Promise as a gesture of good faith and support for the Davis family. The board and I really like how you managed the press storm. They also got a flood of interest from publications wanting to write pieces about how there is a culture of support on campus. I've already suggested you coordinate the efforts. You did good work. You got a little lucky, but that's half the battle in this industry."

I needed someone to pinch me. Was this real life?

"I'm going to give you a glowing recommendation, Miss Matthews. Assuming you survive the remainder of the semester. You've got about seven more games and a few bowl games to go before graduation. But Coach Howard and I have already discussed it. Keep working hard. I'm here if you need me, and I look forward to seeing you at the commencement ceremony."

"Th-thank you," I stammered. I was in shock. I couldn't believe I pulled it off—and I didn't need my father to do it.

"Have a good day." Dr. Haynes hung up the phone, and I did a little dance in my bedroom.

I was so excited that I felt like a kid on Christmas morning. I was bursting to tell everyone I knew. Since Oakley was still at practice, I sent him a text, knowing he wouldn't be able answer for a hot minute.

Amanda: Talked to Dr. Haynes - I'm graduating early!! I still have the job!

I added about five more exclamation points before sending it. Just to make sure he would know how excited I was.

Next, I called my mom. She answered after one ring. It's like she sensed from a thousand miles away that I had something important to tell her.

"Hey, honey, what's going on?" she answered.

"I did it, Mom! I'm going to graduate early with recommendations from both Dr. Haynes and Coach Howard!" I blurted out so fast all my words ran together.

"I knew you could do it! And if those two old farts had given you anything less than that, I would have flown down there to kick them in the balls myself!" she said, a little too enthusiastically.

We chatted for a few more minutes before hanging up. I was surprised to see a text from Oakley waiting for me.

Oakley: So proud, Solver. Meet me at the football field after practice. We need to celebrate!

I started primping immediately, and this time, I wanted Oakley to think that I made the extra effort to look good for him. I went a little outside of my comfort zone and put on some bolder eye makeup with red lipstick. I didn't even need a YouTube goddess this time.

I slipped on a black chiffon tank top and shimmied into

some dark skinny jeans. I put on flats since I didn't know what we were doing. I could still be sexy as hell and wear comfortable shoes. I waited until my alarm went off on my phone, alerting me that practice was done, before making my way to the stadium. I couldn't wait to celebrate—especially if that celebration involved Oakley and me doing the hibbity-dibbity. I wanted him to fill me out like a job application. Glaze my donut. Lock legs and swap gravy. I was gonna sheath his meat dagger and rock those two-person push-ups.

Okay, I'm done for realsies now.

I ran a hand through my hair and walked down the sidewalk. Oakley Davis was mine.

"SOLVER," Oakley greeted with a low whistle before strutting up to me. His hair was wet as if he'd freshly showered. And though he moved like a man that was just forced to do a bazillion push-ups, he looked incredible.

"Coach run you ragged?" I asked with a giggle as he did a slow, sexy sweep with his eyes.

"He rode my ass all practice. But he seemed happy with my skills. He told me to stop wearing makeup and improve my footwork." I laughed while shifting my weight on my feet. I suddenly felt awkward and unsure of what to say. Luckily, Oakley seemed cool and confident. "I bribed a security guard. We got the stadium to ourselves for a few hours. I also ordered us a pizza."

The old me would have mentally calculated the grease content and calories, but the new me smiled. "I hope you ordered pepperoni." One cheat meal couldn't hurt.

He laid a blanket down on the fifty-yard line, and the lights shut off. Somehow, he'd managed to find a couple of flashlights from security guards and set them up like lanterns around us. I sat cross-legged on the ground, munching happily on pizza as he stared at me. "Amanda Matthews," he began. Why did he sound so nervous?

"Yes?" I wiped at the corner of my mouth with a napkin before setting my slice of pizza down.

"You're crazy."

Not exactly the romantic sentiment I wanted, but okay. "Why?"

"The first time we met, you were going through my phone and kicking my ass. I seriously thought I was going to have to get a restraining order."

"You probably should have. I broke a few privacy laws," I replied with a laugh.

"You constantly surprise me. You make me better. I...was a little lost before you. We've already kind of established that you're my girlfriend now. I'm kind of terrified that you're graduating early, but we can face a long-distance relationship when we get there. I just want to ask you a very important question." He started digging around the blanket, and my anxiety spiked.

No. No. Certainly he wasn't going to—

"Why do you look terrified?" he asked, pausing his movements to look at me.

"I like you a lot, Oakley. But if there is a ring somewhere hidden on your person, I will probably freak out and say no and embarrass us both. This isn't a Hallmark movie."

He tipped his head back and laughed, holding his stomach, roaring with humor. "I'm not proposing, Solver. I wanted to ask if you'd be my girlfriend. Officially."

My cheeks flooded with embarrassment, and I watched as he resumed searching for something. Luckily, it wasn't a velvet box he pulled out, but a single rose.

"Your mom said they were the ultimate expression of...llove." He stumbled on that word, and my mouth dropped open. Love? He loved me. Holy cats, he loved me.

"I love you too," I replied in a whisper. "You crazy pain in the ass."

He started laughing, and I reached forward to cup his cheeks for a kiss. His soft lips fit perfectly with mine. God, he was a good kisser, his tongue darting skillfully over mine. I loved this man. I really did. This infuriating, kind, hardworking, protective man.

I gently pushed him down onto the blanket so that he was lying on his back. I positioned my body at his side, wrapping one of my legs around his. My clitorasaurus roared to life.

I took the rose and teased it down his neck. "Time to return the favor," I said in a throaty voice.

Oakley reached up to touch me, but I caught his hand in mine and shook my head. "Can we go somewhere more private?" I didn't want to risk some pervy groundskeeper recording us. A leaked sex tape would probably be bad for publicity. Oakley smirked. "I know just the place."

Oakley quickly got up and grabbed my wrist. Abandoning the picnic, we made our way through a tunnel and to an elevator. "Where are we going?" I asked as he pressed the button leading to the top floor.

Instead of answering, Oakley cornered me, pressing me against the wall of the elevator with his hard body. "Oh-oh my," I rasped when his palm cupped my breast.

His lips landed on mine, and I curled my leg around him, moaning and flicking my tongue against his. I slipped his shirt over his head, and when the doors opened, we left it on the floor while running out of there.

"Welcome to the press box," Oakley whispered, flicking on the lights. As much as I wanted to look around, I wanted Oakley naked more.

I started what I prayed to Aphrodite was a sexy striptease

as Oakley made his way over to a large window overlooking the stadium. He looked so handsome and powerful standing there with his back pressed against the glass.

After I had danced my way out of my blouse and jeans, I unhooked my bra and slowly lowered it down to reveal my nipples already budding with anticipation. Oakley followed my movements hungrily. I loved the effect I was having on him. As I twirled my bra around my finger, his chest heaved up and down.

I dropped the bra and trailed my fingers down his bare pecs and past his sculpted abs, stopping where I could see Oakley's massive erection through his jeans. "I want to make you feel good," I whispered before unbuttoning his pants and shoving them down.

"Oh fuck, this moment is going in my spank bank for all eternity," Oakley rushed out as I dropped to my knees and stared at his *long dong silver* with a hint of trepidation. I was a bit intimidated by his size. Parting my lips, I licked the tip, making him shake.

"Fuck," Oakley groaned as I took him in my mouth. He held my hair back with his hands, jerking his hips with every pump of my mouth. He tasted good, and when I stopped to lick him from the base of his cock all the way to the tip, his entire body shook. "Yeah, I need inside of you right now."

Oakley brought me to my feet and frantically pulled my panties down while bringing me over to a wall. One second my feet were firmly on the ground, and the next he was picking me up and pressing my back against it. I wrapped my legs around his hips. "Fuck, condom," he groaned.

"I'm clean and religiously take the pill," I rushed out. I wanted to feel him with nothing between us.

"I'm clean, too." I gave him a look laced with scrutiny. It was probably bad form to bring up previous sexcapades after a declaration of love and right before he boned me, but I didn't fuck around. "I just got tested. Coach makes us do physicals every month." He looked at me, waiting for the go-ahead, and when I gave him a little nod and a wicked smile, Oakley thrust inside of me.

I've never been with a man coordinated and strong enough to do the whole *standing wall sex* thing, but Oakley Davis held me against him, sliding in and out of me with pure skill. I moaned and whimpered as our bodies moved. Up and down. My legs were shaking while wrapped around him. With his head tilted back, I kissed at his neck, crying out with the crest of my orgasm.

"Oh fuck," I screamed. My body quaked, and I dug my fingers into his back. I really hoped no one could hear us up here. The second I could see clearly again, Oakley set me down, and my legs shook with the aftermath of my pleasure. We both continued kissing frantically as he guided me to the cool tile floor.

I climbed on top of Oakley and straddled him. Being on top of him made me feel powerful. In control. Beautiful. I dipped my head down to his neck and traced long slow circles with my tongue, working my way up to his ear. I tenderly bit his earlobe, and Oakley let out a soft moan. He was so fucking sexy when he moaned.

I was ready to have him again, and when I couldn't take it anymore, I reached down and positioned his cock at my entrance, plunging him inside of me. "Yesss," Oakley hissed. I rode him, thanking God I'd been working on my squats. Being on top was a lot of work.

He moaned and said my name over and over and over again. We climbed that peak of bliss together. Our bodies were slick with sex, and the sound of our panting filled the room. He felt so good, and each gyration of my hips brought us closer and closer.

"Amanda," Oakley cried out as his body went stiff. My

breath hitched as I joined him. We both fell apart on a scream, the rolling orgasm running through my body like a bath overflowing with water. And when we were done, I collapsed on his chest, completely sated and out of breath.

"That was," Oakley began, seemingly at a loss for words. "That was incredible."

I smiled and rolled over to his side, finally taking a moment to look around the room full of desks, computers, and office chairs. "Solver," Oakley whispered while propping his head up to stare at me. He stroked my neck with his fingers.

"Yeah?"

"I love you. I mean that. I really fucking love you."

My heart bloomed. I couldn't believe this man. I couldn't believe we were here. Oakley Davis broke down all my walls and proved me wrong. We were both changed for the better.

"I love you, too."

EPILOGUE

THREE YEARS LATER

"If you want an exclusive with my client, then you better make it worth our while. He's the hottest player in the NFL right now, and if you want him on the cover of your magazine, we need to make sure it represents his brand well," I said while simultaneously typing an email. I was a multitasking goddess.

"We'll send over the concept right away, Miss Matthews," the editor for *Sports Illustrated* rushed out. I ended the call and stretched my arms up. I'd been working all day and needed a break. Being a publicist to three of the top athletes in the US was a lot of work, but I loved every second of it. Although I really needed to study golf a bit more for my newest client. I had no idea what a barkie was and had made a fool of myself earlier. Good thing I was damn good at the other aspects of my job.

"You done working?" Oakley asked. He'd popped his head in the doorway to my home office.

"Yes. I'm so hungry. I need carbs. And maybe a Diet Coke," I pleaded, standing up. Oakley fully entered my office, and I was shocked to find that he was in a suit. "What are you wearing? Shit. Was there an event tonight I forgot?"

Oakley smiled. "Yep. I laid your dress out on your bed. Be ready in an hour?" I casually reached for my calendar, but he reached out to grab my wrist, stopping me. "No working. Go get dressed."

I gave him a curious look before heading to my room. My apartment was in the heart of Dallas, about an hour's drive from the practice stadium. Oakley owned a house nearby, but he basically lived with me. Slowly, he'd been taking over my closet space and bathroom countertops, but I didn't mind. He was a busy man, playing for the Dallas Cowboys and making guest appearances around the world. I was greedy for whatever time I could get.

Three years. Three years of dating and navigating the crazy world of sports together. Three years of romance and humor. He was my boyfriend, but also my best friend. In addition to managing his career, we also built up Daisy's Promise to be one of the largest anti-cyberbullying organizations in the world. Together, we'd brought down numerous videos and assisted victims across the globe.

The dress he picked was long, black, and elegant. It had a slit up the thigh and a heart-shaped neckline that graciously emphasized my curves. I put it on and did my makeup, lightly dusting eyeshadow and powder on before grabbing my clutch and meeting him in my living room.

"Fuck, Solver. You look incredible," he grunted while holding his hand out to me.

"Are you going to tell me where we're going?" I asked. He was always doing this. Surprising me with extravagant dates and taking me out. I loved how romantic he was.

"Nope. The car is waiting," he replied with a smile before leading me out the door.

To my surprise, we took a limo to the Dallas Arboretum.

Daisy's Promise had funded a rose garden here a year ago, and we tried to visit whenever we could. "What are we doing here?" I asked. My intuition was screaming at me that this was big, and I had the urge to pat him down and see if he was packing a little black box. We'd talked about marriage, but every big date usually ended in orgasms and not a diamond ring—not that I was complaining.

It was funny how the first time I thought he was proposing, I was terrified. Now, every time I got an inkling that it was happening, it made me feel a lot of hope.

"I want to show you something," he insisted.

The gardens were absolutely stunning. We strolled along the long, winding paths through trees lit up with twinkle lights that made me feel like I was in a fairy tale. Although the heels on my feet reminded me that I hated the stiletto death traps and wanted nothing more than to murder the inventor of them.

It wasn't until we made it to the beautiful rose garden that my heart completely fell out of my ass. I mean, I wasn't sure if that was actually possible, but that's how it felt. "Amanda Matthews," Oakley said. My strong man was shaking and looked like he was about to puke.

"Are you okay?"

"Yes," he replied quickly.

"WAS THAT AMANDA? DID SHE SAY YES?" a voice asked.

I blinked. That sounded like... "Is my mother here?" I asked, looking around. Oakley quickly reached up and grabbed my chin, forcing me to look at him.

"Be quiet, dear. You'll ruin the surprise," my father said in a whisper-shout. I chewed on the inside of my cheek to stop the bright smile from crossing my features. Tears filled my eyes.

Oakley let out a sigh and shook his head, his own grin breaking out. "Amanda Matthews," he began again.

"Oh! Oh! It's happening," my mother squealed. I couldn't see where she was hiding, but I had to guess she was somewhere behind a shrub.

"For fuck's sake," Oakley grumbled under his breath before raising his voice. "Come on out, Mr. and Mrs. Matthews. Mom, you too," he shouted hopelessly before grabbing my hands. "They're terrible at secrets," he then whispered to me.

Movement to my left grabbed my attention, but my eyes locked on Oakley's the moment he dropped to one knee. "Oh, Crosby. LOOK! It's happening," my mother yelled.

"Amanda Matthews," Oakley began once again.

I shook my head. "Are you going to ask me to marry you, or what?" I teased.

"I had an entire speech planned," he groaned.

"Well, get on with it then," I joked back.

"I love you. I love you more than all the roses in all the world. I love your smile. Your confidence. Your grace. Your determination and grit. I love how you make me a better person. I love waking up with you by my side and falling asleep with you in my arms. I want to have a family with you —one day."

"I can't wait to be a grandma!" Mom whispered.

Oakley grinned. "I love you more than anything. I love every version of you. Every piece of your heart, mind, body, and soul." I was a sobbing mess. Every word made my heart bloom. "Will you do me the absolute honor of becoming my wife?" he asked, reaching into his pocket and pulling out a ring. I didn't even look at the diamond. I reached for Oakley and yanked him up to a standing position so I could wrap him in a big hug.

"Yes, Problem. I will marry you. I love you so much," I cried. Oakley picked me up and spun me around, cheering as we moved in circles.

"I love you too, Solver."

A NOTE FROM THE AUTHORS

Hey there! Thank you so much for reading!

We had so much fun writing this book. It was the humorous distraction we needed during such incredibly difficult times. We hope you enjoyed Oakley and Amanda's story as much as we enjoyed writing it. Happy endings are so important right now—and we don't mean that as a euphemism.

If you enjoyed this story, we kindly ask that you leave a review. Reviews are the lifeblood of an author's career, and every star counts.

Have a happy day,

Carrie and CoraLee

ACKNOWLEDGMENTS

This book would not have been possible without the support and love of Amy March, as well as Christine Estevez with Wildfire Marketing.

We would like to especially thank Casey Allen and Harleyquinn Zaler for beta reading.

We are grateful to all of those with whom we have had the pleasure to work with during this book. We'd like to especially recognize our editor, Helayna Trask. She always takes the time to dive into the worlds we create and make sure they are perfect for you all. We would also like to thank all the dedicated members of The Zone and Cora's Crew. And finally, thank you Dee Garcia for this drool-worthy cover.

ABOUT THE AUTHOR
CORALEE JUNE

CoraLee June is an international bestselling romance writer who enjoys engaging projects and developing real, raw, and relatable characters. She is an English major from Texas State University and has had an intense interest in literature since her youth. She currently resides with her husband and two daughters in Dallas, Texas, where she enjoys long walks through the ice cream aisle at her local grocery store.

www.authorcoraleejune.com

ABOUT THE AUTHOR
CARRIE GRAY

Carrie Gray is a new author who has enjoyed putting her own voice on the page and watching the story she helped create come to life. She grew up in Chicago where she received her Bachelor of Science in Biology and has not science-d since. She lives in the Dallas, Texas, area with her husband and son.

Printed in Great Britain
by Amazon